Lotte R. James trained as an actor and theatre director, but spent most of her life working day jobs crunching numbers, whilst dreaming up stories of love and adventure. She's thrilled to be finally writing those stories, and when she's not scribbling on tiny pieces of paper she can usually be found wandering the countryside for inspiration, or nestling with coffee and a book.

Also by Lotte R. James

Gentlemen of Mystery miniseries

The Housekeeper of Thornhallow Hall
The Marquess of Yew Park House

Look out for more books from Lotte R. James
Coming soon

Discover more at millsandboon.co.uk.

THE MARQUESS OF YEW PARK HOUSE

Lotte R. James

MILLS & BOON

First Published in Great Britain 2022
by Mills & Boon, an imprint of HarperCollins*Publishers* Ltd,
1 London Bridge Street, London, SE1 9GF

www.harpercollins.co.uk

HarperCollins*Publishers*
1st Floor, Watermarque Building,
Ringsend Road, Dublin 4, Ireland

The Marquess of Yew Park House © 2022 Victorine Brown-Cattelain

ISBN: 978-0-263-30158-8

02/22

To anyone who has ever felt trapped.

To Laura, for helping to inspire Galahad.

And always to my mother, Brigitte.

Chapter One

The Most Honourable Henry Walter Fortitude Edmund Spencer, Marquess of Clairborne, was many things. Impetuous was not one of them. Though his devil-may-care smile might suggest otherwise, the Marquess, Spencer to his friends, was considered the paragon of an English lord. Disciplined, dutiful, he never so much as twitched an eyebrow, without having thoroughly considered the move, in view of morality, Society, and the strict behavioural code imparted onto him since birth.

It was a wonder then, that on the morning of May the thirty-first, in the year of Our Lord 1830, he was travelling the final miles along a Scottish loch to his most remote estate, Yew Park House, having left London without a word of warning some three weeks prior. The most surprised by this precipitous departure and subsequent voyage, was undoubtedly Spencer, though admittedly, he hadn't truly realised how out of character the entire escapade was, until now.

Now, at the end of the road.

Slowing his mount to a quiet amble, Spencer drew in a deep breath, and tried to slow his heart, the sheer insanity, the recklessness of what he'd done crashing over him.

What were you thinking?

You weren't.

Yes, that was the problem, wasn't it. For the very first time, he hadn't thought about what he was doing; and the consequences. He'd needed to leave London, and so, he had. He had afforded himself the luxury of *feeling*; the supreme, untouchable luxury, of allowing emotions to rule his decisions.

The breathtaking landscape currently surrounding him magnified the utter stupidity of this conduct. Truly, there was no other word. Here, in the shadow of the mighty mountains, beside the forbidding waters of the loch, surrounded by the lines of sky-reaching trees, in the solitude of the shockingly sunny morning, he felt…exposed. As if the whistling wind, the calls of the birds, the snorts of his own horse seemed to cry out and denounce his foolhardiness.

I couldn't stay, he longed to scream back. *I couldn't stay there!*

He could almost hear the echo of those imaginary words bouncing back, taunting him.

I couldn't stay.

The hopelessness, the panic that had gripped him the night he'd left, hollowing out his chest like a mighty cavern, or rather perhaps only illuminating it for the empty thing it was, returned with a vengeance, and he bent over Simpheon's head, willing the reassuring scent of horse to fill him.

'Breathe,' he murmured, forcing his body to be lulled into comfort by Simpheon's gentle rocking. 'Just breathe.'

Three weeks he'd been on the road, mostly alone, having forced Josiah, his valet, to pack a trunk and follow with the brougham. Occasionally they'd met at stops along the way, first at Enfield, where, when asked, Spencer had simply said, *'We're going North'*. That was all the plan had been at first—*go North*.

Originally, Spencer had thought of visiting the new Thornhallow Hall, Reid, and Rebecca; the only friends he felt might understand his predicament when in truth he didn't even quite understand it himself, but then he'd remembered roundabout Lincoln that she would be nearing the end of her pregnancy, and he would not intrude on that. On *them*.

He'd got well foxed that night, and Josiah's eyes had nearly popped out when he'd caught sight of his habitually very restrained master literally fall-down drunk. No… That night had not been a good one. It had…stirred things. Things which were already stirring, hence the reckless voyage, but not things he needed to dwell on *just* then. He needed to keep moving, and so he had. Because Lincoln *had* also been good, reminding him of somewhere he'd forgotten long ago.

Yew Park House.

His Scottish estate. Where he'd not been in…

Twenty-nine years.

So long, it felt odd calling it *his*. It was his father's. No, not even truly that. Rather, Great-Uncle Jasper's. The smallest estate in the Marquessate, a remnant of Jasper's Scottish roots, it was there, looming at the edge of business always, but never really worth noting. There was only the house, occasionally let, and still inhabited and tended to when not by a small army of local servants. A cottage, almost always let, and two small farms. Numbers were good, well, as good as they could be; problems were dealt with quickly, and reports were succinct.

Yet, once, it had been a happy place. He'd remembered that in Lincoln. Before then, his mind had never allowed him to remember the wonder of it. A place where he'd felt part of a family. Where he'd felt love, and cherished, and *happy*. Things he hadn't felt since then if he was honest. Because he hadn't really *felt* since then.

Since I was a boy of five.

He'd grown up, become who he had to be, and lords like him did not feel.

And as for his family, well… After the last summer here, that is when everything had changed. When the cold had seeped in, and love had been replaced by formality and manners. Not even Mary's birth that year had prevented it. Before, he hadn't remembered the change, merely the icy cold, the loneliness…

Spencer shivered as he drew back from Simpheon's neck and sat properly, his gaze flicking over the surrounding ancient mountains, the great barrier they provided from the rest of the world strangely comforting.

This is why you've come. Peace, and to remember happier times.

Escape.

This was why Yew Park House was perfect. Perhaps he could find what he'd lost. Find some answers, clues as to how to find it all again.

Because he needed to find it again. He couldn't simply continue on, push through, ignore the feelings, and the unrest, and the void inside. That last night in London had told him that. He'd come here because he needed to settle himself. A marquess who had attacks of the nerves in the middle of ballrooms and felt utterly lost… Well, that marquess was no good to anyone. He couldn't be what he needed to be, for all those depending on him.

So he'd left. Naturally he'd made sure to leave his mother a note, otherwise she might've charged the King's Guard to find him, but he hadn't told her *where* he was going, only that he would be gone. For a time. The summer. Perhaps even autumn. She didn't need him. Hadn't, really, ever, save for him to fulfil his role.

And his sister, Mary, certainly hadn't needed him in a long time; if ever either. A bitter truth, one he was reluctant to admit, because he was meant to be her protector, her adviser. He was meant to be needed, to have some sort of say, to have some importance but she was so headstrong, so independent...

Really, they were a family in name only.

Strangers inhabiting the same spaces sometimes. And he hated it, he—

Breathe.

Leave the rest behind. Settle yourself so you can be what you need to be.

So you can...

So he could settle himself for the rest of his life.

The future he'd always known was coming had been there, *right there*, a fathomless pit beyond a precipice naught but a step away, and he'd...panicked. Seeing it, nearly being able to touch it... Had made him realise he wasn't ready. Which is why he'd come here. To think, to find equilibrium before he returned to his life.

Not that it feels like it.

But that was the price one paid for privilege. Duty, and sacrifice, were the price for power. He should know. That lesson had been drummed into him more than all the rest.

Live honourably. Take care of those who depend on you.

Marry well. Beget heirs.

Preserve the heritage for future generations.

Rolling his shoulders as if tossing off the weight of that mantle, Spencer took another steadying breath, and found his heart finally returned to its normal pace. He smiled slightly as the cool air, scented with hints of heather and pine, filled him like a drug.

Rest. Quiet. Peace. Escape.

Spurring Simpheon on, Spencer allowed his fears to be swept away by the wind. Ahead, he spotted the turn leading to Yew Park, and grinning, he pushed Simpheon into a gallop.

Escape.

If anywhere could be deemed an escape from the world he'd decided to quit for a time, Yew Park House was certainly it. Set back slightly from the loch's shore, hidden from the drive by yew and oak, the house was something from a dream. A fantastical, slightly feverish dream.

He'd forgotten how strange it was. Magnificent, grand, yes, but also strange...

That I had forgotten.

The glimpses of memories were like shards of a broken vase, and seeing it now as he and Simpheon slowed nearing it… He couldn't help but laugh. The house was utterly bizarre. Pieced together like those shards of imaginary ceramic; by someone who had no idea what a vase should look like.

Every style of the past two centuries was represented. The main *corps* was strong, square, stone; all that remained of the original medieval structure. From there, the house sprawled along the mound on which it stood, a section there in baronial style, a Palladian wing there, some gothic towers for good measure; a baroque wing and an Italian Renaissance-inspired orangery, disappearing around the back.

It didn't look like a house. It looked like some exuberant confection concocted by a duchess's chef with sugar, fruit, and towers of cake.

And before it all, in the midst of the drive, stood a gigantic five-tiered fountain that flowed noisily, a crowded collection of centaurs and gods frolicking in the glittering spray. Surrounding the house were thick copses of trees, veritable forests to him as a child, though they had those too, along the foot of the great mountains rising in the distance.

And gardens. Gardens of wonder, and just as eccentrically mixed as the house, to make everyone from the Italian masters to Capability Brown proud.

Yes, the perfect place to rest a while.

A thick bunch of fluffy clouds passed before

the sun overhead, and in a trice, that thrill was replaced with a shiver as a shadow forced the colourful house into a spectrum of greys. Something tugged at the back of Spencer's mind, something dark, and dangerous. Something long forgotten.

'Our secret, Henry...'

He tried to shake it off, but when a tinkling of childish laughter danced on the wind, ghostly, and chilling despite the joy of it, the prickling along his spine only worsened, and he actually shivered.

Just a spot of cold. Here, was a happy place.

Yet as he rode on to the door, as the grooms and staff poured out of the cavernous medieval doors to greet him, he couldn't help but doubt his own reassurances.

'Welcome back to Yew Park House, my lord,' the butler greeted in his deep Scots tones, softened nonetheless for his role, dropping into a low bow. Spencer dismounted, tossing the reins to the groom, and made his way to the older man, who was somewhere in his late sixties, with a grey mass of curls tied back with leather cord, thick, deep lines, and a proud bearing that seemed to be more Scottish than *butler*.

Spencer smiled; the blue gaze that met his own sparked memories of a bear of a man, who had spent many hours chasing him through corridors.

Though the man had aged, he'd lost none of his impressiveness, nor the twinkle in those eyes.

'McKenna.' Spencer nodded. 'And Mrs McKenna,' he added, turning his gaze to the severe-looking woman to the butler's left, the housekeeper. Nearly as advanced in age, she too remained the unflinching, daunting woman from his past, though there was a sadness about her he didn't recall. 'A pleasure to see you both again.'

'Ye remember us, then,' Mr McKenna said, his eyes widening in surprise. Mrs McKenna cleared her throat and threw him a look that suggested he not be so bold again. 'Apologies, my lord. Please, follow me. We have prepared the house as requested, though we weren't sure when to expect you. The messenger said soon—'

Again, Mrs McKenna cleared her throat as they arrived in the main hall. Spencer smiled to himself, not that he minded McKenna, in fact he quite appreciated the lack of restraint, so at odds with the staff anywhere else in his houses, but he would wait to tell the man when his wife, as stringent on etiquette as his mother, and himself most days, it seemed, was somewhere else.

'We can have a cold meal brought up immediately, my lord,' Mr McKenna continued, as Spencer gazed about the vaulting expanse above and before him, all dark wood, grey stone, gold-gilded hunting scenes and remains of the hunts, lit with braziers a man could get lost in. 'With coffee or wine… Or a hot meal ready in as long as it might take to refresh yourself. If that is your wish, of course.'

'Thank you, McKenna. I think I shall refresh myself, and then coffee and a cold platter on the terrace. We do have one of those?'

'Aye, my lord.' Mr McKenna grinned. 'Several.'

'I thought as much.'

'Jack here,' the butler continued, waving towards a footman loitering nearby, 'will show you to your rooms, and assist until your valet arrives.'

'Thank you, McKenna.'

'My lord.'

The butler bowed, and made for his wife, who stood in the shadowed corridor behind the stairs. She curtsied and turned away, but not before throwing Spencer a look that chilled his blood. It was filled with an odd mix of anger, resentment, and longing.

Just the light, old chap. Just a trick of the light.

On that note, he followed the footman upstairs, and put anything which might disturb his newly found peace, well behind him.

An hour later, Spencer was clean, redressed in one of his two sets of simple travelling attire—also refreshed and pressed—full to the brim with delectable cheese, coffee, and freshly baked bread, and entirely at a loss of what precisely to do.

Sat on the first of many terraces trickling down

from the house to the loch, he stared out onto the shimmering expanse of water, enjoying the contrast of the crisp breeze and glorious sunshine, and wondered what he was to do with himself.

There were plenty of things he *could* do. He could review accounts, inspect and tour the estate, even meet with the steward. He could do any number of things a smart landowner would do to ensure his property was well-ordered, particularly since he, and to his knowledge, his father, hadn't been here in three decades. He could do anything a lord like himself was to do in the country, like go for a hunt; though he couldn't actually think if it was the season for anything. He could go for one of those invigorating country walks people went on, or even go fishing. Or...

What else does one do in the country?

More accurately, what *he* was *supposed* to do in the country. There were dictates as to what someone like him *should* do, which normally he would abide by. But the whole point of this trip, *fit of utter madness*, was to escape his life, for a moment. To have peace, so that he could find balance; identify whatever it was causing him to feel, *un*settled, and empty.

So it followed that doing what he would normally wasn't the solution. He should instead do whatever he wanted, without concerning himself with what he *should* be doing. Only when one had never had that liberty, apparently one could find themselves at a loss.

Tilting his head up to the sun, closing his eyes and turning his focus inwards, he tried to think of what he would *really* like to do in that moment.

Last stretch of utter freedom. No Mother, no Mary, no Society, no—

No.

Thinking on all that... Was not useful.

I should write to Reid and inform him of my whereabouts so he can send news of the babe—

Damnit. Focus!

But the tinkling of a child's laughter caught his ear again, and Spencer sprung to his feet, his eyes searching the horizon for any clue as to the source.

Were there any children on the estate he didn't know about?

Farmers, and workers, surely, but not for miles, not so near the house.

Could one of the servants be harbouring a child here?

Surely not.

Still, he couldn't accept that he might be dreaming, or worse, *hallucinating*. He would not even consider that; nor the other option, that some ghostly child prowled the grounds.

Indeed not.

With newfound purpose, Spencer made for the next terrace, a Roman inspired mosaic creation, then vaulted over the hedge and banister surrounding it, landing neatly on the lawn. A smile threatening at his own prowess, he then strode towards the expanse of gardens to his left.

He began his search in the sprawling Renaissance gardens. The ankle-height mazes of tidy boxwoods were empty, and no one hid behind Venus or even Apollo. There was nothing in the rockery but the tinkling of a waterfall, and only birdsong in the *roseraie*. Spencer moved on quickly to the natural section, *à la* Brown, and had just rounded onto the path towards a collection of oaks and wildflowers, when he heard the laughter again.

Tilting his head, he tried to determine its direction, and heard something else.

'Elizabeth!'

A woman's voice. So I'm not mad!

And it was coming from—

The Temple of the Four Winds.

'I've got you now,' Spencer muttered, marching off towards one of the many follies littering the landscape, the thrill of the chase coursing through his veins like a drug.

He took a couple wrong turns, but finally arrived at the small clearing which housed a large Palladian temple, complete with Corinthian columns and gilded French doors. He was headed inside when a small creature vaulted out, and ran straight at him, giggling.

He was so taken aback, as was the little devil,

all bouncy brown curls and mussed cotton, that he simply let her run into him, and they both stood there, stunned, as the voice yet again called.

'Elizabeth!'

Slowly, he extricated himself from the miniature female, hands on her shoulders so she couldn't escape, and stared down at her, as she looked up with enormous green eyes. And there was an intense fear in those eyes, which made his heart do a funny little number in his chest, and he forced himself to smile.

After all, he *had* been enjoying the chase.

'So you are Elizabeth,' he said gently, removing his hands.

She was tall, coming to his chest, and he estimated her to be about ten or so, as lithe as a newborn colt. And he thought she might prove to be as skittish, until she quirked her head, studying him, then with all the grace in the world, curtsied.

'Henry Spencer.' He smiled, dropping into a formal bow. 'The Marquess of Clairborne. At your service, my lady.'

'Elizabeth! Oh—'

Spencer and his new friend turned in unison towards the voice.

Standing there was presumably Elizabeth's mother, considering she was staring at them with the same wide green eyes, though hers seemed darker, like forest moss, but perhaps that merely the light reflecting off her dark widow's weeds.

She was only slightly taller than her daughter, and more generously curved; not solely by womanhood, he noticed, when the latter slowly slipped away and positioned herself at her mother's back. He would almost call her *abundant*, in a pleasant way, as if she were altogether overflowing with vitality. A Grecian goddess escaped from statue form to life.

And the mother's hair is lighter, Spencer thought, studying the newcomer, not for any particular reason other than he always studied people, and he felt like he recognised her, and also he was generally curious, and certainly not because he felt a little stab of *interest*.

He put her age around Mary's, or perhaps slightly younger. The mass of unbound hair which reached just below her shoulders was like an autumnal rainbow. There was her daughter's chestnut in there, but also honeysuckle, and copper, even hints of silver and black. Her cheeks were rounder, and red at the moment, like little apples, though the two shared the same button nose, dark straight eyebrows, and adorably long ears.

And those lips...

He certainly couldn't think of examining Elizabeth in that fashion. Her mother, however, it was hard not to notice the generous lips, the wide mouth that he thought would produce a brilliant smile. Her entire being seemed to glow, and he wondered, what it might feel like to bask in that sort of light. To be the sole focus of it, to entangle oneself in it—

What the Devil has got into you?

Elizabeth whispered into her mother's ear, and an iron curtain seemed to be drawn up between the pair of them, and himself. He decided he did not like it.

Not one bit.

'My lord,' the woman said, in dulcet, cultured English tones, dropping into as elegant a curtsey as her daughter. *Interesting.* 'Our apologies. We did not know you were in residence. My daughter wished to explore your gardens.'

'And you grant her every wish, Mrs...?'

Spencer had meant it in jest.

He'd even said it with the smile that had won over more sour Society matrons than he could count. The ticking of the lady's jaw, flash of pure anger in her eyes, and stiffening of her back, told him he'd severely offended her.

'Madame de l'Omont,' she said coldly before he could redress the offence. 'Your neighbour, my lord.'

She gestured towards the southwest, and he understood.

'Ah,' he said as jovially, as welcoming, as he could. 'So you are the new tenant of Willowmere Cottage.'

'Yes, my lord. If you will excuse us, we will disturb you no longer.'

'You may visit the gardens whenever you wish, *madame*,' he said as they turned to leave. 'Any time, *mademoiselle*.'

The lady showed no sign of having heard, simply continued on, though the younger de l'Omont turned slightly and he might've sworn threw him a tiny whisper of a smile.

Though perhaps that too was a trick of the light, Spencer thought as he turned back towards his own house. As he walked back, he found himself hoping that they did return.

How interesting that might be.

Chapter Two

'I'm sorry, Maman,' Elizabeth whispered meekly, and Genevieve's heart twisted. Slowing the punishing pace she'd set whilst trying to escape that man, and glancing at her daughter, she saw the all too familiar dropped head, and stooped shoulders. With a look over her shoulder to ensure they were out of sight, and out of danger, Genevieve stopped. She tugged Elizabeth's hand gently, and her daughter turned to face her, though she did not lift her eyes.

How dare you look at me with that insolence in your eyes, girl!

Shaking off the vicious echoes, Genevieve tucked Elizabeth under the chin, and the girl finally met her eye. The fear and guilt mingling in the green depths so like her own were a knife to the gut, and Genevieve forced herself to smile.

You swore nevermore to see that in her.

'There is nothing to be sorry for, my love,' she

said lightly, though inside she was still rattled; rattled and rattling, and angry, and scared, and— *breathe*. 'Mrs McKenna told us we were welcome. We did not know His Lordship was in residence. Only now we do, we shall simply leave him to enjoy his gardens. We have plenty to enjoy at Willowmere, after all.'

'He said we could come back, perhaps when he isn't there…'

'That would not be wise,' she said sadly.

She hated having to deny Elizabeth the pleasure of those gardens, it had been a long time indeed since she'd seen her daughter so enthused, laughing so freely, but it was the truth.

Unwise is the least it would be.

The worst thing was that her daughter understood precisely *why* it was unwise.

That she'd been forced to rip away her innocence, and explain…

Everything.

'*Oui, Maman.*' Elizabeth nodded, her disappointment nowhere to be seen nor heard.

Another well learnt lesson. Damn him.

Four years they'd been free of her husband's clutches; two years since they'd left London, put the scandal and all the rest behind them, and still, some lessons refused to be unlearned.

Time. It takes time.

Yes. She only had to look at herself to know that. Not that she cared to at the moment.

Peace, and time from the world is why we're here.

'Let's back home, now,' Genevieve said with forced joviality, starting off again towards Willowmere. 'Juliana will be cross as it is, we are quite late for luncheon.'

'Oui, Maman.'

As they continued on towards the cottage, at a slower, more reasonable pace, Genevieve tried to calm herself.

It took a lot now, to shake her. To threaten her composure, her tranquil balance so utterly. Years of practice, first with her parents, then in Society, then with her husband, then with the scandal, had made her strong, and resistant to *unsettling*. But the damned marquess had managed it in less than two minutes. After everything she'd been through, encountering a lord on his own property should be the very *last* thing to unnerve her so profoundly, and yet.

Calm yourself. Or Jules will know something is amiss.

And a thorough questioning would not do. Especially when there was really nothing to be questioned about. She'd been surprised, that was all. Because no, she hadn't expected His Lordship to appear like some manner of woodland sprite because his man of business had assured her he *never* came to Yew Park.

'Not in twenty years, madam,' the old codger had sworn.

Well, apparently His Lordship has decided to remedy that slight. Just my luck.

But there was nothing for it now. He was here, as he had every right to be. Nothing to be frightened of. Nothing at all. She wouldn't ever see him again. Perhaps in passing, in Aitil, though she doubted it, when he had an army to provide whatever he wished at a moment's notice. Even *if* he did visit the town, they would only see each other from a distance. He would have no reason to engage with them. So the chances of him realising who precisely his new tenant was, were slim to none. It wasn't as if they'd been part of the same set in Town. She hadn't known him, and so he wouldn't know her. Even if he had seen—

No.

He wouldn't make the connection. Another reason she'd chosen his lands above others. She couldn't even remember seeing him across a ballroom in all the years spent in Society. Not that she'd been in very many after a time. *Regardless.* He would not know her, *that* was the point. And even if he did somehow discover her, from what little she knew of him, he was honourable. No scandals, apart from his friendship with the Disappeared Earl, or rather, William Reid, Earl of Thornhallow; but then his actions in standing by his friend had been honourable. Not only had he staunchly supported the Earl's marriage to a housekeeper, but he'd fiercely fought for the conviction of Viscount Rochesdale, a despicable wretch who had preyed on not only the newly minted Countess of Thornhallow, but dozens of women for nearly twenty years.

And that scandal did push your own out of the papers...

Nevertheless. Even *if* he discovered her, he was not the sort of man to banish them from his lands simply because of her past. He would not go shouting it on the rooftops for all of Scotland, England, Wales, and Ireland to hear. He would...simply not associate with her. Which they wouldn't be doing anyway, so, a moot point.

Stepping out of the woods that marked the edge of Yew Park grounds, seeing the old stone cottage, the loch, and the mountains rising before her, Genevieve felt a weight lift from her shoulders.

All will be well.

They had found peace here, and nothing had changed. Nothing would change.

All will be well.

Though the swarm of locusts that had taken residence in her belly contradicted her as they refused to cease their fluttering.

Better admit it, Genevieve thought wryly as they took the slower path along the water. *It isn't only fear of discovery that troubled you.*

No, galling as it was to admit, *the man* had troubled her.

It was preposterous that she'd even noticed

he was a man. She'd not thought that was possible, not since her girlhood had ended and she'd become a wife. There were no *men*. There were lords, and farmers, and chimneysweeps; solicitors, and fishermen, and coach-drivers, but they were not men. Not in *that* sense, which reminded her that she was a woman. Not a wife, not a mother, not a trophy, not the dirt beneath someone's shoe, not a doll, and not a—well. She'd never been a woman before. *Only* a woman. She'd skipped that step somewhere along the bumpy road of life, and never really given it much thought.

Until now.

Damnation, and dashed inconvenient really.

Odd, too.

Admittedly, the Marquess was handsome. Once she'd recovered from the fear of seeing Elizabeth with a strange man; once she'd realised who he was and that he meant neither of them harm; once the initial panic had subsided, her mind, much against her own volition, had noticed the fact that he was undeniably attractive.

Tall, long-limbed and lithe, but with enough of everything to nicely fill in those plain, but perfectly fitted, *so perfectly they seemed sewn on*, clothes. She hadn't *wanted* to notice any of that. Nor the head of artfully dishevelled luminous blonde locks, and strangely delicate face, with a neatly pointed chin, complete with a dimple of a cleft. Not the sharp, high cheekbones, Greek nose, straight brows, and certainly not the deep set, powder blue eyes as cold as the loch in winter, and yet discomfitingly inviting. They drew you in, just like the bloody loch, and she would drown in them about as easily as in the water itself.

Which is why she truly shouldn't be noticing any of anything that made up his person. Only she had, and it was odd, because she'd never felt… interested. At least not that *immediately*, that viscerally, as if she not only saw him, but *felt* him, calling out to her. Once upon a time, she'd felt stirrings of desire, *yes, deny it all you like, but that is the word, Genevieve*, but those had been the first flittings of youth. When any handsome face made your heart flutter and your cheeks heat, and you felt giddy with possibility. And once upon a time, yes, she had felt *something* for her husband, but it hadn't been so very…

Primal.

Impossible.

Yes. That's what it all truly was. Impossible. No matter what she felt, or saw, or thought. Because even if she were ever to allow herself to discover her own womanhood, even if she were ever going to trust herself with another man, well, it would certainly never be him. The Marquess of Clairborne was one thing she would not only deny herself; he was one thing she wouldn't even allow herself to want.

Quite right.

* * *

'Apologies for our tardiness,' Genevieve said as she and Elizabeth entered the warm, safe confines of Willowmere's kitchen, which smelled delectable thanks to Juliana, as always. Jules, her dearest, *only*, friend and companion; her rock, who was currently sitting at the kitchen table, mending a sheet. As Genevieve hung her and Elizabeth's things, and the latter washed up for luncheon, she glanced down to find a basketful of bed linens, and scraps of cloth. 'Didn't we hang those this morning? Dare I ask?'

'That demon found a way out of his pen again,' Jules said, blowing a stray curl of raven hair out of her face as she leaned over to cut a thread with her teeth. 'Proceeded to find a way to bring down the washing, and devour it.'

'Demon is certainly not a euphemism,' Genevieve laughed, tidying up the scraps of linen as Jules folded her work and set it in the basket. 'I swear that beast has the powers of Lucifer.'

'Galahad is a sweetheart,' Elizabeth protested. 'You simply don't understand him.'

'I'm sure Hades said similar things of Cerberus,' Jules muttered as she rose and stashed away the basket.

'He was likely bored,' Elizabeth continued, undaunted. 'You know he hates being cooped up in that tiny pen.'

'That tiny pen takes up half of what land we

have left,' Genevieve pointed out, as Elizabeth took the delectable smelling fish pie from the stove and set it on the table. 'And you were not being so defensive of your sweet knight yesterday when he availed himself of the trim on your dress.'

'He was only hungry, and left it alone when I gave him milk.'

'You're spoiling him,' Genevieve admonished as the three of them sat, and Jules served them all healthy portions of her creation. 'It is no wonder then that he escapes to devour the linens if he believes there is milk in it for him.'

Jules raised a brow and gave Genevieve a look which perfectly communicated her thoughts on Genevieve accusing Elizabeth of *spoiling* people, or in this instance, a goat.

Not the same, Genevieve told her silently.

'So, did you get lost in those gardens then?' Jules asked.

Elizabeth looked to Genevieve, and though she might've liked to avoid the discussion, Genevieve knew there was keeping secrets. Not from Jules. Not ever.

Not as if there is anything noteworthy anyway.

Genevieve nodded, and allowed Elizabeth to recount their…

Adventure.

'We met His Lordship in the gardens,' Elizabeth said.

'The Marquess? But I didn't think he would be

in residence. Ever,' Jules said with a frown, glancing at Genevieve.

It really was annoying when a friend knew you so well. Knew you'd be scared because a lord dared return to his own castle.

'Yes, well, he is,' she replied smoothly, turning her attention back to her delicious fish pie. 'Which means no more expeditions onto Yew Park grounds. We'll need to be even more mindful of Galahad.'

'Ginny—'

'It's nothing.' She smiled, utterly unconvincingly she knew, but it was an attempt. 'Absolutely no need for alarm.'

Juliana looked as though she wished to say more, but she didn't push. They all returned to their meals in silence for a while, and Genevieve thought she'd escaped.

'So…what's he like?'

Damnit, Jules.

'Much like the rest of them.'

Liar.

'Indeed. He was the one involved with that business last year, Thornhallow, and Rochesdale, wasn't he?'

'You know very well that he was, Jules.'

'Hm.'

'If you have something to say, please do,' Genevieve said, rather harsher than she intended.

'Merely being curious, Ginny. I hadn't realised

the newly arrived Marquess was such a delicate subject.'

Genevieve glared at her friend for a long moment, before offering Elizabeth a reassuring smile, and then turning back to her food, for which she no longer had any appetite.

Delicate subject indeed.

'May I be excused?' Elizabeth asked a short while later.

Nodding, Genevieve ceased pushing her pie about, and put it back into the pot instead. Elizabeth rose, cleared her plate and the others, and once she had disappeared, Genevieve rose and went to the window.

'You're worried about him,' Jules said, slipping her arm around Genevieve's waist as she came to stand behind her. 'Why?'

'I don't know. I have this…strange feeling. That this will change everything. Ruin all we've built.'

'How? We shall have nothing to do with him. He'll never know.'

'You're right. I know that,' Genevieve sighed.

If only it *felt* like that.

Not like somehow everything *was* about to change, like it or not.

'Whatever happens,' Jules said soothingly, as she pulled away to begin the washing up, dropping a kiss on the top of Genevieve's head, something which always reassured her even if it was aggravating how easy it was for her Amazonian friend to do so. 'We'll face it together, as always.'

'I know.'

And she did.

No matter what, she would always have Juliana. Compared to all they'd faced in the past, this was nothing. Together, they were formidable. What was one marquess against two women who had scraped and clawed their way back from darkness and oblivion?

Absolutely nothing of note.

Chapter Three

A week since his arrival, and Spencer was, for lack of a better expression, having fun. Much like *impetuous*, fun was a rather foreign notion. And it was, admittedly, just as thrilling, *panic-inducing*, as impetuous. In fact, he thought as he wandered the walled apothecary gardens, enjoying a welcome ray of sunshine, letting your emotions and wants drive you was rather more work than he'd have ever thought.

But it is worth the fear—the panic.

It would be. It was, already.

In fact, it was the only way to solve the problem he'd discovered plagued him.

The morning after his arrival, and subsequent meeting with the intriguing neighbours, he'd awoken feeling rather excited about the day, and all it had to offer, and that feeling had lingered until he'd washed, dressed, and broken his fast.

Habitually, he would read his correspondence,

then the papers. He would plan his day, and speak to his mother, and Mary about anything they needed. Typically, those conversations would arrive at the same point, *'You need to marry, Henry'*, then he would go to his study, and deal with whatever business was on the agenda that day.

Ever since it had become clear that Mary was irrefutably, *on the shelf,* though not for lack of trying nor advantages; his mother's attempts to marry *him* had increased a hundredfold. He'd always been jealous of his sister for that; Mother had simply stopped badgering her after a time. He, on the other hand…

Got it worse with every passing day.

Regardless. Today, there was no pestering mother, no Mary, no correspondence, and no papers. He'd felt the solitude as he'd broken his fast, which was odd, considering most of the time he felt alone regardless. The rain as it pelted on the windows had been the only sound, and he'd realised, he was again at a loss of what to do. So he'd settled himself in the study with coffee, as he normally would, and examined his problem as he would any other.

With logic, and reason.

Problem: I am not myself. I fear the future that was always certain, and feel restless; an emptiness inside.

Solution: leave London, find tranquillity.
Remember happy times, and who you are.

New problem: Tranquillity cannot be found.
Emptiness cannot be filled as... I do not
know how to make myself happy. I do not
know what I want.

As he'd written those words, a realisation had
struck him, like some great bolt of lightning from
the Heavens.

I do not know what I want, for I do not know
who I am anymore.

It had stolen his breath, that thought, knocked
him as senseless as a man's fist might.

I do not know who I am.

He felt empty, because he *was* empty. A shell,
a construct of his upbringing and his position.
He was Henry Walter Fortitude Edmund Spencer, the Marquess of Clairborne, but *who* was
that? So many years he'd spent creating a face
for the world, becoming what he'd been born to,
that he'd lost a sense of who he was in his heart.
He'd learned the lesson of doing away with emotions so well that he didn't truly know *how* to feel
anymore.

There were some things he did know.

That despite the distance between them, he
loved his family as much as a man could. That he
had a sense of duty; that he had friends, and was

loyal to them. But as for himself, what he liked, and wanted, he didn't know. Because it had never factored before.

It seems to factor now.

Yes, it did. Because he didn't want to be an empty shell. He didn't want to just pass through life without purpose, or rather, with only the purpose he was supposed to have. To be the best man, the best marquess he could be, he had to be… *someone.*

This was why he'd balked when the future had presented itself in the shape of a most suitable potential bride. Because to offer another a life, one which he'd always promised would not be cold, and unfeeling, and devoid of colour, as that of his parents had been, he had to have something to offer, other than money and a title. He wanted a wife who would desire more from him than that.

And so, he had determined something else.

Solution: to find yourself, you must find what you want and like. Therefore, you must try everything you haven't before.

Spencer had consequently set about doing just that.

If there ever was a place for it, it was here.

For inspiration, he'd begun with a tour of the house; just as eclectic inside as out. There were rooms of ancient weaponry, parlours with stuffed trophies, and exotic rooms full of baubles taken from the furthest corners of the globe. There was a bathing room plucked from Arabia and a room of *cabinets de curiosités* that would enchant anyone of a scientific *penchant*. For those of that inclination there was also a laboratory, filled with more specimens and grimoires. There were so many portraits, paintings, and books, one could live a lifetime and not sample each of them. There was the enormous orangery and two conservatories of exotic blooms, fruits, and other things he wasn't really sure how to catalogue.

And after the day of exploration, he'd settled himself in the library with a tray of sweet treats and read a romance, something he'd never done before, lounging on the rug before the fire like a child. He'd awoken the next morning, on that very same rug, and decided he wanted *more*. Of everything.

Much as a proper landlord might, he'd visited his tenant farmers, only, much *unlike* a proper lord, he'd insisted on helping with the work. He had helped de-horn calves, irrigated potatoes, and tried his hand at haymaking. At first, the farmers had looked at him as though he were mad, and perhaps he was, but he'd felt…*good*. The respect in their eyes at the end of the day, had felt good. He couldn't really say that he now had a particular desire to be a farmer, but he knew he didn't particularly *like* certain aspects, and that was something. And he knew how good it felt to lay your head on the pillow after a day of physical labour, and he understood better the fears, travails, and demands of those who worked the land. Which he'd always *known*, but never understood.

After that, it was the servants who began to think him mad. He'd found a book of botany in the library, and set about following the gardeners, helping them, and asking them myriads of questions.

Josiah had arrived on the fourth day along with the rain, and his man had related the rest of his tumultuous journey—obviously a raise was in order—and supplied a few of the London, and northern papers. Spencer didn't even glance at them, knowing he would find the same as always: news of business ventures, elopements, and various other assorted glittering Society happenings.

Instead, he took to following the servants in the house. He'd helped the scullery maids, much to their distress, before turning his attentions to those doing the laundry, and learned how precisely one washed and pressed, and prepared, well, everything. They'd been troubled as well, but amiable and encouraging, returning to their idle chatter as he scrubbed linens against a board. Josiah had found him not long after, and so Spencer had latched onto the man; forced him much against his will to show him through the duties of his day. Again, he found that he had no particular keenness for stain-removal, or scuttle bucket emptying, but he did find that he appreciated it all more. That evening, he'd allowed himself some old pleasures, trouncing Josiah at billiards before being trounced at darts.

Days five and six were full to the brim of adventures. He found a volume on entomology, along with some old cases of beetles and butterflies, and wandered the garden in search of more; not to capture and pin, simply to appreciate. He found he quite liked knowing the names of various insects, and the thrill of discovering one thriving on his lands. After that, he'd gone for a very refreshing swim in the loch.

He'd spent hours at the pianoforte, something he'd never been allowed to learn, though Mary had shared her lessons with him sometimes; on the rare occasions they were granted time together. He was dreadful at it, but he enjoyed himself, singing along loudly to his own off-kilter tunes.

He'd also tried needlepoint and watercolours—the latter another of Mary's accomplishments—and though he himself had no natural talent nor clue of what he was doing, he found the passing of the brush on paper soothing, and satisfying. He ended up with a very unclear picture of the loch, and a tangle of threads best left unmentioned, but he felt an odd happiness at having *created*.

With every new activity, his hunger for experiences, for *life*, grew. He'd never had passion for anything before, horse-riding perhaps came the closest to that description; and now he was finding he could have passion for life. He tried foraging with the groundskeeper, and all aspects of tending horses with the grooms. He read every type of book he'd never thought of before, simply for pleasure.

Spencer knew he should feel guilty. Guilty because he was being irresponsible. Neglecting his other affairs, though he knew very well that his men of business, solicitors, even Mother and Mary, were more than capable of handling it all for a short time. He should feel guilty because yes, he'd left so abruptly. Abandoned his mother and sister in the midst of a duke's ball. But the more he discovered, about the world so near that he'd never quite seen, and about himself, the more he knew that he was on the right path.

Could a man properly lead, guide, and counsel others if he knew nothing beyond the miniscule world he dwelled in? Yes, there were rules, edicts, laws, and morals which kept society from chaos. But without experience, how could one have wisdom?

That night in London, Mother had arranged a meeting with a duke's daughter. Lady Laetitia. It was understood that if all parties found each other suitable, if arrangements could be made, there would be wedding bells in Spencer and Laetitia's future. But standing there beneath the glittering, dripping candelabra, staring at Laetitia, her parents, and his own mother across the marble, he'd literally panicked. Been unable to breathe, to think. He'd seen his future clearly; he and Laetitia, married, their perfect children decorating their perfect house, and it had been the nightmare he'd sworn never to accept. He'd been terrified of who he might be if he took that step, and continued on precisely as before.

There had never been a question that he would marry, and beget heirs, and that though he would have a say in his choice of bride, certain criteria would be essential. Love, would never factor. And he'd accepted that, been grateful for all the rest life offered him. But he'd always resolved, that if he could not have love, he would have partnership. Though he'd not remembered the happy days of his childhood here, subconsciously, he'd yearned to find some measure of the happiness he'd known once; to build a family such as that he'd known. He'd promised himself a match of warmth, and mutual need, respect, even desire. Only, he couldn't have that, he realised, if he had none of that to offer himself.

That was why he'd panicked. Deep down, he'd known he was…

Lacking.

He'd felt it for some time, the imbalance. At first he'd thought it *ennui*, but then Reid had returned after ten years of absence and Spencer had been forced to face…

An upending of the status-quo.

Possibilities.

The man had had the damned nerve of falling in love with his housekeeper to boot, and *that* had tickled some dark, hidden part of Spencer. Awoken some desire long buried to have what his friend had. A *loving* wife. A life not dictated by Society's rules and regulations. The ability to choose his destiny, and forge his own path.

But Reid was always that way.

Yes. And Spencer…wasn't. And it was one thing for Reid, who had no one but himself to think of, no sister, no mother—*may they rest in peace*—to do as he pleased, and say *Hang Society*, and another altogether for Spencer to. As it was, it had taken all the power Spencer and his mother wielded to keep Reid's scandal under control. To keep the worst at bay, and to get that swine Rochesdale convicted. However, that power came at a price.

Respectability. Honour. Stalwartness. Sacrifice.

And really, he could dream all he wanted, it wasn't as if he were in love, pining for a beautiful girl. There was no one he would even begin to think of in terms of *I'd do anything for her even destroy my life and that of those in it.* So he could want the kind of love Reid had, but in truth, even if he ever found it, he doubted he would be able to show the same courage to forsake all else.

Still. I can have...

Companionship.

But only if I have enough of myself to offer another.

Because though Lady Laetitia might be a lost prospect, his departure irrevocably destroying that possibility, a duke's daughter never lasting long on the Marriage Mart; there would be another.

There must be. And you...

Must be whole.

Hence, this escapade.

So...

What will it be today?

Spencer knew what he *really* wanted. Or rather, who he really wanted to spend time *with*. Only his captivating neighbour and her daughter hadn't returned. He'd been walking the gardens regularly, when the weather meant they might visit, but he'd seen nor heard no trace of them. He had a feeling they wouldn't return. She was...wary of him. Which he could understand, only, he wasn't used to it. And he found, he certainly didn't like *her* nor little Lizzie being wary of him. Because...

I like them.

Their meeting had been brief, but he'd felt...a connection to them. Inexplicably. Something he'd never felt before, not with anyone, that instantaneous understanding that went beyond knowledge of a person, and became a sort of recognition.

Hogwash.

Likely. But then why couldn't he keep them from his thoughts? His attraction for Madame de l'Omont, which he couldn't deny, odd in itself considering it usually took him knowing a woman for more than five minutes to develop such…ardent feelings, was not all that kept them lurking in his mind. It wasn't just his physical interest in *her*, but the desire to be part of whatever they were. To capture their vibrancy, their joy, and take some for himself, *selfish bastard that you are.* There was also some mystery about them, something that didn't quite fit, and for someone like Spencer who usually knew within an instant who someone was, a mystery was always tantalising.

He'd asked McKenna about them, but he'd only shared that the de l'Omonts, and a companion had moved in two autumns ago, and were a pleasant bunch. Spencer could've learned as much from his own records. *Mrs* McKenna had, after he'd told of his encounter with them, confessed she'd been the one to invite them to enjoy the grounds. That disquieting look had been in her eyes again, though it had only been a flicker before she'd taken herself off into the shadows, as seemed to be her habit. There was something…disquieting generally about the housekeeper now. His memories might be very vague, but still she seemed so altered…

And now you're wondering about your house-keeper and being utterly fantastical.

Only it wasn't just her. That shadow, that chill he'd felt when he first arrived… It seemed to permeate his dreams, creeping into the otherwise pleasant, unremarkable things, conjuring images, feelings, that seemed almost memory. And then the images would fade, and all he could recall was…

Dread, and fear, and loss.

Manifestations of your other troubles.

Yes, that's all there was to it. His mind was finding ways to cope with the impending sense of doom as he hurtled ever onwards towards his future, and his concerns for his family, his estates, even Reid and Rebecca and their unborn child.

So more distractions are in order, Spencer thought as he decided to perhaps go for a ride or see how Josiah fared at chess.

Only, just as he stepped out of the old stone walls, he heard a quiet murmuring that gave him hope.

My prayers have been answered.

'I hadn't thought you would accept the invitation to return,' said the smooth voice Genevieve had prayed she wouldn't hear. *Not ever again.* She and Elizabeth both turned from the statue of Per-

seus they'd been admiring, to find the Marquess
who had invaded far too many of her waking,
and sleeping, thoughts, smiling an undoubtedly
charming smile, complete with dimples. She mentally chastised herself for noticing how well he
looked in his much more fashionable, and colourful clothes today.

*He looks every inch the lord he is, lest you
forget it.*

Though she couldn't remember admiring someone before for sporting a lilac waistcoat and forest
green coat, but then, she couldn't remember ever
seeing anyone wear such a combination and still
look so incontestably handsome.

But he is a lord, and dangerous, never forget it.

Even if that smile seemed less practised today.
Less *charming*, and more *charmed*.

Even more dangerous.

Really, they shouldn't have come. She'd had
every intention of remaining true to her own decree, and never coming back. Only, they'd been
cooped up with the rain, and she'd had to neglect
Elizabeth whilst she finished some lace orders,
and she'd seen those longing looks her daughter
had cast in the direction of Yew Park when she
thought no one was looking.

Denying Elizabeth was not something she could
do. The Marquess had been quite right; though it
was not simply the over-indulgence of a mother.

So she'd relented, and surprised Elizabeth

with another visit here, but she'd hoped against all hope they would remain unnoticed, and that she wouldn't be faced with the man currently bowing to her and her daughter.

Marquess, not man, she reminded herself, dropping into a curtsey.

'My lord. We have disturbed you again.'

And will leave immediately, she was about to add, but the Marquess spoke before she could finish; with enough haste that she knew *he* knew very well what she was about to say.

'Not at all,' he said with a seriousness that was rather more troubling than feigned excitement or politeness would've been. 'I'm glad to see you.'

Frowning despite her usual ability to conceal whatever she felt, Genevieve took a moment longer than she should have to move past that remark.

Don't look in his eyes. They are ensnaring.

And confusing. His genuine words were confusing her, and flustering her, because she knew men like this, *charming, debonair, shallow*, and she'd reassured herself with that the past week, yet now, up close, he didn't seem like all those smooth veneered lords. The ones who toyed with words, and knew just how to manipulate those around them, how to make them feel less, *nothing*—

Elizabeth shifted beside her, bringing her sharply back to the moment, and reminding her that she hadn't said anything in far too long.

'Elizabeth believes your grounds as magic as

Brocéliande,' she admitted, hoping her daughter
would forgive the revelation. Only, she had no desire to lie. *Not to him, though you lie with every
breath.* 'I did not have it in me to deny her discovering its wonders.'

'We are quite devoid of great sorcerers, though
it is said we have Fair-Folk. And there is a most
enchanting grotto,' the Marquess added with what
could only be described as a very cheeky smile,
and when Genevieve turned to Elizabeth, she realised her daughter's eyes were full of a light she
hadn't seen in, well, a very long time; if ever. It
was a light of youthful excitement, and the shadows of concern and fear were swept away. The
Marquess caught it too; she noticed his own smile
broaden. 'Shall I show you?'

'You need not trouble yourself, my lord.'

She could feel Elizabeth's disappointment, but
then, she couldn't just say, *yes, please, do show
us about your gardens, my lord.*

Because…

Because.

'It is no trouble, I assure you, *madame,*' the
Marquess said, with that same serious tone that
really made everything worse. 'In fact, it would
be an absolute pleasure.'

I believe you.

So, despite her better judgement, despite all
that could be utterly ruined, *my life, Elizabeth's,
Jules's,* Genevieve nodded.

She felt that moment in her bones. As if she had just signed some great pact with the angels above, or perhaps the devils below. As if, she had just veered off the path she'd been on her entire life.

Which was absolute and utter nonsense.

Still, that was how it felt.

The Marquess looked as if he wished to offer his arm, but, sensing her general reluctance, simply gestured towards the path leading north, and together they fell into step as they made for this grotto of his.

We'll simply go see this grotto, then be on our way.

It is neighbourly. To refuse too adamantly would rouse suspicion.

Liar.

Through the gardens they went, past the house, all the way to the other side of the grounds. Genevieve was even more reluctant, but for Elizabeth's sake, she said nothing as they continued, heading into fashionably wilder areas. The trees were more closely arranged, and if Elizabeth had thought the other side Brocéliande, well, Genevieve wondered what she thought of these darker, mysterious forests.

Veering onto a smaller path, the Marquess led them to a rivulet running down from the mountains, and that too they followed for a while, the tinkling of water over stones, the thickening of the air, transporting them into a different world altogether. Finally, they reached a tiny pool, and at its end, tucked into a man-made mound, was a little gated entrance.

They tread carefully along the narrow path, Elizabeth safely tucked between the Marquess and Genevieve. With a resounding creak, the Marquess opened the gate, and bowed for Elizabeth to step inside.

'Won't it be dark,' she asked tentatively, and the Marquess smiled reassuringly.

'Do you trust me?'

Genevieve was about to protest, say something, anything which would put the damned marquess back in his place—*she trusts no one, and neither do I, we are leaving*—when her daughter nodded, and she swallowed the lump that formed in her throat.

'Then step inside Lady Lizzie,' he said gently.

Her daughter did as bid, carefully, but with none of her usual reticence.

The Marquess waited for Genevieve to precede him, and as she passed, he offered her a nod of acknowledgement that seemed to say, *she can trust me, and so can you*.

The fact that Genevieve believed it, without knowing anything of him, whilst heading into a dark cavern at the edge of his property, was entirely disconcerting and yet, soothing. Her mind said she was mad to trust any man, least of all a *lord*, ever again, but her instinct told her she could. It was incomprehensible, and she was so lost in thought that had Elizabeth not gasped, she might not have even noticed the incredible surroundings, only the damp cold that seeped from the earth surrounding them.

The short passageway opened onto a circular room, as large as the mound itself, adorned with shells. Hundreds of thousands of them, all arranged in neat patterns, some geometric, some depicting scenes from folklore. She could see them all perfectly, for the room was lit by holes in the ceiling, rather like skylights, around which had been arranged mirrors and pearlised shells that reflected the light down below.

She and Elizabeth both stood there, stunned, taking it all in, and she noticed there were more passageways leading presumably to other chambers.

'I'd heard of such places,' Genevieve admitted breathlessly—*breathlessly? Honestly*—as the Marquess came to stand beside her. 'But never seen one.'

'Great-Uncle Jasper oversaw the landscaping of these parts,' the Marquess said with a smile in his voice. Though Genevieve would be damned if she turned to witness it. *Literally.* 'He refused to undo all that was done in ages past, but was also a great follower of new trends. The grotto I'm told was one of his pet projects. His lady-love was fond of one she'd visited in Kent, so...'

Genevieve felt the Marquess's gaze, and this time she could not help but glance at him.

There was that cheeky grin again, though it seemed to mask the look of hesitancy in his eyes. The look that asked: *will you judge him?* Since she was the last person to cast stones, she merely raised an eyebrow, challenging him to finish, and trust *her*.

Playing with fire...

'He was hopelessly in love with another man's wife, truth be told. Died in a duel for her heart.'

The flooding of emotion that took hold of her then was entirely unexpected, and Genevieve had to clench her jaw hard to avoid betraying any of it. She wasn't sure what it was, the tragedy of it, the romanticism, the mere idea of love, or the impossibility of it; maybe it was the emotion in the Marquess's own voice, a sort of wistful longing, or admiration. Whatever it was, was unwelcome.

Luckily the Marquess misinterpreted her reaction, though there was disappointment along with casual amusement in his tone as he continued.

Better he think you judged, than to know what a simpering mess you are.

For no justifiable reason.

'Yes... He was one of the black sheep of the family, the reason I am now lord of the manor so to speak. Jasper died without heirs, and so my father became marquess,' he added conspiratorially.

'We've had a few, black sheep,' the Marquess continued, thankfully leaving her side to wander the room. 'And we latest Spencers have been bearing the brunt of those lesser ones. Duty, the family name, that is all that matters,' he added, almost bitterly. 'Though the greatest dishonour belongs to my ancestor, who had the temerity of being a tradesman before Charles II elevated him and restored the title lost before the war.'

The Marquess seemed to remember himself, and laughed, shaking his head as he turned back to her, what she now recognised as the veneer of charming complacency now back in place.

Though how she knew the difference, she dared not even question.

'I bore you, *madame*, with my tales. I apologise.'

'You do not, my lord,' Genevieve said, though why she felt the need to invite, or encourage such intimate talk, for banal though it may seem, it *felt* intimate; again, was a question she dared not ask.

Just as was the question of why she was standing there, staring into the Marquess's now warming eyes, smiling like some beatific innocent. She was saved from having to answer any when Elizabeth's voice brought them sharply back to the room.

'*Maman*, look! A dragon!'

Elizabeth emerged from one of the passageways ahead, grabbed her hand, and dragged her to the next chamber, smaller, but just as impressive and intricate.

Genevieve felt the Marquess at her back, a wave of oddly enveloping warmth she wished would never leave, as he looked over her shoulder, or head perhaps, as he was more than able to, at the dragon Elizabeth had indeed found, cowering at the bottom of a wall, beneath a very knightly-looking St George.

'Ah… You have found George. I rather confused George and the dragon as a boy,' the Marquess said softly, nostalgia tingeing his voice now. Genevieve turned ever so slightly, and watched his own eyes dance with as much pleasure as her daughter's over the rough edges of the mural. 'Would you care to see the ice-house,' he said after a long moment, moving back abruptly, a shadow flitting across his face, as if whatever memories he'd conjured weren't so pleasant and idyllic after all. 'It is in the style of an Egyptian pyramid.'

Elizabeth gave her a hopeful, and pleading look, which Genevieve wouldn't have been able to deny in a thousand years.

'Very well.' She smiled. 'To the ice-house, my lord.'

With a bow, the Marquess led them back out of the grotto, and though she knew this was a very, infinitely, incontestably bad idea, Genevieve couldn't help but feel strangely at ease. More so, than she had in a long while.

One afternoon. One tiny moment in time will not endanger the future.

As long as you mind yourself.

As he led the intriguing Madame de l'Omont and her daughter back through the west gardens, Spencer found that he could not stop smiling. A little smile, the kind that lingered on one's lips, because one was content. He was used to smiling; it was a weapon, a piece of the mask he always wore, but only rarely was it genuine, and even rarer than that, was one such as this, that felt unstoppable.

Spencer was not so fool as to deny that he was enjoying his time in their company. Hence why he'd suggested a visit to the ice-house, and once they'd found it, this escapade to the stone circle— another folly, not built by the ancients.

Why he was leading them at a slow amble, not only so they could take in the sights, but because he wanted to prolong their time together as much as possible. He found that he wanted to give them every reason to return. Every reason to trust him enough to return. And trust, he knew, was something these two did not do lightly.

Which is probably why he'd felt a queer little flutter when Lizzie had given him hers, if only for a moment.

Now for your mother. I wonder what your name is, my most mysterious madame...

One of many things he wondered.

Perhaps it was only because she and her daughter were offering him another new experience. Rarely did he spend time in the company of children; and widows, well, only slightly more often, and never in such a relaxed, free setting.

Habitually, he cared to know about others only what would give him clues as to how they might behave; or even how they might serve. In this case, he found he simply *wanted* to know. Wanted to know who this woman was, who could loosen his own tongue so easily, without any prompting whatsoever, other than the invitation that seemed to linger in her eyes, to confide in her. That she was a sort of safe harbour where one could come with all their troubles, to lie down and rest. Truly rest.

Well, there is really only one way to get to know someone...

'McKenna tells me you've been here some time now,' he began, thinking that was a good way to begin indeed. Lizzie was a little ahead, and her mother seemed slightly more relaxed now, almost as if she were enjoying herself, and not about to take flight at the earliest opportunity. 'How do you find it? Was it France you came from? I detect no accent, and yet, your name, and Lizzie calls you *maman*...'

'It is wonderful,' she said, a wistful smile on her own face as she took a deep breath, and took in all that surrounded them. 'Peaceful. Elizabeth enjoys the freedom, and wildness.'

He noted she called her daughter by her full name, though he heard no reproof of his own abrupt and oddly instinctive shortening, and indeed, the girl herself seemed to take no umbrage.

And I note you do not answer my questions, madame.

'There was not much countryside where you are from?'

'Plenty, my lord. But we were not to enjoy it.'

Pain flitted across her face for the briefest instant before surprise replaced it, and she turned to look up at him, those wide green eyes telling him she hadn't intended to say all she had; just as he hadn't earlier.

'She is a quiet girl,' Spencer said, nodding towards Lizzie. 'There is a fear in her eyes… And yours. Your husband was not a kind man.'

Madame de l'Omont stopped, and so did he, turning to face her. He could see surprise, outrage, and trepidation in her now, though she held her ground, with all the ramrod straightness and pride of the most English matron.

'You are very direct, my lord.'

Never. Until today.

He always abided by the rules of politeness. He always said something in the most diplomatic way, spoke without speaking, as everyone in his world always did. But today, here, with her, he found he didn't want to be anything *but* direct. He wanted to cut to the heart of the matter, not dance around with pretty words, and learn nothing of import.

Callous, and tactless, perhaps, but it was also...

The wisest course of action. For I have little time, I think, to know you.

'Not habitually. Forgive me,' he said, though he meant only to apologise for causing her alarm or hurt. 'You came to begin again, and I shan't pry, if you wish to forget. But you may speak freely. Should you care to. It will go no further.'

'I barely know you.'

'Yes. I suppose that is true,' he conceded. *Though that is not how it feels, extraordinary as that may be.* There was an ease beneath the unease; an ease between them that spoke of old friendship. Still, it would not do to spout such poetic nonsense, indeed he couldn't quite believe his own mind had conjured such thoughts. 'Yet strangers are sometimes the easiest to share burdens with.' Madame de l'Omont eyed him for a moment, before finally nodding. They began walking again, Lizzie smiling at them as she waited a little ahead. 'May I ask, at least, why here?'

'It was as far as I could go,' she admitted with a small wry smile.

That tiny gesture told him the thaw had begun.

He felt more pleased than by rights he should; not pleased with himself as he had been so many times before, for breaking down barriers, conquering the toughest opponents, but pleased, because it was as if a door had opened a crack. He could almost see it, there in the gloomy darkness, shafts of light pouring out from the infinitesimal breach. He'd never cared so much to see what lay beyond a door, but now, it was all he could think of.

Opening doors and old friendships, truly old man, you're losing your grip.

Really, he was just curious. She was a novelty, a *divertissement*, something delightful to experience. Granting her any more importance was not only foolish, it was bewildering.

And beguiling.

'And what do you do with your time then, *madame*?' he began, clearing his throat and mentally shaking himself. 'When you are not indulging in trespassing that is?'

'My companion, Miss Myles, and I teach Elizabeth. Tend the garden. We make cheese. And I make lace,' she offered with a brightness that surprised him.

'So that is your pleasure, then?'

'That is how I make my living, my lord.'

He nodded, in acknowledgement, and apology, willing her to understand, he did not judge her.

He *did* judge whoever had arranged her widow's portion, and made her settlements, but her, he could not. Society, his mother, might have very distinct notions about women who worked, but he didn't. Never had. Anyone who worked in any fashion to advance themselves, or simply survive, deserved respect, not scorn. Hence his comfort around people like his friend Freddie, who'd been born with nothing, and built himself an empire.

If things had been different, Spencer would never have become Marquess of Clairborne. He too might've had to pave his own way, buy a commission, or become a clergyman, had his great-uncle not perished without proper heirs. Yes, he'd been raised knowing his duty, his future, but in the back of his mind, there had always been that sense of *what if.*

A taunting, haunting, sense of *what if.*

'I blame no one for my situation,' the widow said, as if reading his thoughts, her smile, and brightness intact. 'I am happy to make my own living, lucky to have a talent which grants me independence. Which puts food in our bellies, and clothes on our back. When one has been deprived of freedom, having agency once again is...'

'Priceless?'

'Dizzying.' Madame de l'Omont nodded with a soft smile.

'I can only imagine.'

'*Maman*! Come and look!'

Both he and Madame de l'Omont were torn from the moment, and looked up to find Lizzie standing before a house.

ral cadence. *No reason to spoil a perfectly good day.* 'A proper one. Much more interesting than the stones I cannot seem to find.'

Seemingly satisfied by his apology and offer, Lizzie began to make her way to the promised horticultural amusement. Madame de l'Omont however did not move, and he felt her gaze, studying him, and it was as if she knew, not only that his outburst had been completely out of character, but that there was something more, beneath it.

Something he refused to give word to.

'My lord?'

Spencer shook his head, banished all thoughts of the old house from it, and offered her his very best smile.

'To the maze, *madame*,' he declared with false joviality, waving them back onto the path.

And so they went, though he could tell she was fooled by neither his smile, nor his convivial mood.

But then, he thought vaguely as they walked on, Madame de l'Omont seemed to see that smile he wore all too often, that mood he donned all too often, were illusions. Brittle reflections that if gazed upon too intently, would shatter.

And what a freeing experience that would be.

Chapter Four

'Are you certain you won't stay for dinner,' Spencer asked, none a little coaxing as they stood at the edge of the loch, below Yew Park House. He could see Willowmere, even if the shoreline was not a straight path to it, dipping into a tiny cove about halfway, the perfect place to depart from for a swim, as he'd discovered.

He didn't want to see Madame de l'Omont and Lizzie disappear along that path; didn't want her to refuse dinner again as she had his offer to walk them home.

Twice.

He was being a bit of an ass, only he really did wish for them to stay, to share a meal with him, to continue what had been in his view, a rather glorious day. They had explored the maze; spent at least an hour trapped within until they'd finally found their way to the gazebo at its centre.

After that, they'd made their way back slowly,

discovering this hidden statue or pond, and now it was growing late, the light changing to that warm glow that radiated across the landscape like magic just before sunset.

'I will happily send to Willowmere for Miss Myles.'

'Thank you for your kind offer, my lord,' Madame de l'Omont answered, and disappointment truly did taste bitter. 'However, we must again refuse. Thank you, for today,' she added with a soft smile that washed the bitterness away.

She had that same vibrancy, that same vitality he'd noticed that first day—*was it truly a week ago?*—and damn him if it wasn't magnetic. Intoxicating, addictive really. There was a light in her eyes, and it was as magic as the light that shone on her. He wished to see it there always, and to be the one to put it there. Always.

Nonsense.

Only, it pleased him to make her, *and* her daughter, happy. Lizzie had opened up today, and the sound of her laughing through the maze, the sight of her smiling, no shadows in her eyes, well, he found it…

It felt good.

'It was truly my pleasure, *madame*,' he said, bowing before her, and Lizzie in turn. 'I hope you will not remain strangers, and visit again.'

The smile she offered this time held a sadness that told him that was unlikely.

That for some reason, she would not come again.

That she would keep her light, and her secrets, to herself.

And though he hated that, Spencer also saw the wisdom. Saw that whatever it was that fascinated him, whatever it was he felt when she and Lizzie were around, whatever it was he felt when he looked into her eyes…was dangerous. Not to be cultivated. Like a weed, closeness, familiarity, had no place in a proper lord's garden. And some things, were better left unexplored.

For everyone's sake. Soon, you'll be gone, old chap.

So in the end, he did watch them disappear on the path. But he stayed, through to the sunset, and watched them re-emerge on the banks by the cottage. Watched them disappear again into Willowmere, but not before he might've sworn, *she* looked back.

Only then, when they were both safely indoors, did he move. He knew he was smiling as he slowly meandered back up to the house, but he couldn't help himself. Memories of the day flitted through his mind as he made his way through the lawn terrace, the monastic terrace, the Greek terrace, the Roman terrace, the Versailles terrace and finally the *palazzo*-style terrace. It had truly been an afternoon of sheer, constraint-less pleasure. Simple pleasure.

He'd not known that kind in a long time. Well, until recently, but even then.

Today, had been different.

He'd known other pleasures. The pleasure of winning an argument in the House, or dancing with a pretty woman. The pleasure of taking tea with his sister, or spending a day with Freddie at his warehouses, full of extraordinary finds from across the world. He'd known the pleasure of an excellent liquor as it smoothly ran down your throat, or the pleasure of riding across the bright expanse of the Sussex Downs. He'd known the pleasures of the flesh, certainly, when a respectable option presented itself for a discreet liaison. It was expected.

But the simple pleasure of living…

Well, not that.

Not like today.

The only thing that had marred the day had been that house in the woods.

The memory of *it* was a putrid stain, and he had to focus very hard to push back the feelings that rose again at the thought of it. There was no Madame de l'Omont and her bright light to chase them away so easily now; no laughing Lizzie to chase away the chill.

It's only a house.

Only that house reminded him of Thornhallow, as it had been when Reid and he were young, not that luckily he'd spent much time there. Only

on occasion when he'd go to fetch him. He could
readily understand the man's hatred of it, after all
that had happened there, and he barely knew half
of it, Reid only confiding bits over the years. But
this house, it had not seen what Thornhallow had.

Had it?

Yet there was no denying, there was…

Something.

And he was now determined to find *what.*

In a calm, collected, rational manner. He would
not let disconcerting feelings, and odd pricklings
of the mind deter or confound him. He was a rational man. He would uncover the mystery of that
house in a logical manner, beginning by examining the estate reports. If the house had been neglected, there must be some reason for it.

Certainly not lack of funds.

What then? He couldn't remember giving any
orders to abandon it without care, so perhaps his
father? But again, why?

No use speculating until you've investigated.

Quite right.

Striding inside, he made for the study, rang, and
within seconds, a footman had come and gone,
with the promise to return with cold supper, a hot
brew of coffee, and Josiah.

Spencer went to the bookshelves laden with
ledgers, pulled out piles of them, then installed
himself at the desk and pulled out all the corre-

spondence and reports he could find; everything he'd promised not to look at whilst on his *retreat*.

I must know.

'My lord,' came Josiah's voice, and Spencer peered around the tower of ledgers. 'You called for me?'

'Have a seat, Josiah.'

His valet did so, with a questioning frown, as the footman who'd been following tried to lay out the dinner tray and coffee on what little space remained. Once the footman had finished, and left again, Spencer helped himself to a cup of coffee, and without thinking, passed one along to Josiah, who took it, slightly flustered.

'Everything in order, my lord?' his valet asked carefully.

He'd repeatedly asked the man to call him Spencer, he considered him more a friend and trusted companion than a servant, hence bringing him here to begin with, but the man wouldn't budge, even despite the peculiarity of the last few days. Not that he didn't understand, he himself was typically a stickler for the rules, but in the past year or so, he'd been testing *bending* them. On small things; in private.

Come to think of it, his behaviour the past few days was simply…

An extension of that process.

'I need your help, Josiah,' he sighed, setting that thought aside for later. 'We need to go through all *this*,' he said, gesturing to the mess he'd made, and the shelves surrounding them. 'Find anything referencing the dower house. Repairs, or lack thereof. My kingdom for any information on why there haven't been.'

'The dower house?'

'Yes. We came upon it today. The place is completely neglected, and I need to know why.'

'Of course, my lord.'

Spencer could tell Josiah had questions, but thankfully he kept them to himself, and simply pulled a box of correspondence closer.

I must know why.

Across the way, at Willowmere, Genevieve was working as hard as Spencer, though not in search of answers, rather, in the vain hope of distracting herself from thoughts of a certain marquess. She'd been sat there, scrunched over her table by the fire, for hours; ever since she'd tucked Elizabeth into bed. Jules had thankfully made herself scarce after suppertime interrogations, which Elizabeth had been all too pleased to answer with gleeful responses.

Only, industrious solitude wasn't working. No matter how intricate the pattern, how difficult the manoeuvres to get the lace *just perfect*, she simply couldn't shake the pesky, useless, dangerous thoughts that kept popping into her head.

It was maddening.

And madness.

Her lacework had always been there, the only thing to keep the darkness away. The only thing that had the power to make the world fade away. When she lost herself in her work, she was soothed. There was nothing but the beauty created by her own hands. Nothing but the growing piece; proof that she wasn't worthless. Proof that she could do *something*. That no matter what anyone said, no matter what her husband said, she *was* something. The lacework calmed her mind, and was a balm to her broken soul.

But not today.

One afternoon, that is what she'd promised herself. And she'd been given that. Elizabeth had been given that. A wonderful, *fun*, afternoon, in the company of a thoughtful, kind, man. An afternoon like they hadn't had…ever, perhaps. An afternoon where *all* her concerns melted away. Where she lost herself in the dream that it could always be so. That there was a chance, she and Elizabeth could have what she'd never really felt was missing before, because how could she, when she didn't even know what that was or looked like.

A good man in her life. In my life.

And that was precisely the problem. Among other things.

It was that he *was* underneath the safe sheen of a typical lord, kind, and fun, and easy to be around. It was that he saw too much; that he had

the formidable ability to read her, instantly. To
see the cracks in her walls and armour, to see the
weaknesses and exploit them. Society had taught
him well; he knew how to wield words like dag-
gers. Never had a man presumed to be as direct,
but she knew that had he not been, her own words
would never have slipped out. Every little thing
she gave him, he kept, she knew it. He was piec-
ing her together like a puzzle, and if he saw the
whole picture...

Do not think on that possibility.

To make matters even worse, he was attentive
to Elizabeth, and that doubtlessly made her heart
softer. He called her Lizzie, and she let herself be
called that, enjoyed it, Genevieve knew, when before, it had been reminiscent of another time. A
sad, terrible time, when the last of her nurses before Juliana had been as cruel as her father, even
gone further, and—

Breathe. Do not think on that either.

Not to mention the Marquess had been attentive
to her, and when he was... It yet again reminded
her of what she'd never been. Of what she wanted
but couldn't have.

That was the *other* problem. If he'd simply been
attractive, that was easy enough to resist. But what
he saw, and the way he made her feel...desirous,
desired... Well, it gave life to meanderings of the
mind, little daydreams that were not only fanciful,

and time-consuming, not to mention inappropriate, they were…

Tempting, Genevieve. Tempting beyond measure.

She'd never felt that gnawing longing at the pit of her stomach. Like she wanted to tear out of her own skin and run naked across the land in moonlight, and—

Oh bother.

Sighing, Genevieve set down the bobbins, and tried to untangle the mess she'd made.

Another reason to banish him from your thoughts.

If only she could manage to do that. Except a flash of that smile in her mind's eye, that broad, boyish, smile he'd had when they raced through the maze, getting lost nearly at every turn, and she was thinking about what else could make him smile. What else those lips could do. She'd think back and see his hands pushing aside a branch, and she would see those long fingers, trailing across her skin, along her collarbone, and—

Damn it, Genevieve.

Frustrated, she turned to the fire, wondering if it might hold any wisdom.

It didn't.

The heat of the dancing flames made her think of wild and wicked things she had no business imagining, and where her mind had even delved to find such thoughts of sumptuous silky kisses by firelight, she truly wondered. It wasn't the thoughts themselves that troubled her, at least, not beyond what they made her feel, *too warm, jittery, alive, and awake as never before*, it was the fact she couldn't stop them.

It had been like this in the beginning, when she and Elizabeth had first tasted true freedom. When they'd been released from their cage, her husband well and truly out of their lives. Before they'd freed themselves of most of the shackles in their own minds; merely managed to move past old habits. When Genevieve had moved past numbness; past anger, and resentment.

She remembered the first time. They'd been walking along in Edinburgh, and they'd seen and smelt the most glorious looking sugary buns. Golden, sparkling, decadent. They'd both felt it, or at least, Genevieve thought it had been similar for Elizabeth.

The initial desire for the pastry.

A desire to sink your teeth into that fluffy deliciousness, and feel the oozing sweetness dribble down your chin, and the rich spices teasing your tongue—

Then came the reminder that such things were not for you.

Such treats were for wives who gave their husbands sons, and did not shame them by breathing. Such treats were for children who were silent, and obedient.

So they'd walked away, that desire gnawing, the image of those buns indelible; their imaginings of the gloriousness of the sweets, the scent in their nostrils, the only things they could ever have. They'd continued on, and Genevieve had spent the next two hours fantasising about those buns. Imagining herself and Elizabeth biting into them, over, and over, until finally, she'd stopped. She'd remembered that if they wanted pastries, they were allowed to have pastries. They had coin to spare, that day at least, and no one would shame them, punish them for indulging.

She had remembered, they were allowed to *want*.

Back to the bakery they'd gone, and their buns they had purchased, and eaten with all the reverence in the world, stood there on the street, onlookers curious but amused. Those had been the most delicious buns ever made, and that night Genevieve had felt something within her break free. Shackles forged by her own self to preserve her and Elizabeth, had clattered to the ground, and after that, provided it was in her means, and some days, when even though it wasn't, Genevieve had allowed herself, and Elizabeth, anything they wanted. Over time, the guilt, the pain, the fear, associated with *want* had lessened. As they allowed themselves more, so the gnawing longing had lessened.

Until now.

But the Marquess is just that. Today's golden bun.

Comparing lords to sweets. She was losing her mind now.

Why? You know he would likely taste as sweet, and rich, on your tongue—

'Enough,' Genevieve muttered angrily to herself.

Enough.

The Marquess was not a pastry. He was flesh and blood. And if she did indulge…

Yes, Genevieve, what? What will happen if you indulge?

If he truly were open to…an indulgence, if they crossed that line and became lovers, what then? What did she imagine came next?

Pleasure, certainly.

Yes, something told her, he would know how to offer the sublime she'd never reached in her husband's bed, only in those darkest moments of the night, by herself. But what then? They would simply pass whatever time he had here together, and then Elizabeth might get attached, and when he left, well. It would not do.

No, it will not.

And there was something, in the current that flowed between the Marquess and her, beyond the attraction, it was…

Potential.

Already when she'd seen those shadows in his eyes, seen the pain flicker on his features when he'd seen that old house, even in the grotto, she'd felt a pang in her own chest. A desire to make it better, and that was not good. That was caring, and wanting to make another happy, and it led to—

Impossibility.

Best to live with this horrible longing. Indulging would lead nowhere, and she'd been nowhere before. It was a cold, terrible place of heartbreak and rage and horrors. So yes, she would live with it, and it would be fine.

As long as she stayed far enough away from *him*.

Genevieve tore herself away from the flames, discreetly rubbing away the little tears that had formed in her eyes, from staring too long at the flames.

Not from anything else. Because she didn't cry. Not anymore.

Not for years.

Her eyes glanced over the clock on the mantel, but it wasn't until she was staring again at the messy lacework that her mind fully processed what her eyes had seen.

Past midnight.

Tiredness swept over her all of a sudden.

Tiredness, and sadness.

There would be no more working tonight. Tomorrow, she would ask Jules to untangle the mess she'd made; her friend was supremely talented at that.

And we are to Aitil tomorrow, Genevieve thought as she took care of the fire and lamps.

A day in town. What a good idea.

No marquesses in town.

And on that disappointing and blissful thought, she went up to bed.

Chapter Five

'I heard you were asking about the dower house, my lord,' Mrs McKenna said, her commanding voice piercing through the haze of foggy exhaustion Spencer was currently suffering from. He and Josiah had spent the entire night—the first few traces of light grey appearing on the horizon before he'd finally forced himself to bed—searching through the estate's records, to no avail.

He'd been so frustrated, and exhausted, but this morning was a thousand times worse. Because he not only had the lack of restful hours to contend with—without fault, he woke at the disgustingly unfashionable hour of seven—he'd also been plagued by nightmares during those few moments he'd been afforded sleep.

These were not the same as before. These were much worse.

Childlike, in their terrifying quality. Monsters seeking to devour him; demonic things with claws of onyx steel, dripping with blood. Maidens locked in towers, screaming, and dragons devouring them. And he, he'd been a boy again, wanting to save the maidens, and escape the monsters, but unable to. He kept running, running and finding himself back before a bright yellow door behind which there was no more comfort. He'd cried for his mother then; he wouldn't be surprised if he'd truly done so for all the household to hear, so vivid it all was, even the raspy dryness of his throat.

Coming here was a bad idea.

The nightmares dampened all the goodness he'd found.

Except for Madame de l'Omont and Lizzie.

The only bright spots. The only light.

God how he'd wished for the widow's light last night…this morning. He'd wished… That she'd been there beside him, to comfort him. That he could fall into her light and softness and forget the dreams, forget the lingering feelings gnawing at him, and only think of her. Only *feel* her.

Only you cannot, and she isn't here.

'My lord?'

'Yes, Mrs McKenna,' Spencer said, dragging his mind back to the room, and his gaze towards the housekeeper rather than his untouched breakfast. 'My apologies, you spoke of the dower house?'

She looks tired too, he noted, his eyes travelling over the impeccable woman, who somehow exuded the same energy he felt.

Tired.

The lines at the corners of her eyes and lips were more pronounced today, and though every hair, every button, was right where it should be, she seemed somehow…

Dishevelled.

'I heard you were asking about it, my lord,' she said, straightening.

'Yes, Mrs McKenna.' He nodded, taking a healthy gulp of honeyed coffee. 'I wondered, what happened to it?'

'Nothing, milord.'

'Quite, Mrs McKenna. That is precisely what I wonder about. Why has it been left to ruin?'

The energy in the room changed instantly; already tense it became so thick one would have difficulty cutting through it with a cleaver. Mrs McKenna stiffened, and that flash of anger and resentment reappeared.

Hell, even the footman tensed.

What the Devil am I missing?

'Because His Lordship your father ordered it so,' she said coldly.

'And you have no explanation as to why, Mrs McKenna,' he frowned. *Doubtful.* 'No inkling as to why my father would order it, when as far as I recall, he had no particular ties to this place?'

The housekeeper flinched, and in that moment, Spencer knew two things.

One, she knew *precisely* why, and second, she would never tell him.

Likely not even if the Almighty himself commanded it.

'Did something happen there?' he asked nonetheless, unable to stop himself.

'His Lordship's reasons were his own,' she answered, her jaw clenching so hard he thought she might injure herself. *Whatever happened, she was involved.* 'It is not my place to question.' Spencer nodded. 'Will there be anything else, my lord?'

'No, Mrs McKenna.'

With the angriest curtsy he'd likely ever witnessed, she left.

Spencer waved away the footman as well, and pushed aside his plate, his appetite gone; not that he'd had any to begin with. He rose, sipping his coffee as he strode to the French doors that overlooked the loch.

Something definitely happened in that house.

Reid had told him of the tower he and his father had kept untouched after his sister's death. Could it be that someone Spencer's own father had cared about was tied to the dower house, and it was a similar situation? But who?

No sister, no brothers.

Which is why Spencer's future loomed so steadily; unless the Marquessate was to go to some *very* distant cousin, it was up to him to provide heirs.

A mistress? A lady-love like Jasper?

Doubtful. Despite everything, his father had been a fervent abider of fidelity. There had never been even the hint of a mistress, that Spencer had ever heard, and those things were never kept quiet long; and besides, he knew the estate books well, as well as his own father's accounts. Nothing had ever stood out as possible cover for the expenses of a mistress, but then, one never knew for sure.

What else could it be?

And strange though it may seem, he felt like somehow, he knew what the mystery was. Like the words to a song you had on the tip of your tongue, remnants of a tune you'd heard once and long forgotten. Whatever had passed there, if he'd witnessed it, if it was that which plagued his unconscious self, he'd obviously forgotten it. Short of miraculously remembering something from nearly thirty years ago, when he was five, he had to find another way to discover what it was.

Asking Mother was out of the question; even if he hadn't been loath to advertise his whereabouts, he had a feeling that if she knew, she would be as tight-lipped as Mrs McKenna.

But not everyone might be...

He could ask Mr McKenna, or better yet, the villagers. There was always an old gossip here or there, who'd heard some whisper of something that had happened in a lord's house. Someone who could give him clues...

Perfect.

He rang the bell, and the footman who'd been attending earlier reappeared in seconds.

'The McKennas hail from Aitil, do they not?'

'Yes, my lord.'

'Please have the stables ready my horse and one for Josiah.'

'Yes, my lord.'

Off to Aitil we go.

The town of Aitil was small, but vibrant, full of history, and well-served thanks to its fortunate situation at an important crossroads. Having played a vital role during the various wars, it now played host to two mills, as well as two inns, having become a popular stopping place for the well-endowed visitors making their way through the picturesque landscapes.

It was a place where those who lived off the land mingled with those who had turned towards the looming future of worldwide trade and industry. A small selection of shops had popped up on Main Street amid the rows of whitewashed cottages, offering both the essentials, and luxuries such as sugar, or fishing poles.

As much as Genevieve enjoyed Willowmere's isolation, she had to admit, having Aitil within reach was reassuring. It reminded her of the world beyond, which, though she could never truly be a part of it again, marched on with reassuring steadiness. And Aitil also provided an escape route; something Genevieve vowed to never be without again.

Though the land provided most of what they needed to survive, now they'd learned how to cultivate it properly, Aitil also provided what they couldn't make or grow themselves. Books for Elizabeth, threads for her lacework, even little treats, like sweets or a bolt of cloth from Glasgow. Most of the shopkeepers accepted lace or goat's cheese in return for these luxuries, which she wasn't entirely sure would be possible elsewhere, allowing them to live within their meagre means. Every penny saved was a blessing, offering possibilities for the future.

Though what that future looked like, Genevieve wondered. They'd come here because, yes, it was as far as she could go. As far as she could flee from the past, whilst ensuring they had a roof over their heads. They'd thought about moving to a city, where work could be found, but with her lacework, and initial help from Jules, who'd saved her salary over the years, they'd been able to make the decision that it was not the life they wished to lead. Genevieve knew she was fortunate to have that choice. Many did not, and she was grateful that though they still worked hard, she had time for Elizabeth. To teach, and learn with her, to simply, *know* her. But as for the future...

Decisions would need to be made eventually.

Elizabeth had a world of possibility waiting for her, so long as the past did not become known. She could choose whatever life she wished for; and that meant leaving Willowmere someday. They could not remain hidden here for ever.

Not that they were hiding.

But possibilities were limited here. The closest towns, like Aitil, were connected, but still, small. Elizabeth deserved more than to be cloistered here, years of hardship and perhaps a husband and children begat too early her only options. Those weren't terrible options, Genevieve did not look down on those who lived such lives, but above all she wished for Elizabeth to have a choice. Something which she herself hadn't; the very reason she'd done what she had. If Elizabeth wished to live here, marry, and have twenty children, very well. But she would not grow up thinking that was *all* there was for her.

She won't.

Taking a deep breath, Genevieve turned her thoughts back to the present. The streets were busy, and the sound of childish laughter rang up from the riverbank a street over, even though carts, horses, and well-appointed carriages bustled along the road. Before the shops, people stopped and chatted, and as Genevieve and the others walked along, as always, she caught the suspicious, disapproving looks which reminded her of just *how* small Aitil was.

Tourists, the locals endured. A strange *sassenach* widow living up here, was an entirely different matter. It wasn't that they weren't welcoming; many had shown them kindness. Still, there was a distance. Not solely because they disapproved of Genevieve's loose concern for propriety; *exempli gratia* when Elizabeth sported breeches and played with the boys at the last fair. It was also as if they knew there had to be some dark reason for two Englishwomen, alone with a child, to come live here. Genevieve wondered whether they would actually care if they ever found out the truth. Or if, they would simply take it in their stride, as they did so much.

Here is not London—and for that I am grateful.

'I should get these parcels sent off,' Genevieve said, tearing away from her musings, and turning to Jules with a smile.

'I shall to the grocer's. Elizabeth?' Jules asked. 'Whom do you follow?'

'You.'

'Shocking,' Genevieve said wryly. Her daughter threw her an innocent look before taking Jules's hand. 'When Mrs Bates offers you toffees for poems.'

'I have memorised Wordsworth for her today.'

'I'm sure she will love it.' Jules grinned, and Genevieve chuckled.

'Shall we meet by the church in an hour or so?'

'Agreed.'

Tucking a stray curl back into her bonnet, Genevieve watched as Jules and Elizabeth strode off, then went off on her own way.

Yes. For this life, I am grateful.

Spencer's brilliant idea, meanwhile, was turning out to be utterly short-sighted and, frankly, stupid. In coming to Aitil, he'd counted on people's love of gossip. Anywhere he'd ever been, from his tenant farms in Sussex, to the clubs of St James's, he'd found one common thing. People liked to talk.

About themselves, their neighbours, about the man sleeping with the vicar's wife, or the duke who smelled of cheese. All he had to do, was casually engage someone in conversation, prove to be a good listener, which he was, collecting facts as others collected rare specimens, and they would tell him everything he wished to know; and often everything he didn't.

Today, not so.

For Spencer hadn't counted on people's loyalty. He'd considered it, that some might be reluctant, but he'd also thought his position as figure of authority and landowner in the area, might give him some leverage.

Not so.

If anything, the fact he was an *English* lord, with only vague droplets of Scotland in his blood, made people more tight-lipped. A feat considering how tight-lipped they already were. Oh, people talked to him, particularly when he spoke what little Gaelic he knew. They just wouldn't speak about what he wanted to know.

Mrs McKenna.

If people's loyalty hadn't been so frustrating, it would've been heartwarming.

Perhaps Josiah has been more fortunate.

Though I doubt it.

'We'll have tae wait till St Swithun's,' the boot-maker said as they stood just outside the shop door, Spencer's new boots in hand. Not that he needed any, but he'd thought that dropping coin might loosen lips. It had; though not regarding the McKennas. 'If it rains, then 'twill be wet till September, ye'll see.'

'I shall bear that in mind,' Spencer said politely, his gaze straying to the passers-by.

He was just about to excuse himself when a familiar laugh sounded, and he looked up to find Lizzie playing piggyback with whom he supposed must be Miss Myles across the road.

Madame de l'Omont followed, laughing, whilst anyone about either smiled or shot disapproving glances. Not that the ladies seemed to notice, involved in their own revelry as they were, Lizzie shouting *'Giddy-up!'* every so often.

Spencer grinned, and raised his hand in greeting.

'Good day, Lady Lizzie,' he hailed, unbecomingly loud. But really, he was glad to see them. *'Madame!'*

The trio stopped, Miss Myles frowning and turning to Madame de l'Omont.

The widow looked about as pleased to see him as one might upon encountering a troll. She bowed her head ever so slightly, then ushered Lizzie down, and before he could even think to take a step, they'd rushed off, Lizzie shooting him an apologetic look and tiny wave before disappearing.

He stood there for a long moment, bewildered, and nursing the pang of disappointment.

'Ye'd know the widow,' the bootmaker said, drawing Spencer's attention. 'Rents yer cottage. Strange business, that.'

'How so?' Spencer asked.

If he couldn't get answers about Mrs McKenna, perhaps he might get some about the woman who had captured each and every one of his other thoughts.

'Pretty *sassenachs*.' The bootmaker shrugged thoughtfully. 'Ladies, no mistake tae be made. But they let the little one run amok, do as she pleases, little hoyden.'

Spencer stiffened, affronted on their behalf, and the man raised his hands in defence.

'Nice lasses, the lot of 'em. Mean nae disrespect. But mark me words, somethin' ain't right. Ye have tae wonder what they're doin' here.'

'Good day, Mr Ross,' Spencer said simply.

The man bowed, and shuffled back inside.

Spencer stood there a moment, looking back at where the ladies had disappeared. Though he would never admit it, the man was right. One did have to wonder what had forced Madame de l'Omont here. Wonder what she was hiding from. Who she was, beneath the widow's weeds. He'd had glimpses, but he wanted more.

And if he was really truthful, he would admit it was because he envied them.

He wondered if they could teach him, how one became so free, one could play piggyback in the street.

Chapter Six

'Good day again, ladies,' said the very last man Genevieve wished to encounter.

Yet ever since she'd first heard the sound of hooves, she'd known that naturally, given her luck, it would have to be *him*. It would *have* to be the Marquess who found them *in distress*; well, with the cart entrenched in mud, and themselves, covered in it after quite literally tumbling into it as they attempted to dislodge said cart. As if witnessing their revelry in town wasn't enough—not that she cared—but really, the last thing she needed was more judgement, or anything more to do with him at all. Still he invaded her dreams, and—

'Might we be of assistance.'

'No, thank you, my lord,' Genevieve said, shooting a warning glance at Jules and Elizabeth as she prepared to heave again.

The last thing she needed was actually to be indebted to the Marquess. Debts gave others power, and it would just be an excuse for him to insinuate himself into their lives, not that he would ever wish to, not after that spectacle in town, and really, that was good—

'*Madame*, I'm afraid I must ignore your refusal. You cannot simply expect Josiah and I to ride on, and abandon you here.'

Yes, I bloody well can.

'My lord,' she sighed, attempting to remain as dignified as she could, considering her current state as she turned to face him.

And there he was, in all his *lordly* magnificence atop his stride—stifling a laugh?

The worst part was that suddenly she felt the urge to laugh too.

This situation was rather—

Incomprehensible.

Quite.

At least his companion, Josiah, who appeared only slightly older, quite handsome in a rougher, more weathered way, with silver-streaked russet hair, and onyx eyes, had the politeness to look unconcerned with their state.

'We are not damsels in distress, my lord. These are not dangerous roads, and Aitil is but two miles back. We will not detain you from your business.'

'*Madame*, you are my business,' the man had the temerity to say, approaching with a smile as took in her mud-soaked figure, and it might've been chocolate for all the hunger in his eyes. *Not good.* 'Josiah and I will see you delivered soon enough,' he said, all gentleness, urging her yet again to drop her defences. But she didn't want to, she couldn't, and she certainly didn't need saving—'There will be no debt.'

And now he could read her mind.

Bollocks.

'*Maman,*' Elizabeth said quietly, and Genevieve relented.

Stubbornness was only acceptable if others did not suffer for it.

'Ladies, if you would please retire to that grassy bank just there.' The Marquess smiled as Josiah dismounted and tied their horses.

Unable to do anything but obey, Genevieve, Jules, and Elizabeth crossed the road.

The men removed their coats, and Genevieve pointedly did not admire anything whatsoever about the Marquess so divested. They emptied the small bags from the cart, and handed the ladies back their own coats, which they slipped on, the damp cold of the mud now seeping through.

And then they proceeded to do as the ladies had, heaving, and pushing, whilst also digging and setting sticks and branches where possible, only *their* efforts were successful with much more rapidity. Within minutes the cart was firmly back on the drier part of the road, their bags loaded, and, *thankfully*, the men had put their coats back on.

'The wheel at the rear is a bit loose,' Josiah said as the ladies joined them again.

'I shall see to that,' both the Marquess and Genevieve said in unison.

They both stared at each other for a moment, whilst Jules and Elizabeth chuckled.

'Do you know anything of cart wheels, my lord?'

'No. Do you, *madame*?'

Damn. She was about to retort something but he was quicker.

'I thought not. I shall see it set to rights.'

'We can bring it to Aitil ourselves—'

'I shall see it set to rights at Yew Park.'

'My lord, you need not trouble your staff on our account—'

'*Madame*, I shall trouble them, but not solely on your account. I have a hunger to learn, you see, and cart fixing will be something new for me, so in fact, I should thank you for the opportunity.'

Oh, but he was quick with his words, and full of guile.

It was much easier to see that, than it was the kindness; and to question the rest of what he'd said.

'Now, *madame*, Lady Lizzie, and Miss Myles, I presume?'

Oh, but dash it all.

Manners flown to the wind, along with the rest of her damned mind.

'May I present my companion and Elizabeth's

governess, Miss Myles,' Genevieve said assuredly, as though making introductions in a salon, not the side of the road. 'Miss Myles, His Lordship, the Marquess of Clairborne.'

The Marquess bowed, and Jules curtsied.

'A pleasure,' he said, before turning to gesture at his companion. 'Josiah, my valet.' The ladies dropped into curtsies out of habit as he bowed, and both men smiled. 'So,' he continued. 'As this wheel is loose, I think it best perhaps you not ride in it. Josiah is an excellent driver, and if you do not object to riding astride, perhaps you might be more secure atop the horses. Lizzie, perhaps you could ride Simpheon with me?'

And there he was, charming her daughter again. As if she could say no to that hopeful look in Elizabeth's eyes.

Not that she wouldn't try.

'We are a mess, my lord, your clothes, Josiah—'

'Will not be alone to tend to them. I know how to do laundry now.'

And with that, he walked to his mount, Lizzie on his heels, leaving her and Jules to stare after him, wondering what the devil sort of marquess this was.

Leaving Genevieve to wonder, how she could stop herself, *liking* him.

So, there was to be a bright spot to his day after all. After leaving the bootmaker's, Spencer had been further disappointed on reuniting with Josiah, who had, unsurprisingly, no more luck regarding the McKennas. Everyone vaunted their praises as *good people*, but when speaking of *secrets* or *tragedy*, they closed up tight as oysters.

Which suggests there are secrets and tragedy.

Josiah had tried to look at the parish registry, but the records from 1801 had mysteriously disappeared. Along with the minister from that time. His trusty valet had offered to go on the hunt—but Spencer had declined. What was the point? If the minister was still alive, he would surely be as secretive as the rest.

No, he would have to ferret out secrets by looking closer to home. Josiah had been ordered to keep an ear to the walls, and Spencer would think on another way to solve the mystery of the dower house. In the meantime, he would set himself to another task.

Delving into the mystery of Madame de l'Omont.

Because…he was a curious lout, and because she and her daughter were good company, and completely different from anyone he'd ever known before, and…

That was all really.

It was important to know one's tenants, wasn't it? One's neighbours, temporary though they may be? The short time they'd spent together already had been…delightful, and unwise though it may be, he would fully take advantage of any further moments he was granted with them. Even if *madame* seemed less than eager.

Or perhaps that was simply the current circumstances. Finding them entrenched in the mud, firmly set upon delivering themselves from it. Though she was certainly not embarrassed, not that she should be, he admired them for endeavouring to solve their own predicament. No, she'd seemed angry if anything at his arrival and subsequent *rescue*, if it could be called thus.

He at least liked to think so, and his riding companion seemed to be enjoying herself. Glancing down at Lizzie sat across his lap, safe in his arms, he smiled as he caught her gently petting Simpheon's neck as they ambled slowly down the road. Madame de l'Omont and Miss Myles shared Josiah's horse, while the latter followed behind, and Spencer was making a concentrated effort not to glance over too often and admire the way the widow sat proudly atop the mount, Artemis herself, wild, and showing none too little ankle.

He'd never been mad for a glimpse of an ankle, but today, somehow—

'How is it you know how to do laundry, my lord,' Lizzie asked, tearing him from his most improperly pleasant wanderings of the mind.

'I fancied learning,' he said, glancing down at the girl. She pondered this for a moment, and he continued. 'I realized I did not know many things when I came here, and I thought, why not widen my gaze?'

'So you will repair the cart yourself?'

'Well, not solely by myself, unless I can find a manual in my library,' he said, wondering if he might just. 'I shall ask for help from those who know, and do as much as I can.'

'What else have you been learning?'

'Elizabeth,' her mother began, about to quell the questioning, but he glanced over and smiled.

He did not mind; quite the contrary.

And if it somehow brought him closer to this bunch, he welcomed any interrogation.

'Let's see,' he said, turning back to the road. 'I have tried gardening, farming, I have learned Josiah's duties, and those of my other staff. I've found quite a passion for entomology, and I tried watercolours, and needlepoint—'

'You tried needlepoint,' Lizzie laughed, and he chuckled.

'Yes, I did. Suppose it does sound quite mad.'

'What did you make?'

'A mess.'

Lizzie laughed again, and he joined her, feeling buoyed by her amusement. He glanced over at the ladies, found Miss Myles chuckling as well, and Madame de l'Omont trying very hard not to.

Will you not let me make you laugh, madame? You did, not so long ago—

'What will you try next?' Lizzie asked.

'You mean apart from cart wheel mending?' The girl nodded, and he pondered the question seriously for a moment. He'd been so involved with solving the mystery of the dower house that he'd quite set aside his own decree to explore *more*. 'I think I should like to try my hand at cooking,' he finally decided.

All his life, he'd been served, and wouldn't likely last a day in truth if he had to fend for himself beyond picking berries. Even then, without a book he'd be liable to find the poison ones.

Rather sad; for a man to be unaware of how to feed himself.

'You should come to Willowmere,' Lizzie said excitedly, and his heart skipped a beat. 'We could teach you how to cook, Jules is very good at everything, and *Maman*—'

'Elizabeth,' Madame de l'Omont interjected, and immediately Lizzie's face fell, along with his own heart. He glanced over to find the widow looking rather more panicked, than appalled. 'I am sure His Lordship has far better teachers than we could ever be,' she said a little gentler.

He shouldn't do it.

He *really* shouldn't.

'You are being modest, I'm sure, *madame*,' he said smoothly, and he rather enjoyed watching her eyes widen, and those luscious lips part slightly as she was rendered temporarily speechless. *Really shouldn't, old chap.* 'Unless you have any

other objections, I would be honoured if you ladies would bestow your wisdom on me. Just name
the date.'

There. He'd done it.

Only, he really *did* wish to spend time with
them, get to know her, and Lizzie, and Miss Myles,
and if he had to play underhanded tricks to achieve
it, well, he would. If she truly despised him, or his
presence, he would step aside, but they'd had fun
together before, hadn't they? She and Lizzie had
trusted him, *somewhat*, and so likely some of her
reluctance was born of the impropriety of their
encounters until now.

Yes. That was surely it. He could fix that. So
that the widow could not misunderstand his intentions. Which were *honourable intentions*, no matter what some parts of him argued. What his own
mind argued when he wasn't conjuring up nightmares, but instead delectable sensations of the
woman in his arms, of what that luscious mouth
might taste like, of what it might feel like to lose
himself in the dark green of her eyes—

'No other objections, my lord,' the lady said
evenly, thankfully tearing him from those *im-
proper* thoughts yet again.

'Tomorrow, then?' Spencer offered. 'I shall
bring back the cart. Should I bring anything else?
Supplies?'

'Tomorrow, my lord,' the widow agreed with a
strained smile. Lizzie beamed up at him, and he

saw the widow's smile soften into something true. 'You need bring only yourself.'

'I shall look forward to it,' he said, dipping his head in thanks.

For he was thankful.

To be allowed in, even only a little.

'What should you like to cook, my lord?' Lizzie asked.

The rest of the journey was spent discussing menus, and plans, and when he'd delivered the ladies back to Willowmere, Spencer couldn't help but feel excited again.

Tomorrow, he thought, could not come soon enough.

Chapter Seven

Taking a deep inhalation of the pine scented air, Spencer pushed away the remnants of last night's nightmare, and focused instead on how glorious the sunshine was. How beautiful the veritable treasure trove of wildflowers before the simple two-storey stone cottage was, and what an admirable flourishing expanse of vegetables and fruit there was to the left.

He would not allow whatever was haunting him to mar all that he'd found. For now, the ghosts and demons that chased him at Yew Park, would remain at Yew Park.

He'd already managed to sneak the horse and cart back into the little stables, all much better for their stay in his own. Repairing the cart had been an adventure, and he'd enjoyed his time with the stable lads. They seemed the least wary of him, and his interests, and even jested about the lengths Spencer was going to for a lady.

Only it wasn't simply for a lady, it was also for himself.

Just as this cooking lesson was—it was for them all. To get to know each other. To spend a nice time together. To try something...

Different.

Glancing back up at Willowmere, Spencer strode forth, entering the ladies' realm. He didn't recall the cottage from his childhood, but he knew a garden such as the one before him could not succeed on its own.

Perhaps, madame, you breathed some of your life into it.

Perhaps...

Spencer shook some sense back into himself and went to the door.

Honourable intentions.

He stood before it a moment, basking in the sun, enjoying the pleasant murmur of voices drifting out from the open windows, and Lizzie's laugh, mingling with the gentle buzzing of the bumblebees and the—

Strident bleat of a goat?

'What the Devil?' Spencer muttered, turning towards the unexpected sound to find a devil indeed behind him, munching on his coat. 'Behave yourself you foul creature,' he commanded. The animal paused, and cocked its head. 'Release me,' he ordered in a tone usually reserved for heated debates in the House. The demon's jaw's opened, and his coat was released. 'Thank you.'

'Galahad!' Lizzie exclaimed.

Both Spencer and the goat looked to the door, where Lizzie stood, a disapproving finger raised, framed by her mother, and Miss Myles, who both looked outraged—whilst trying to fight a bout of laughter.

'Remarkable name for such a terror,' Spencer remarked wryly.

'Apologies, my lord,' Lizzie said, dropping a hint of a curtsey before stepping forth to grab the vicious knight's collar, and dragging him away. 'We've discussed this, Galahad,' she continued gently. 'No eating people's garments or no milk.'

Spencer smiled despite himself and turned back to the rest of his captive audience.

'Good morning, ladies,' he greeted, doffing his hat. 'Quite the welcome committee you have.'

Miss Myles snorted, and Madame de l'Omont blinked.

The former recovered first, curtseying then moving aside. 'My lord,' she said sweetly. 'Won't you come in.'

'With pleasure.'

With very much pleasure.

'My lord,' Genevieve said, dropping into a curtsey as he passed her. The man truly had the ability to keep her on her toes, that much was certain.

With every moment he surprised her, and that really wasn't good. She thought she knew his measure, but every time she learned something more, she was drawn in further. A marquess who did laundry and repaired carts? *Madness.* A marquess who laughed at being devoured by goats? *Madness.*

This whole day was madness—she'd tried and failed to stop it—but the man was too good. And what he wanted with them... She wondered. If she'd thought there was anything nefarious beyond his calculations to get their company, she would've shut the door and bolted it, but he seemed to genuinely...

Want to spend time with us.

Which was odd, and nice, and—*oh my Lord I am standing here like a ninny in the corridor and staring.*

'The kitchen is straight ahead, my lord,' she said, *finally,* ignoring the man's dimples flashing in her direction, a boyish sort of hesitancy about him, all mussed hair, and impeccably tailored clothes, a strange combination of pale green and burnt orange today; though the coat had suffered Galahad's valiant attempt at guarding the house. 'Would you care for tea?' she asked as they arrived at their destination.

'No, thank you, *madame.* Ah, the cart and your horse are returned home.'

'Thank you, my lord.'

And then he was looking at her again, and she was caught in that bright blue gaze, and why was it so hot in this kitchen—

'As you see we've prepared everything,' Genevieve said, waving at the laden table for lack of anything else to do.

The Marquess smiled, though he didn't even glance at the table, not that she believed for one moment he hadn't seen everything in this kitchen. Why was he so silent? And why was her mind going suddenly blank? Certainly not because of that dashed smile, and those eyes—

I should apologise. About his coat. The goat.

'I must apologise,' Genevieve said, shaking herself back to a semi-composed state. 'About Galahad. He seems to have a fondness for clothes. You must send us your tailor's bill.'

Elizabeth chose that moment to reappear, and Genevieve felt herself relax a little when the Marquess turned his gaze to her daughter, and his smile broadened.

'Lady Lizzie,' he greeted.

'Apologies for Galahad,' Elizabeth said, coming to stand before him. It was troubling, how comfortable her daughter was with this man. Yesterday when Genevieve had seen them riding together, it had seemed so natural, so easy, and...

And nothing. Show him how to cook a pie and be rid of him. This is dangerous.

'I cannot believe he listened to you.'

'Does he only listen to you then?'

'Yes. We understand each other.'

The Marquess nodded, as if that made complete sense, and Elizabeth showed him the table again.

'We shall all make pies together,' she said, and to his credit he showed more interest this time. 'And for dessert, gooseberry jelly.'

'Actually, if you don't mind,' Jules said, reminding everyone that she was in the room, 'I have some mending to do, and this kitchen is rather small, so…'

'Not at all, Miss Myles. Until later. We shall have a feast ready for you.'

Genevieve shot Jules a look that said *stay and help me.*

'I look forward to it, my lord.' She smiled, and then left with a curtsey.

Traitor.

'Well then,' Genevieve said, turning back to the others, reminding herself that this was absolutely, entirely, unquestionably normal, *all of it*, and that it would all be just fine. 'Shall we begin?'

Madness. The whole day was in fact incontestable madness. And Genevieve had enjoyed every last second. Once they'd begun the actual cooking, Genevieve had let herself simply be. There wasn't much choice, really, but to let the day take her away, to stop thinking, and to let herself go along with whatever it was they were all doing together.

And just as she had that day in the gardens, just as they all had, they'd had fun.

The Marquess was anything but a talented cook. His attempts at pastry were miserable, more flour ending up on him, Elizabeth, and Genevieve, than in the actual preparation. The man had even had the indecency of lobbing some directly *at* her and Elizabeth when they commented on his blob. Not that the ladies hadn't retaliated.

So there had been a food fight.

Somehow they *had* managed to make the pies after that, and the gooseberry jelly. Elizabeth had been an excellent teacher, and while they *cooked*, they had delightful conversations, about anything and everything. The country, politics, art, philosophy...

When the Marquess listened to her or Elizabeth, he *really* listened. And when he spoke to them, he did so without guile, or condescension, or even reserve. He seemed so open, and *interested*, and there had been times in that tiny, warm kitchen, when she'd got that little bit too close not to notice the freckles along his forearm, in his rolled-up shirtsleeves as he was. Got too close not to notice how easily her own smiles came when he glanced at her, or asked her to inspect his work. Not to notice his heady scent, *bergamot and pine and everything else delicious and fine*, and the hypnotic allure of the blue-green depths of his eyes. *Yes, blue-green today, with specks of silver light.* So close she could nearly count how many flecks of silver there were—*three in each eye...*

Over the course of the day, they had stopped being *the Marquess* and *madame.* Simply, a man, a woman, and her child. He'd been so open, and for a moment, she'd let herself be too. Not thinking on the past, but simply being. She'd laughed, *really* laughed, until her belly hurt. She'd let down her guard, and—

It can't happen again.

As they'd all sat at the table, eating their creations, Genevieve had realised that. She'd realised she truly *liked* him. She liked that for whatever reason, he seemed intent on learning about gardening and gamekeeping. She liked his presence, and how she was around him. She didn't care much *why* he was there, only that he was. She wished to know more, to have more time, and that was bad.

Very bad.

Whether her instincts were correct or not, and she *could* trust him, which was absurd considering she could never trust anyone again, she *didn't want to*; the fact was, she couldn't. Her armour, her walls, had been crafted for a reason. And what a fool she would be to begin dropping them at the first softening of her heart. Terrible things happened to women caught off guard, and terrible things would happen if she let herself be party to whatever madness this was.

Which is why she had to make sure this day was the end of it.

'My lord,' she said, as they made their way to the door. He'd already said his goodbyes to Jules and Elizabeth, and the two had gone off to have a music lesson. 'I wondered if I might have a word.'

'Of course, *madame.*'

She nodded, and showed him into the drawing room that hadn't really seemed so small until now.

Until his eyes were flitting about it, resting on the simple furnishings, and opened books, and discarded pieces of mending peeking out from the baskets. The Marquess advanced a few steps, then stopped, hands behind his back, not really looking, merely perusing. Genevieve took a tentative step further from the door, though why, that was a mystery. Eventually his gaze settled back on her, and there was a long moment before either said anything, the echoes of Elizabeth's music from above filling the space between them.

Not that it felt like there *was* much space, only half the drawing room, which was tiny, very small actually, when someone looked at you with a softness in their eyes so like the enchantingly dangerous loch, and chuckled lightly as he did now, an awkward but endearing little laugh that made her smile.

No, then, it really didn't feel like there was any space at all.

'Lizzie is very talented with her harp,' the Marquess said finally.

'Indeed.'

'Does she play the pianoforte?' he asked, care behind the mask of nonchalance that was a very potent drug indeed. Everything about the man was potent, and there she was, being drawn in again. 'There is one she might use at the house. Tomorrow evening, perhaps. You could come to dinner. I promise I won't cook.'

She smiled despite herself, and just like that, the spell was broken. The reminder of the chasm that must at all times remain between them, was as sobering as a bucket of ice water.

'I fear I must refuse again.'

'Why?' he asked bluntly.

The tender amusement was gone, and it was not harsh, but simple, stark curiosity in him now. Somehow that was even more disconcerting. Harsh would imply he was offended, *not that he actually bloody well cared why I keep refusing his delightfully tempting invitations.*

'And don't tell me you are otherwise engaged,' he added as Genevieve made to open her mouth to say just that. 'We both know you have no engagements.'

Genevieve flinched, and the Marquess's brow furrowed.

Do something...say something...

'It would not be wise, my lord,' she managed

to say in a passably even voice, when really, she just wanted to scream at him to leave her alone, or perhaps also, beg him to stay. 'There is enough talk as it is.'

There.

For a man whose name meant everything to him, despite his rather outlandish behaviour recently, that should do the trick. The mention of *talk* to an upstanding, dutiful gentleman like himself, should be enough for him to say *jolly good, tally ho then, have a lovely life, say toodle-loo to Lizzie for me.*

'Talk.'

'I can only imagine what you heard in town yesterday. There would be much more.'

The Marquess nodded, and turned his gaze to the window for a moment. And for that moment, Genevieve thought she was safe.

But no.

'There is talk you do what you please,' the Marquess said as he turned back to her, with a grin far too dangerous and knowing and suspicious. Like a cat who'd not only got the cream, but all the mice in the kingdom as well. 'With no regard for convention. And yet, you would refuse for the sake of convention?'

The way he asked, it sounded absolutely absurd.

But then, yes, looking from the outside, she supposed that is what it appeared.

I wish I could explain—
But you cannot.

Genevieve was aware of the fact that she was currently opening and closing her mouth as if performing the role of *guppy gasping for air* in some theatrical, and so she forced it closed one last time, and looked down at her hands for inspiration.

Why do you even need inspiration? Just rid yourself of him and be done with it.

'Elizabeth cannot get attached to you, my lord,' she said.

And that was true. Neither of them could.

'Why not?'

Bloody hell.

'It is complicated,' Genevieve sighed.

Weak, at best, yet it was all she had.

She glanced back up only to find the Marquess right before her, scandalously close. Did lords have special shoes made which were silent on rugs so they could creep up on unsuspecting females?

Likely.

She should certainly move away. He was trying to set her off-balance, so she would answer his questions. It would've been nice if she'd been able to say in no way whatsoever did his proximity put her off balance. In no way did the warmth emanating from him make her want to sink into it, and abandon all hope of resisting. Make her want to tell him everything, *everything*, from every sordid detail of her past, to all she thought about in his presence, like those imaginings she had right now of his lips closing the infinitesimal distance between them, or tracing the hollow of those dimples or tasting—

'Aren't you tempted?'

His voice was but a whisper, but considering how close they were, their breaths mingling, in time, well, she heard him perfectly.

And that was precisely the problem.

She *was* tempted, beyond measure.

To give into temptation, and for one moment to lose control, to let go of that final barrier of rationality that had helped her survive so much.

'It's complicated,' she breathed, willing him to see that this wasn't easy.

Willing him to see that in another life, yes, she would gladly give him anything he wanted, but in this one, she simply couldn't do it. There was no lying anymore, no manners, no polite platitudes, only truth.

I want what you offer but I cannot so please leave me.

'Tell me.'

'It will not unravel the complexity.'

'Why will you not trust me with even the smallest piece of yourself? I would keep it safe.'

I know you would.

Because she nearly did tell him everything then. She opened her mouth and the words nearly came spilling out.

I am divorced.

That is why we cannot see each other, why we should never have come this far to begin with.

To the world I am an adulteress, the Great Whore of Hadley Hall, and my life is steeped in shame. My husband was not kind, but neither is he dead, and I fear so much, for myself and my child. We came here for peace, and so I should like it again, and if you were smart you would run, far away, lest you be tainted by the filth I have been soaked in.

But coward that she was, she could not. Because even if she had been sure he wouldn't repudiate her right there and then, throw her off his lands, the truth was, she didn't want to see him look at her with disgust, and scorn. There was something, sweet and lovely, and the thing of dreams between them, and when she was in her dotage, and alone, she could think back on it, and think on the possibilities there might've been had her life been different. She could warm herself with imaginings of something more, something she'd never thought she could dream of ever again, and so she could not bring herself to ruin that.

I keep a little something for myself.

Tears that could never fall pricked her eyes, and though she wanted to turn away, to hide them, she couldn't. He begged her, silently, in turn, to let go, only Genevieve understood now, clearer than ever, why the answer had to always be *no*.

Because if she trusted him with one small piece, the floodgates would open, and she would trust him with everything. If she did, all her strength would go with it. She would be released, and the armour she'd crafted would disappear like smoke, and then where would she be? How could she carry on without it? How could she ensure Elizabeth's future, and even Jules's, without it?

And more terrifying than that, more terrifying even than his potential rejection, of her return to *nowhere*, was acceptance.

That he would take her nonetheless, all that she was, and—

'Elizabeth has finished,' she said, pushing back every slash of emotion, and taking a much-needed step back. Away from him. The echoes of Elizabeth's music had faded into silence, just as the echoes of any future with this man had faded into nothingness. 'You should go. And I would thank you not to return, my lord.'

'Thank you for today, *madame*.' He nodded. 'I shall never forget it.'

The same sadness and resignation that lived in her heart, she saw reflected in his eyes.

Or perhaps, she was simply being fanciful. Perhaps, he did not feel the same as she did, as if something monumentally wonderful had been snatched away by a cruel and vengeful God. Perhaps he was simply disappointed to be deprived of some *divertissement*. After all, he would be gone soon, back to Society, where he belonged, to continue on the course charted for all men of his ilk.

She truly wished that was the case, and that he didn't feel even a speck of what she did.

For she would never wish that bitter, brutal pain on him.

'We came here to start over,' Jules said, coming to stand with Genevieve at the window. She hadn't been able to stop herself going to it, vaguely thinking it might be cathartic, to literally watch *him* walk away from her, from Willowmere, from Elizabeth, from them all; but in the end, it had only made everything worse. Because then she'd longed to rush after him like some simpering lovesick fool, which she wasn't, because he was really nothing to her.

He was long gone now.

Still, she remained, staring out onto the garden, thinking it was strange that someone who meant absolutely nothing might leave such a gaping void.

'We didn't come here for you to bury yourself, Ginny.'

'I'm not burying myself,' Genevieve retorted, hoping the words might become true if said enough. 'We're building a life here. A sustainable one.'

'A safe one.'

Genevieve glanced back at her friend, pain morphing into righteous defensiveness.

'There is nothing wrong with that.'

'There is if your fortress is yet again shut so tight no light can enter.'

'Fostering a closeness with him is dangerous,' she sighed. 'You know that.'

'I think you are putting the proverbial cart before the horses,' Jules mused, and Genevieve frowned. 'I'm only saying, he seems kind enough. Elizabeth likes him. You like him, deny it though you may. You need not deny yourself a laugh, or a smile, or two…'

'The truth…could hurt him.'

'Don't play that card, Ginny,' Jules scolded. 'You're scared. And that is normal after all you and Elizabeth went through,' she continued, softer now, in that loving tone that would for ever be Genevieve's downfall. 'What Stapleton put us all through. But you are free of him. So, do not deny yourself another friend simply because you fear a future which isn't even a whisper.'

'To what end, Jules?' Genevieve asked, all her resolve melting away to reveal the hurt underneath.

The hurt of not being able to enjoy a man's company, a man's attentions, because the best you could ever hope for would be to be a mistress. Not even that. Men of Society such as the Marquess chose their bedfellows based on reputation as well. And hers was so blackened there could be no redemption. She might have permission to remarry, she might've fought hard for it, to feel well and truly free, but even if Stapleton hadn't besmirched her as he had, remarriage would never be possible. Even if a man were able to forgive her past, any man who married her would have to accept being scorned by Society. And a man such as the Marquess... Well. He could never.

Even if she wanted such things, which she didn't, because to give a man control like that again, to be subsumed into another...

No.

'What's the point, Jules? Elizabeth is already getting attached, and I...'

'So are you.' Genevieve nodded. 'The point would be happiness, even for a tiny moment.'

'A tiny moment steeped in lies.'

'You could always tell him the truth.'

'I thought about it,' Genevieve admitted quietly. 'For a moment, I was ready to. That's what scares me. How easily I would relinquish everything if he asked. How much I want him,' she choked out, turning to her friend, all semblance of excuses gone. Only the hard, terrible truth, she knew Jules, of all people, could understand. Her friend's past was a secret—apart from the fact that once, her own desire had nearly destroyed her. 'How much I would want *of* him. I don't understand, how I can feel so much, in an instant. It is... Beyond like and lust.'

'Ginny... I cannot explain this away. I wish I

knew why we forge such strong connections, in an instant. But I do not,' she stated, her own sadness tainting the weak smile she flashed. 'I understand, the fear. But we left one prison, we should not build another. No matter the noble reasons for doing so.'

Genevieve nodded, unable to say anything else.

Instead, she watched the wildflowers dance in the summer breeze, trying to convince herself that Jules was wrong.

A prison, could not be so beautiful.

Chapter Eight

It shouldn't hurt this much, Spencer thought as he set off towards Yew Park. He needed to pull himself together. This was unusual behaviour for him, and useless behaviour at that. Crying over spilt milk and such. After all, merely his pride was wounded. Nothing else. There was nothing else that could be wounded. He was simply disappointed. Yes, that was it.

Disappointed, and a little offended, frankly, and why shouldn't he be, after all. He was a good man; a polite, well-bred, man. Whenever they spent time together, he, Madame de l'Omont, and her daughter, it was wonderful. Cooking with them... had been, extraordinary. Special. Full of something he couldn't name, but that felt like part of what he'd been missing, and he didn't quite understand why she wouldn't want to spend more time with him.

Actually, that was a lie.

He knew bloody damned well why she wouldn't.

It was there, always, in the air, in the space between them.

Attraction.

And he was being a bloody liar by saying he didn't want more than friendship and time. He wanted those, but he also wanted for the first time in his life to surrender to attraction. To see where it could lead. Because the attraction between them, it had undercurrents of something more. Something brilliant, and invigorating, and—

She neither wants nor needs it, and you should respect that.

Leaving them be is the smart thing to do.

It was the smart thing to do, and he did respect it. Only that didn't diminish the sting. She'd been hurt by a man, as had her daughter. They didn't trust easily, he understood that. They didn't know each other—what right had he to demand trust?

None.

But he wasn't *demanding* it— he'd asked for it. Begged for it. And he knew she'd wanted to give in, that she did in tiny moments, that she wanted to trust herself to him, but then that damned wall had been drawn up between them again, she'd raised her shield, and shut him out, and *that* hurt.

His pride.

Naturally.

You shouldn't even be wanting their trust and company.

After all, what could they all ever be to each other?

Nothing.

The widow was right. Elizabeth couldn't get attached to him, nor he to her, to either of them, because he would leave, and then there would be only hurt. For all of them. And he wouldn't hurt them, not in a thousand millennia.

Best to leave it here, old chap.

Spencer kicked a pebble, and watched it soar into the air then tumble back, rolling until it disappeared into the loch.

I just—

I'm just—

Frustrated. Angry.

Not at the widow, but at himself. For breaking the tenuous link they'd created.

Broken the fragile trust they'd had—all because he'd craved more. Needed more. Like a man deprived of water in the desert. Madame de l'Omont and Lizzie brought light into his life, and now he'd lost that, all because he'd grasped too hard. Like trying to grasp water, they had simply slipped through his fingers.

This wasn't like him.

He was smart. Clever. Never made a move without knowing every possible outcome and weighing the risks and benefits. Never made a move without knowing with certainty what his opponents' would be. And yet he had. He couldn't quite read her, though she seemed more than able to read him, and that was…

Exciting, novel, terrifying.

He'd rushed in, eager, and *wanting*, and now he had nothing to show for it, but the same desolation he'd been so eager to leave behind.

Idiot.

What was it that had him behaving so? Could he blame it on the same restlessness that had forced him here to begin with?

No. It is something…other.

The craving he felt for Madame de l'Omont went beyond the flesh—beyond that which he'd felt for other women in the past. It was…a craving for only that which she could provide. A craving for a connection. His want was not only for her body, it was for her company. Knowledge of her in the utmost sense. Her trust, *her*, in her entirety. He wanted her in his life so badly he'd nearly said *damn the consequences* and—

Why does that sound familiar?

I need to write to Reid.

Spencer nearly ran the rest of the way. He made straight for the study, settled himself behind the desk, set his pen, ink, and parchment before him, and…

Nothing.

Tapping the pen against his cheek, he tried to

find the words which would accurately describe his predicament, and formulate his questions adequately. He'd never been in such a disquieting position before. Never spoken, asked such things of anyone. Likely because he was not *supposed* to be asking such questions in the first place, nor *feeling*, well, at all really.

Reid, I have a problem.

No.

Dear Reid,
I have a problem I hope you may assist me
with.

No.

Dear Reid,
I find myself in a situation—

No.
Coffee. He needed coffee.
So he rang for some, and sipped on it once it had arrived, recommencing his attempts.

Dear Reid,
I hope this letter finds you and Rebecca in
excellent health.

Better.

*I look forward to hearing the news of your
child's birth, then to meeting the little one
when they arrive.*

Well he wouldn't hear news unless he explained
where and how to write.
Quite.
Actually, an excellent way to bring that up;
likely Reid had already heard of his precipitous
departure, mother having doubtlessly interrogated
him for her wayward son's whereabouts.

*You will no doubt have heard of my de-
parture from London. Please find my current address below, so that you may share
the happy news as soon as you can.*

Awkward, but it would do.

*I am loath to trouble you in this time, but
I find myself in need of assistance regarding a rather delicate situation.*

A situation which shouldn't be delicate or troubling or which forced him to ask for assistance,
but, well, here he was.

I will be honest, Reid, I don't know why I am writing to you about this.

That much was true. Why the Hell was he writing this letter? Making an absolute huge affair of something that was absolutely nothing at all.

It's not nothing and you bloody well know it, old chap.

Back to the letter.

I don't know why I am writing to you about this, troubling you in a time which should be full of nothing but the wonder of your wife.

'Wonder of your wife?'
Moving on.

I find myself...interested. In a woman.

Putting it mildly.

To a degree which I find... I am not accustomed to.

Putting it *very* mildly.
Obsessed, entranced, fascinated, rendered dumb; slightly more accurate.

I find myself behaving rather uncharacteristically. Unable to accept her clear re-

*fusal of my polite company, which is most
ungentlemanly and boorish. Perhaps because I feel she is as...interested as I.*

*She is a widow, I should specify, and I be-
lieve has suffered in the past. I don't know
why my mind cannot let this matter lie—
indeed, soon I shall be returning to London,
and searching for a suitable wife. There can
be nothing more than friendship between
this woman and I, for a limited amount of
time, but I find... I want the time.*

*I find myself feeling as though I am wast-
ing what little time I have been given with
her, and her daughter, whom I think your
wife would like very much for some reason,
and I know that would be a terrible waste.
Something I would always regret.*

*Which is why I am writing. I am trying to
understand—*

No.

I need to know—

No.

*I am lost, old friend. That is the truth,
plain and simple. Coming here... Some days
I think it a mistake. Other days, a blessing. I
thought coming here would give me peace,*

*and certainty, instead I find none of that,
save in very rare moments.*

With her.

With them.
*We have lived very different lives, you and
I. I have never told you this, but I envy you
your courage, Reid. Your freedom. I suppose I wonder now... I ask for your counsel.*
*How did you find your way in those dark-
est days? How did you know when to take a
risk, when to gamble all you had, when to
keep on the same path, and when to change
direction? How did you know you wished to
take the great leap with Rebecca, knowing
all you would face?*
*I remember, Reid, telling you that you
could not make her your Countess. Then
you did, not knowing whether anyone would
stand by you; not knowing what kind of life
might await you.*

Where did a man get such faith?

*Where does a man get such courage? To
venture forth into the unknown, devils be
damned? Forgive me, Reid, I seem to have
become philosophical with time. Or perhaps*

it is this place, so full of simplicity, and wild-ness.

Regardless, there you are. Any thoughts you have on my frenetic ramblings would be most welcome.

In the meantime, all my very best to you, Rebecca, and the babe.
Yours,
Spencer

PS: My apologies if my mother has been ha-rassing you, however, I beg you, do not dis-close my whereabouts.

Spencer did not re-read the letter. He did not edit it, fix any turns of phrases, or do anything he normally did. He simply powdered the parchment, folded it, addressed it, and gave it to Josiah to be posted before he could change his mind.

Wandering back to the window, he felt lighter. No answers had miraculously come to him, but somehow, the hurt, the confusion, had lessened.

He would step aside.

Let the de l'Omonts be.

Feeling as if he could master time by grasping at things too tightly, was what had cost him. Now, he would simply try…

To enjoy the time you have here in whatever small ways you can.

Chapter Nine

It had been two days. All of two days. And Genevieve was officially losing her mind. It was all
Jules's fault. Jules and her words of *wisdom*. *'Do
not deny yourself another friend simply because
you fear a future which isn't even a whisper.'* She
made it sound so easy. So uncomplicated. But
what Genevieve had said to the Marquess was
true. It *was* complicated.

Case in point, it should've been easy to move
on. To stop thinking of him once she'd asked him
to leave and never return, then avoided his lands
like the plague, much to Elizabeth's chagrin.

*I will have Jules take her around the grounds
sometime...*

The problem was, she *couldn't* stop thinking of
him. The man had upset the status-quo. They had
a good life here. Quiet, tranquil. They were well-
fed and left to their own devices. There were good
people around, and they had what they'd never

had in their lives before. Independence, choice, freedom, pleasure. And then *he* had arrived, and it felt…

Like something is missing.

Which was preposterous, because, as stated previously, they had everything they needed.

If only I could stop thinking of him.

It was making her restless, and distracting her. How many times had she been too involved in her own thoughts, and not heard a word Jules or Elizabeth said? How many times had she made another utter mess of her lacework? She was becoming inattentive because her mind was too busy conjuring images of him.

Again.

It would begin innocently enough—a return to his gardens with Elizabeth. But then, they would be alone, and he would ask again, *'aren't you tempted?'*. There would be a stolen kiss. A brush of his fingers against her own. Another kiss, more ardent, passionate. He would hold her close and never let go—

And that is precisely the problem.

Precisely why she'd taken herself outside on this grey, wet day. Volunteered to feed Galahad and the chickens, and after that, gone on a walk. Not too far, just far enough to expend some of this frenetic energy. No amount of reassurances that she'd made the right decision, was being smart, and careful, that she was better off never see-

ing him again, was enough to quash this feeling
that her skin was too small to contain her. That
there were locusts travelling in hordes through
her veins, making her jittery, and jumpy, and it
certainly did not quench this burning need for
his touch.

Which was absolutely preposterous as he'd
never touched her, only got too close, in every
sense, and yet, she ached for him. Hungered for
him. She would fantasise about his taste, his heat,
what he might feel like inside of her. The past two
evenings, alone in her bed, she had taken liberties
with herself, hoping to relieve some of the tension.

It hadn't worked.

It wasn't enough.

She felt wrung, and wrung out, and nervous,
and miserable. As if she were some forlorn maiden
in a book, yearning for her true love.

It's just animal. Lust.

Which was driving her mad.

Madder than the pastries.

*The Marquess is not a pastry. We've been
through this.*

Indulgence would not be good.

She would tell herself this, endlessly, but then,
Jules's voice would come into her head.

'*We left one prison, we should not build another.*'

But why shouldn't she? This prison happened
to be supremely comfortable, and full of freedom,

and beautiful wildflowers. And safe. It was not a prison. It was a sanctuary. She'd given everything to build it. What was its purpose if she flung open the doors to all and sundry?

No purpose whatsoever.

Yet there was another voice, that grew stronger with every second of every day.

Why not indulge?

A discreet and honourable friendship with a man who treats you with kindness.

Because she couldn't trust herself, that was why.

Because there was an attraction, and friendship might be what they said they wanted, but her body demanded more. His eyes demanded more when he looked at her. Demanded everything she had to give.

And? You need only give that which you wish to.

What if you could have a discreet tryst with a friend?

After all, you know there can be nothing else. That he will leave soon.

It is within the bounds of what's done.

Why not indulge?

Her protests were growing weaker with every cycle of thoughts.

In the end, the voice would whisper, *you indulged in the pastries, and that is how you cured your desire for them.*

Giving in to temptation may be the path of the sinner, but it is a most delicious path.

'The Marquess is not a pastry,' Genevieve muttered angrily, pulling her shawl tighter as she forged on, crunching twigs and squishing through mud.

On she went, trying to drive the tempting madness from her thoughts and the thrumming need from her body by exerting herself on the landscape.

It didn't work.

Not solely because she was entirely certain *nothing* would work, but because she got carried away, and went literally too far. Marched herself right onto the Marquess's grounds. Still, it might've worked had she immediately walked herself back home. Only, the flickering of flames caught her eye, and she turned to find a bonfire raging on the loch shore, there in the midst of the little cove.

And so, her attempt at distracting herself from the Marquess failed miserably, because a moment later, the man in question rose from the waters like a young Neptune.

In that moment, Genevieve knew she would indulge.

Once. Just this once.

Your craving will be satisfied, and you can move on.

It was the final thought to cross her mind before all thought fled, and instinct prevailed.

Dazed, or more aptly, hypnotised, Genevieve walked towards him, leaving the confines of the thick, dark wood, for the open expanse of the cove. He saw her then, as she emerged from the trees, and stopped his own progress for a brief moment. Their eyes met, and she felt a calm certainty in her heart. That this was always how it was going to end.

That everything would be all right, because this was where she was meant to be.

Not so much fate, but a confluence of the decisions she'd made up to this point.

It gave her the courage to continue forward, until she'd reached the fire.

Just like in my dreams.

In her dreams, however, he hadn't been glistening wet, his hair slicked back, his sharpness cutting against the hazy grey background she couldn't see for he was all she could, and wished to see. She watched as he resumed his progress, sure, and steady, every inch of him visible, covered as he was only in old linen breeches. They clung to him, *every part of him*, reality surpassing imagination. Her hunger grew as she watched him move, sure, and slick in every step. He moved with as much ease and grace on land as he must in the water, until there he was, standing before her.

Her gaze followed the reverse path of the droplets that slid down his abdomen, followed them up past the lines of muscle, past the slope of his chest, the dip of his collarbone, the bump of his Adam's apple, along the bristly lines of his jaw, until she met his gaze.

There was no hesitation in the blue depths she was already drowning in.

No question, no shock, no surprise.

There was only need. Heat, and a steadiness, she could cling to.

They stood there, gazing at each other, breathing together, for a long moment.

The light of the fire danced across him, making his wet skin glitter, and sparkle, until he seemed to glow. A droplet slid from his hair, and Genevieve raised her hand, hesitant for a brief second before she allowed herself to follow it, and its brothers' paths with a finger.

The Marquess's skin was cold, but heat radiated from within. His eyes never left her as she trailed her finger along the lines of his face, then down his throat, there to that dip, and gooseflesh appeared as she continued down, over his left breast, over his heart.

It wasn't enough.

She needed more.

She let the rest of her hand continue the exploration, down further, along the slope of his belly, to the line of linen at his hips. It was so rough in comparison to *him*, and she savoured the contrast as she ran the palm of her hand along it. He shivered slightly, and she stepped closer, into his circle, into his heat, into his world.

Everything else disappeared. There was only this moment, in this cove, sheltered from the world. Invisible, but to the Heavens. There was no rain, no birdsong, nothing but the sound of their breathing.

One of his hands came to rest on her arm, and trailed down, forcing her to release the shawl she still clutched. It fell away, not that she noticed, too distracted by the glide of those fingers as they made their way to her own. They tangled together, and her other hand trailed upwards again, feeling every ridge, every bump of gooseflesh, every bristle of unshaven stubble until the tips of her fingers rested just beneath the ridge of his cheekbone. Her gaze went to his lips, which parted slightly, in invitation.

And then he was curving into himself slightly, lowering, just enough, his entire body a shield around her as she rose to her tiptoes, and met his lips with her own. It was a soft, somewhat clumsy brush, and so she tried again, gently raising herself, pressing her lips against his. Briefly, before doing so again, further along the seam of his lips, testing, tasting. She could taste the loch on him, fresh and bitter, and a hint of him, but nothing more.

Not yet.

Inhaling deeply, she revelled in his scent, as her lips continued their initial exploration along his mouth. There was no bergamot today, but somehow he still smelt of pine, musky salt and hundreds of her favourite things. The briskness of winter, warm chocolate, and sun-kissed carriage rides. There were a thousand comforting notes to his scent, all underscored by that essence that had no match, but was simply *him*.

The next time she kissed him, she took his bottom lip between her own, swiping the tip of her tongue against it, marvelling at the tiny ridges in the softness. The restraint the Marquess had shown, the control he had, *for me*, wavered, and his hand still in hers, he twisted her arm around, careful not to cause her pain, so that he held her across her waist, their hands resting, playing at the small of her back. His other hand cupped the nape of her neck, pulling her in close to continue what she'd started.

Her own hand slipped over his neck, fingers tangling in the wet strands as the kiss changed from sweet, tentative brushes, to intent sampling. There was mastery in his touch, as he explored her in turn, and she could feel it, his own passion, his own desire, barely restrained, though he let her take the next step.

So she did, taking one of his breaths for her own, letting her tongue slip into his mouth, searching for his. She needed to know his taste, needed to find that missing piece, drink from the waters her body craved so maddeningly. His grip tightened when she found him, nothing between the length of their bodies now but her dress, and the thin fabric of his breeches.

He was better than she'd imagined. She'd never tasted any delicacy so delicious, so perfect it seemed to enchant her anew with each stroke. There was sweetness, and boldness, like a sun-ripened peach, and it quenched her need even as it stoked it. Vaguely, she was aware of a sound humming in her throat, but she couldn't seem to care, couldn't seem to feel anything but the places where they connected.

He must've heard however, for in a second the mastery he'd been wielding vanished, and then it was only instinct. He was devouring her, curving over her until she thought she might fall, but she didn't care, because he was holding her, keeping her steady even as he tempted her with sweet oblivion.

Yes, please.

Spencer had thought she was a dream. A figment of his imagination—a trick of the Fair-Folk that he hadn't believed in until he'd seen her emerging from the misty woods as if conjured by his own desire. He'd tried to chase her from his thoughts, tried to move on, to find pleasure and purpose elsewhere, but he'd failed. Even his swim had not helped but to tire out his body.

Though he wasn't tired now. He was afire, alive again, or had he ever been alive?

When he'd seen her, realised she was real, he'd known.

We were not meant to part.

The flicker of surprise had faded, because he'd known that they hadn't reached their end, that every circumstance which brought them together had been blessings, and everything within him sang with joy. He couldn't think, didn't want to; didn't want to be reasonable and wonder on the consequences, the after. He'd been gifted this moment, and he would cherish every second.

There had been hesitancy in her eyes, a flicker, along with resolve, as she'd stood before him, the firelight making him wonder if she were not truly Artemis, and he'd known, somehow, that she needed something from him, needed *him*, and so he'd let her take. She could have everything he was for all he cared.

It was always hers to take, he amended when she first touched him.

He should've been freezing. Some parts of him definitely were affected, for a second at least, before she touched him. But then everything was alive inside, his skin, his nerves, his heart, everything waking as if it had laid dormant all his life.

It had.

I have.

The tentativeness of her touch, of her explorations reached an unknown, tender part of his heart. He'd understood, what a leap she was taking with him. He doubted she'd been with anyone save her husband, and what had that man shown her but cruelty? She was trusting him, with herself, and he vowed not to break that trust. He'd promised her he would keep any part she cared to share safe, and he meant to.

God, she is intoxicating.

Her scent, lavender and firewood; her taste, silky smooth like caramel, and something bittersweet, uniquely herself; her heat, the light pulsing from within, seeping into his bones, loosened the leash he held on himself. She was everything he'd dreamed of, and more. Reality surpassing imagination. He couldn't help but ask for more, seek more, losing himself as their tongues tangled together, and he held her close, so close. She fitted perfectly, though he could do without the scratch of her dress between them.

Never mind.

He had her fingers tangling with his own, soft but calloused, and he had that mane of hair he adored, wild and as velvety as down. And he could have more.

He shifted, releasing her mouth to take a breath, and turned his attentions to the satin skin of her cheeks, and her jaw, and her neck. She arched back for him, offering whatever he wished for, and he decided that he could live here, for ever, in this moment. There was no past, no future, no world outside, nothing but them, and nature. Fire, water, air, and wind. All there was at the beginning, and all there would be at the end.

He slid his hand from her neck to pull down the front of her gown, much too high for his liking, and proceeded to explore the creamy expanse beneath, offered up by the marvel of a corset she wore. Generally, he hated the things, but today he made an exception.

He nipped slightly at the abundant, yet disappointedly minimal flesh offered up for his delectation, and her fingers tightened in his hair, pulling him back. He obliged, moving back to gaze into her eyes. There was a flash of pain waiting for him in the green depths, and a request. He nodded, kissing the tip of her nose before returning to where he'd made his mistake, laving the spot instead with his tongue, and finishing his apology with a tender kiss.

Releasing the hand he'd kept trapped behind her back, he made to go for the buttons of her dress, *past time for that to go*, but she stopped him again, this time with a hand to his chest. He drew her up straight, then released her entirely, and stood, waiting.

I want it all, madame, but today, take what you will.

A dip of her chin, and a tremble at the corner of her lip told him she was grateful for that. Her hand still on his chest, over the heart that beat for her, she pushed him back slightly, moving him to where his clothes lay waiting. Another slight pulse of pressure, and he was sitting down on the discarded things, his eyes refusing to leave hers. Even if he'd wanted to, he wouldn't have been able to. There was an unexplored universe in them, *in her*, and he was lost in it.

Happily.

Then she was lifting her skirts, and settling atop his thighs. Nimble fingers went to the tie of the fabric still preserving some semblance of his modesty, and he rose as she divested him of that final piece. Sliding herself closer, she wrapped one arm around his neck, and he took hold of her waist, stopping her for a moment, to ensure she was certain. He was, God knew he was, but he needed to know she would not regret this. So he asked her silently, searching her eyes for any hint of hesitation, but there was none.

Only vulnerable certainty, as she took him in hand, and guided him inside herself. She was ready for him, so quickly, receiving him with slick heat that nearly made him lose his mind. His other arm went around her, until he was holding her as close, as tightly as he could. Their lips met, and the frenzy of the kiss belied the kindness, the compassion, the care within. She rose and fell, slowly at first, her hips, her body moving in a rhythm as old as time. He held her tight, guiding her a little when she faltered, unsure, as if seeking that which she'd never known.

Perhaps she has never known it.

And he...

Had never known anything like this. He'd never known it could be like this—beyond the heat, the sweaty stickiness, the maddening pleasure. He'd never known you could feel the ripples of each stroke in your chest, in your heart; that you could feel each brush of lips carving your soul, reshaping it into something other.

And he wanted more, Hell he wanted it all, all of her, laid bare, nothing at all between them. Not the dress, and not that wall that still shielded her soul from him. It was still there, in her eyes, he saw it for a brief moment as she pulled away from the kiss. He asked her to lower it, but instead she lowered her head, burrowing into the crook of his shoulder.

One day.

She clutched him tighter, her breath unsteady against his neck, her nails digging into the skin of his back and scalp. Her pace quickened as she sought that peak, and he let one of his arms fall from her waist, trailing it under her skirts, over her wool stockings, up until he found her innermost self, just above where they joined.

Tighter still she held him, as he caressed the

dewy bud, repeating certain strokes when he felt her breath hitch or her legs tremble. Higher he sent her, as he himself climbed right behind her.

A quiet cry sounded at the back of her throat as she stopped, her inner walls clenching him so wonderfully he had to bite his lip to stop himself from spilling inside her. He held her close, revelling in her heat, her pleasure, as she crested, then fell. Once she had, he slid his hand from her sex, under her buttocks, gently lifting her so he could remove himself from her depths.

It was torture, not the exquisite kind, everything within him shouting that he was leaving the place he belonged, truly belonged, but it had to be done. Still, he held her as close against himself as he could, his other hand gently stroking her hair, soothing her. He felt her radiating a sweet sort of pain, that which comes with the little death, complete surrender and freedom, but also something more.

Something he wanted to soothe, wanted to fix, wanted to mend, if only he could.

But she would not let him.

Perhaps she felt the shift in him—from lover to *lover*—and so she began rocking again, brushing herself against his unfinished self. And he let her, gripped himself as she helped him reach his own completion.

He would've been lying if he said it didn't feel good, if the pleasure wasn't delightful, but it felt, *incomplete.* He felt incomplete somehow. As if for the briefest second, he'd touched her soul, glimpsed beyond the veil, only for its shining brilliance to be taken away.

They sat there, entwined, for a time after, basking in the glow of the dying fire, the drizzle steadily washing away the heat, the scent of their togetherness, until there was naught but cold between them again.

And all he had found with her was snatched away. The woman who had been with him, the nameless woman he needed more than air, was gone, and in her stead was Madame de l'Omont.

Who released him, and rose, and ran, before he could do anything to stop her.

Chapter Ten

No, no, no, no, no. It wasn't meant to be like that.
The pleasure—yes, that was what she'd sought,
known she would find with him. But the rest…
the rest was precisely why she'd stayed away. Why
she had denied herself the temptation, why she
should've ignored the little voice telling her to indulge because the Marquess wasn't a *goddamned
pastry.* He was the most dangerous being she'd
ever encountered, she'd known that from the first,
so why hadn't she stayed away?

Pusillanimous feather-brained dimwit.

Genevieve cursed herself with a hundred more
insults as she ran, as fast, and far as she could,
from the Marquess. It numbed the hurt a little,
the hurt not of injury, but of healing.

The worst kind.

The pain in her legs, in her ribs, the pound-
ing of her heart, the shortness of breath, they distracted from the searing pain of parts of her soul

mending. Only the distraction didn't last long, in an instant she was back at the edge of Willowmere. She stopped, and braced herself against a tree, unable to go inside, to emerge from the forest, just yet. She had to…

Pull yourself together.

Yes. That.

You're letting your mind and heart run away with you.

Yes. Precisely.

It was only scorching pleasure.

Yes. The novelty had…stunned her. Discountenanced her.

Just so.

All her life, her desires had been designated as *unimportant*, and so she'd quashed them. Her desire itself, her carnal fire, had been deemed *shameful* by her husband, as well as society. It was not for her to want. So having a man not only allow, but *encourage* her need, welcome it, revel in it, was…novel.

Liar.

If only it were that simple.

Clutching the tree as she'd clutched *him*, letting it support her as *he* had, Genevieve forced herself to take in long breaths through her nose, slowly releasing them through her mouth. Jules had taught her that, when she'd begun having attacks those first months, when the proceedings had begun, and Stapleton had initiated his ultimate act of cruelty and humiliation. When she'd had a choice: crumble and be defeated, or stand strong.

It helped a little, though it did nothing for the tempest in her breast.

She'd known there was more than lust between them. She'd felt it, from the first touch, and she should've run then. But it felt so *good*, to be desired. It felt *good* to be protected, and cared for, and listened to, and worshipped, and to be given control. To feel like a woman, a being, in and of herself, independent of name, rank, title, even role. To be given power; to be given leave to take. She'd been so drunk on it, on him, on how it felt to hold him inside herself, to truly connect in body, and in—*say it, Genevieve, heart*—that she hadn't been careful. She'd thought she could easily separate her heart from the rest—whilst knowing that with another, perhaps she might've, just not with him. She'd let him in, let him seep into her, let his touch stitch back minute pieces of herself.

It wasn't up to him to do that. She shouldn't have allowed it. His tenderness, his sweetness, his attentiveness, she wished now that she'd never known it.

Liar.

Yes.

It was a lie. Her heart cried that she'd never wish to unknow that. Though she did regret it, because she would never have it again. It was not better to feel as if magic and wonder were within reach and lose, than to never know any of it. She'd been just fine in her little prison, there was enjoyment there. She'd been just fine in the darkness—like Eve before the Fall.

Fine is good.

Good enough.

People underestimated contentment. Contentment was better than living death, better than despair. Contentment was sufficient to get through life. But how did one go back to *contentment* when the possibilities of more existed?

With him.

How did one go back to being *mother*, and *friend*, when one could be fulfilled, a whole person not solely defined by their roles? No matter how fulfilling those roles might be, they weren't who she was in her entirety. But they had been enough for so long. Hinging her happiness, her satisfaction on Elizabeth's, had been enough. Society, the Church, they said that was her purpose. What she'd been created for. Indeed, she felt that truth, and the privilege it was to be *mother*.

But now, it didn't feel like enough to complete her, and that was wrong, wasn't it? Being a mother should be enough. Being a friend on top of that, should be more than enough. For so long, it was all she'd wanted. Wanting more, was greedy.

Wanting to be a whole person independently of others is neither wrong nor greedy, the pernicious, troublemaking voice whispered.

Isn't feeling a whole person thanks to another's touch undermining the concept of independence?

'Bugger,' Genevieve muttered, annoyance slowly overtaking the heart-wrenching healing.

If she could think philosophically, then her reason was returning. The haze of pleasure was fading, though she might've sworn she could still feel him, taste him, smell him. As if he'd been woven into the fabric of her being when she'd stitched back pieces of herself.

Nonsense. Just an exceptionally good bout of rutting.

The stab in her heart disagreed, but it had no say on the matter.

Because really, she had no way of knowing whether what they'd shared was anything *but* an exceptionally good bout of rutting. She'd only lain with her husband before, experienced some stolen kisses before that, but who was to say that the way the Marquess felt inside her was special? That there wasn't some other man out there who might feel just as…as…magic. Just because it hadn't felt like that with her husband, didn't mean anything.

He'd been a right selfish bastard, particularly in bed.

And that had been different. A marriage. Lying with each other to beget a child.

Not pure, unadulterated passion.

Yes. Right. Quite.

Be grateful for the gift you were given.

Be grateful for a thoughtful, kind lover, to have shown you what you'd never known.

Be grateful for having experienced connection and trust beyond what you thought possible.

And move on.

He would.

Soon.

Be grateful for that too.

Chapter Eleven

'There's nothing in there, my lord,' Josiah said as he climbed back out of what would've been the dower house's dining room window. 'Nothing but traces of wild things,' his valet added as he dusted himself off, and came to stand before him. 'Even the wall furnishings were stripped. I'm sorry.'

Sighing, Spencer nodded, his gaze still on the wild, forbidding house.

It had been a gamble. He'd known it would likely win him nothing, but he'd had to try. He'd been intent on going in himself, but Josiah wouldn't hear of it. *'Much too dangerous,'* the man had said, citing the likelihood of rotten floorboards and other such hazards, and in the end, Spencer capitulated. Though it was less the prospect of bodily harm which forced him to cede; more the fear of what he might see, feel, *remember*, inside.

Cowardly, perhaps, but then, he was not ashamed

to admit it. He *wanted* to remember, Heavens knew he did, but taking that step, going in *there*... There was only so much a man could take in a matter of days. Going in had seemed a good idea at the time he'd had it, but once he'd stood before the house again, he'd let Josiah sway him into remaining here, staring at the overgrown grey stone, the wind whispering the words he'd heard when he first arrived over and over.

'Henry... Our secret...'

Spencer shook his head, literally shaking himself back to the present, chasing away the whispers of the past.

'My lord,' Josiah began tentatively, taking up a post beside him, staring up at the old house as well. 'May I be so bold as to ask, what is it you are looking for? You've seemed troubled since we left London. Before then, even.'

Long before then, Josiah.

'I don't quite know.' He shrugged, turning away, and making his way through the vegetation back to the path. 'Answers to old questions I never thought of till I came here.'

Spencer glanced over at his valet, who, rather than look as perplexed as Spencer felt, simply nodded pensively.

'I'll keep looking, my lord,' Josiah said after a moment. 'Though I think, perhaps, the answers may need to be demanded by yourself.'

'Do you think me cowardly if I admit I seek other ways so I won't have to?'

'No, my lord.'

Spencer raised an eyebrow, wondering if the man's dissent stemmed from his urge to serve, and not offend.

'You may speak plainly, Josiah,' he assured him. 'You have served me, what, ten years now? You know me better than most, I think,' he said, realising the truth of it in that moment. The extent of it. Distance was something one was taught to maintain between master and servant. Yet those who served saw more of his true, inner life, than those called friends. *Even family.* 'Seen me through good times, and trying times. I believe we have reached a point, found a place, a moment in time, when we can be honest, and speak as men.'

'My answer remains the same, my lord,' Josiah said with a smile. He stopped, and Spencer followed suit, waiting for whatever wisdom the man might share like a beggar waiting for mercy. 'It isn't easy, for anyone, to confront another. To demand the truth, when we know before we hear it that the truth may hurt us more than ignorance ever did.'

'You think the truth will hurt me?'

'I think,' Josiah said carefully, studying the trees over Spencer's shoulder. 'That if there was nothing to hurt you, we would've discovered it by now.' Josiah met his eye, and Spencer nodded.

'But that is not all that troubles you, my lord,' he continued. 'Since we speak as men.'

'I thought coming here would settle me,' Spencer admitted, as he began ambling on. 'We all have parts to play, in life, don't we, Josiah?' The man nodded, and he continued. 'Mine has always been very defined. My path, certain. But I began to feel…apprehensive, I suppose. Hence our sudden departure from Town. I thought distance, time, new experiences, might help me regain my bearings. But it seems to have made matters worse.'

'Has this anything to do with the widow?' Josiah asked, and Spencer stopped, eyeing the man with surprise. 'She is very beautiful, my lord.'

Understatement of the century.

She was more than that. She was a lighthouse in the harbour, beckoning him. She was sensuous, and lovely, and—

She left me.

Two days. Two days since she'd come to him, and he could no sooner rid himself of her scent, her touch, the feel of her taking him within herself, than he could stop breathing. The other reason he'd been forced on this expedition to the dower house. Without her…

The past returned with a vengeance. The nightmares worsened, and nothing could chase the fear, the confusion from his breast. When she and Lizzie were around, the rest faded away. Seemed…less important. Without them…

There is no light.

He'd waited endlessly, for the widow to come to him again, to send a note, to say something, to say what had passed between them meant as much to her as it did him. It had taken so much for her to come, he knew that, just as he knew she needed time, to come to terms with it, hence why he hadn't gone after her as soon as he'd recovered his senses. He'd made the mistake of grasping too tight before, and he wouldn't again. But then, the doubts had begun creeping in.

What if she hadn't felt the same way?

What if she'd simply used him to experience that which she hadn't before?

What. If.

'The widow certainly has a part to play in my confusion,' Spencer said finally.

A starring role, really.

'An unusual interest for you, my lord,' Josiah said with a wry, knowing smile, and Spencer chuckled. *Another glaring understatement.* 'What is it you want from her?'

'Time,' he said without hesitation.

Time to discover what binds us.

Time to discover who you are.

Time to discover whether certain things are possible.

Time to simply be as I never have.

Josiah nodded, seemingly understanding all that was left unsaid.

'And the lady will not give it?'

'The lady giveth, and the lady taketh away.' Spencer sighed, and rubbed his jaw, determined to out with it all. 'I admit, I begin to doubt if she truly is so different from the other women I've known.'

'She has lost, my lord,' Josiah said slowly, conscious of his position as Devil's advocate. 'I suspect, someone like that, would be reluctant to… get attached again. Her presence here suggests diminished circumstances. I can see why she might be uneasy, trusting someone so far from her reach. After all, my lord, other than time, what can you offer?'

Spencer's heart twisted a little and he grimaced.

With a simple shrug, Josiah set off again, and a moment later, Spencer followed.

What can I offer indeed?

But perhaps, if that was all, it could be enough.

For us both, madame.

After returning to the house, Spencer had done some more thinking. Something which he was doing a lot of lately. Which was good, but odd. He always thought, measured, weighed various plans and stratagems, but he never truly *thought*. Examined his heart, his desires. Hence, coming here.

He'd come to the conclusion last night, a conclusion cemented this morning after yet another tantalising dream of Madame de l'Omont, that it was time to be a man about this situation. She'd come to him, and they had shared…

Something extraordinary.

In his opinion.

Perhaps it was only pent-up passion. Perhaps it was nothing more than a quick tumble. All he knew, was that it wasn't, not for him. And unless he spoke to her, confronted her, declared in plain terms what he wanted, well, he would never know.

All he knew, was that he would regret silence.

And so it was, that he found himself travelling the path to Willowmere that bright afternoon, so full of sunshine, fluffy white clouds, and promise.

Or so it seemed.

Once at Willowmere, Spencer did not have to look far to find his quarry. He found the confounding woman at a table on the lawn behind the cottage, those nimble hands that haunted his dreams furiously twisting this way and that as she worked on her lace.

At least, that is what he guessed it was. He'd never seen anyone make lace, and he thought, even if he had, it wouldn't be quite the same. He remained there, watching her for a long moment, her dedication, speed, and talent hypnotising. But then, everything about the woman seemed to keep him spellbound. She could be doing nothing at all, and he would be spellbound.

A giggle broke his reverie, and he spied Lizzie playing with the demonic goat a little away, where the point jutted out into the loch. She spied him too, and waved, but he pressed a finger to his lips and she nodded, continuing on with whatever game she was playing.

They all made a pretty picture, he thought, even the horrid, coat-munching goat.

And that desire to be part of it somehow, even if for a moment, returned.

Which is why you're here.

Right.

He strode onwards, his purpose renewed, and quietly planted himself at *madame*'s side, dropping the shawl she'd forgotten in her haste to literally run away, at the edge of her table.

'You've been avoiding me,' he said after a moment.

He knew she'd noticed him; far more alert to her surroundings than she seemed, but perhaps she'd hoped he might just whisk himself away from whence he'd come.

No such luck. You will not be rid of me so easily this time, madame.

After all, he did deserve an explanation, at least.

Quite so.

'I have not,' Madame de l'Omont said stiffly, though she faltered on a twisting of her bobbins and a small part of him cried out in victory.

You lie, madame.

'You have been busy, then,' he offered.

'Very.'

'I see.'

'Was there anything you needed, my lord?'

'Would you believe me if I said I missed you?'

And there goes another twist. What do you call that? A stitch?

'If you are concerned I shall ask for something more, you need not be.'

Ah, so she doesn't believe me, but would like to.

If she'd looked up then, she might've seen him grinning like an idiot.

'What if I wished for more.'

God, do I wish for more.

'I have no interest in pursuing an affair.'

'Who said anything of an affair? I simply wish to know you better,' Spencer said, hoping she could hear the truth, for still, she refused to look at him. 'I like you,' he admitted. There were thousands of pretty words, but he knew she would believe none of them. Now simplicity, unfettered truth, *that* he could give her. 'And Lizzie. I like who I am with you.'

'We both satisfied a need,' she said coldly, her grip on those bobbins so tight he could see her knuckles whitening. His own fists tightened, along with his heart. *So it was nothing more to her.* Had he truly been so wrong? Felt something that wasn't there? 'There can be nothing more.'

'Satisfied a need,' he repeated dully.

'Do you deny it? There was an attraction,' she

said, as if speaking of the damned weather. 'We succumbed to it. Surely you are well versed in such trysts. It is the way of Society.'

'To use and discard people? Indeed,' he spat, unable to contain the hurt, despite knowing that was very much her intention.

'There can be nothing more.' Not, *'I don't want there to be anything more.'*

'But it is not my way.'

'Is it not,' she retorted, finally, *finally*, setting down her work, and rising to face him. 'You are so entrenched in that world's rules I imagine you select mistresses as one would a stallion. Deal with them coldly, but respectfully. Only fulfilling a need, in an acceptable fashion, until such time as you find a young bride so like you in every way she too shall fulfil your needs and think of England as she breeds your heirs.'

What hurt most was that she was right.

That every word, every accusation, was true, in every possible way, and he hated that. Hated that all she said *had* been his way. *Would* be his way, if he continued down this path he was on.

Only, that isn't what he wanted, he never had, and he had to make her understand, that was why he was here, *goddamnit*, only his hurt spoke before his mind and heart could catch up.

'And what of you? You speak of using people, but did you not do the same? You float about, doing whatever you please, without care nor consequence. Without care of who you hurt—'

'Are you saying I hurt you? Perhaps your pride, because I dictated the terms—'

'Madame—'

Whatever he was about to say, was swallowed by the scream that rent the air, quickly followed by a splash.

Lizzie.

They both turned to where she'd been, but she was gone, as was the damned goat.

'Elizabeth,' Madame de l'Omont screamed as they both tore off towards the last spot she'd been. 'Elizabeth!'

Madame de l'Omont blanched and Spencer's own heart had stopped in his chest.

'She cannot swim,' Madame de l'Omont yelled as they drew up to the edge, her terror palpable.

And I share it.

There were ripples a short distance away, and his dread grew ten-fold. The water was deep here, a straight cut down from the steep bank.

'Neither can I.'

The admission mattered little; Spencer was already devoid of his coat and shoes, and in the water. He didn't register the cold, only the horror of not being quick enough to save the girl. It took the longest few seconds of his life to find Lizzie, but then finally he felt a push of water towards him and he threw his hands in that direction. A brush of cotton told him he'd found her, and he grasped it tight, pulling the material towards him until he had the girl in his arms. She thankfully ceased her own battling, and he pushed up to the surface.

They both took large gulps of air, and Spencer carefully wrapped his arm around her shoulders to keep her calm, and above the water. Holding her close against his chest, he looked back up to the bank, and saw Madame de l'Omont shaking, clutching herself tight, and she nodded to him gratefully.

Lizzie coughed and spluttered, and he made his way to where they could come up easier on shore.

'It's all right, Lizzie,' he whispered soothingly, Madame de l'Omont following their progress to meet them. 'I've got you.'

'Galahad,' she muttered, and Spencer couldn't help but laugh, the relief washing over him and making him dizzy.

He glanced around and found the irresponsible knight already waiting for them, munching happily on grass.

'He is fine. And soon, so shall you be.'

Always, he promised silently.

For no matter what had been said, or done, no matter what happened in life, he knew he would be there for her. *Had* to be there for her. Whatever he could do to bring her joy, or ease her way in the world, he would. If he failed everything but that, then, his life would at least have had a purpose. And what a glorious purpose it would be.

Chapter Twelve

'I'm sorry, Maman,' Elizabeth said for the hundredth time, as Genevieve settled the blankets up to her daughter's chin. Elizabeth had finally stopped shivering, having been warmed in the bath, forced to drink at least two pots of hot tea with honey, and redressed.

I will not lose her today.

Genevieve, on the other hand, couldn't stop shaking. She tried, so very hard; she didn't want Elizabeth to see and feel worse, but the terror that had coursed through her veins was still there, bubbling and boiling her blood, and the more she tried to stop it, the worse it became.

How she wished she could cry, just fall down right there and cry away the fear, the relief she'd felt when the Marquess had come up with a spluttering Elizabeth. When she'd known for certain she hadn't lost her daughter. How nice it would be to release all of that, to let it go, only she couldn't.

Strong. You must remain strong.

Even if she truly, truly wished to, would her body even remember how to cry? She felt the salty signs of weakness prick her eyes sometimes, but they never fell. It had been so long; fifteen years, probably more. The tears had gone when she'd built her armour; when she'd learned to hide the hurt, to numb herself until she felt nothing at all. *Showed*, nothing at all.

A lesson taught by her parents but that had served her well with her husband.

'Please don't hurt Galahad, it wasn't his fault.'

'I won't,' Genevieve said, though she wanted nothing more than to flay the beast.

If the Marquess hadn't been there—

Stop. Do not think of what might've happened.

Easier said than done. It was all Genevieve *had* done since she'd learned she was with child. Worried what might happen to the one being she loved more than life. The being who had given her a reason *to* live again.

'Promise,' Elizabeth ordered wearily. 'It was my fault for playing too close to the edge, he didn't mean to trip me.'

Sighing, Genevieve settled herself into the chair by her bedside and looked down into the pleading green depths—her downfall, always. Particularly when her daughter looked altogether so small, and—

'I promise,' she said begrudgingly. 'I will not hurt Galahad.'

Elizabeth relaxed and her eyes finally fluttered shut.

It really wasn't the beast's fault after all, Genevieve thought as she watched her daughter fall into peaceful slumber, as she had so many times before. It was, for a long time, the only time she'd been able to see Elizabeth, Juliana sneaking her into the nursery. Sometimes she would lie beside her and breathe in the scent of her hair. The most comforting scent in the world—the most wondrous. Mostly she would just sit there, as she did now, watching the rise and fall of this small being's chest, so mesmerising. This part of her, that she would do anything for.

Yet you failed her today.

If it was anyone's fault, it was her own, for not watching Elizabeth properly. She'd looked away, let her mind wander for the briefest second— and this was what had happened. For days she'd dreaded the Marquess coming here, for days she'd hoped he would just *let it be*. Satisfy himself with what she'd given. She had armed herself, prepared for battle in the eventuality that he did, but then he'd said those things...

'I missed you.'

'I like you. And Lizzie.'

The cool, unaffected demeanour had slipped, he'd chipped away at her armour again, and she'd

had to fight so hard against that irresponsible heart
of hers crying ceaselessly as it had for days, *yes,
yes, stay with me, keep us close, be with us*.

So she'd pushed through the temptation, and
lashed out, lost her temper, and then the man
hadn't even had the decency to fight as dirty as
her, to prove he was unworthy. No, he had to attack with painful truths, and so she'd lost her
focus, and with that, she'd nearly lost that most
precious to her. If she lost Elizabeth, she had nothing. She was nothing. Elizabeth was the only thing
that kept her going, and without her…

There was no purpose to anything.

So she could not afford to be distracted again.

She could not risk her own emotions taking
her off her guard.

You know what you must do.

Yes, that she did.

Already, things had gone too far.

This, *this*, was the price of indulgence.

'His Lordship is standing guard in the corridor,'
Jules said as she slipped in some time later, a tonic
ready for whenever Elizabeth woke, to stave off
fever. The darkness in the room was the only sign
time had passed. Jules looked down at Elizabeth
with as much love in her eyes as Genevieve, and
she knew her decision was the right one. 'It took
all I had to force him to take care of himself—he
was beside himself with worry.'

Do not tell me that. You'll only make this harder.

'We owe him a great debt,' Genevieve said hollowly.

She might know her decision was right; still, it seemed to carve something out of her she didn't think she could be without.

'It's not your fault, Ginny,' Jules said gently, which stung all the more. 'It's not anyone's fault. It was an accident.'

'I know,' she lied. Jules looked ready to protest, but Genevieve rose and gave her a convincing enough smile. 'I should speak to him. I'll be back in a short while.'

'Take your time,' Jules said, though there was wariness in her eyes, as if she suspected Genevieve was about to do something she wouldn't agree with. *It isn't your decision to make.* 'I'll stay with her.'

'Thank you.'

Taking a deep, steadying breath, Genevieve glanced down at her hands before she opened the door.

Shaking no longer. Proof that this is what must be done.

And so, she left the room, to put an end to what she'd begun.

Before it's too late.

'How is she?' Spencer asked, pulling himself up from the floor as Madame de l'Omont finally emerged. He'd sat there in vigil for however long it

had been since he'd drunk the tea Miss Myles had
provided, and redressed once his clothes were on
the dryer side of damp. He couldn't be sure how
long precisely that was, time slowed to a gruel-
ling pace as he waited for news.

'A good night's sleep, and she will be right as
rain,' Madame de l'Omont said quietly.

'My offer to send for the doctor still stands,
should she develop a fever—'

'Juliana and I will keep an eye on her tonight,'
she said reassuringly, and he nodded.

Of course they would.

She was Lizzie's mother, and he was…

Nothing.

They would take care of their own, and that
was the way of it, but after all he'd felt, after that
promise he'd made in the water, he couldn't deny
he hated the fact that he wasn't part of *their own*.

Madame de l'Omont gestured towards the corridor, and he understood. They began walking
back downstairs slowly, both aware of all that remained unsaid; all that needed to be said before
he took his leave. Which was why she led him
back towards the kitchen, and prepared another
pot of tea. He sat down, and watched her, the only
sound that of her preparations, and the crackling
of the fire.

She looked so…

Tired.

Beautiful still, to him, perfect, and wonderful, but tired. Though she stood as proud as ever, it felt as if today's ordeal had bled her dry of her strength. She felt brittle, as if a gentle breeze might knock her down, and all he wanted to do was take her into his arms, and give what strength he had. She could take it all, leave him with nothing, and he would be content.

But he could not.

There was still a barrier between them. Thinner than ever, like the veil between worlds, and yet as impassable.

'Did she say what happened?' he asked as she set down the tea, and served them both, cradling her own cup in her hands as if attempting to revive herself with its warmth.

Take my warmth, take it all, I give it gladly.

'Galahad tripped her,' she sighed, not meeting his eyes, lost instead in a world of her own. 'I would kill the creature, but she has forbidden it.'

Madame de l'Omont shook her head and set down her cup. He watched as the frustration turned into hesitancy, and she began stroking the handle of the delicate china before her distractedly.

In the light of the fading sun, she seemed to fade away herself, into its rays, and it terrified him.

'I will have a fence erected,' he said gently, hoping to keep her here, with him. *Do not fade away.* 'So it can never happen again.'

Her lashes lowered, and she took a deep breath before raising her eyes to his.

There was a universe in them, as there always seemed to be, but this one was full of the emptiness he'd felt himself not so long ago. He swallowed hard, the recognition terrifying and heartbreaking, and was about to reach out to her, rules be damned, when finally she spoke.

'Thank you,' she said, in a voice that was not a whisper only because of the force of the emotion beneath the words. 'Thank you,' she repeated.

And this time, he did reach out.

He reached across the table, reached across the chasm between them and finished the bridge she'd created. He took her hand in his own, gently rubbing his thumb across the back of her knuckles.

He'd thought for a moment she might reject him, tear herself away, but instead she gazed down at their hands, and he could feel her, taking what was offered.

'I would say there is no need.' He smiled, somehow more at peace in that moment than he'd been his entire life. 'But I know you need to speak the words.'

She nodded, and he took the opportunity to test his luck. He leaned over, and raised her hand to his lips. Still, she did not recoil.

'In case I wasn't clear before, I should like to spend time with you,' he said softly, laying their hands back on the table, but refusing to relinquish the connection. This wasn't the best time to broach the subject, but he knew he wouldn't get another chance. 'Get to know you both.' A faint smile danced across her lips, and there was a flash of hope in the evergreen depths of her eyes. 'When Lizzie is well, perhaps I can teach her to swim. Teach all of you.'

'I would like that,' she breathed, and Spencer smiled, hope invading his own heart. Until he saw the light fade in her again. 'But I cannot accept.'

She drew her hand away slowly, the loss chilling him to the marrow.

'Have I given you cause to doubt my motives?' he asked, his need to understand so desperate he didn't care if she saw. He wanted her to see; see how deeply she affected him. 'Do you find my company distasteful? For I'll admit,' he said, leaning back in his chair, trying to think on *what* could be stopping her now. From accepting what Fate had declared was to be theirs and being joyous about it. 'I cannot understand why else you would refuse a…friendship,' he said, at a loss for a better word. He did want friendship, that and so much more, but if it was all he could have, damn him, he would take it, and be fulfilled by it. 'I am unattached. You are a widow, and though still in mourning, there is nothing unseemly about our spending time together. Despite what happened between us—'

'I'm divorced.'

The words were like a shot in the dark.

Everything stilled, until Spencer couldn't even hear his own heart beating.

If it still does.

He stared at her, trying to understand, trying to make sense of the words which were like stones, preventing him from breathing, from thinking.

'I'm divorced,' she repeated, the veil that had been for the briefest moment swept away, back in place. There was such distance between them then, and she put it there. To preserve herself. *From me.* 'Not a widow.'

And in that moment, Spencer understood.

All the pieces of the puzzle came together, and he knew. Why he recognised her. Why she was afraid of recognition. Why she was so removed from any society. He realised *who* she was.

Oh God.

'Lady Stapleton,' he breathed.

'De l'Omont was my grandmother's name. I am the Great Whore of Hadley Hall.' She nodded, a challenge in her eyes, and Spencer flinched, unable to meet it. 'Catchy little moniker, isn't it? So you see… Should anyone discover who I am… Our association…'

Her voice trailed off, but her gaze and countenance were steady.

How could she be so steady when he was there, tumbling through a void, his entire world slipping away from beneath his feet? How could she be so calm, and cold, as she revealed the depths of her deception?

He wanted to scream, to demand how she could've lied to him all this time, he wanted to scream at himself for not listening, to her and his own instincts, and staying far, far away.

Only no words would come.

'It is not for myself that I refuse, but for you. Not only would you suffer, but your entire family,' she continued, stating things as if he did not know very well indeed what all this meant. Being publicly attached to a widow would've been scandalous enough; but a divorcée… *Ruin. Impossible.* 'You said nothing mattered more than duty, and your good name. Don't risk damaging it for a fleeting fancy that will wither and die like a flower in the frost.'

Damn but the woman is masterful.

That final stroke, a kill strike, did its work, and did it well. It felled him, tore into him like shrapnel, sweeping away all that had been light and good for the tiniest moment, and turning it to ash.

'A fleeting fancy.'

Spencer didn't know how he managed to draw in another breath, and rise, steadily onto his own feet. He felt as if he would be ill, as if he might tumble onto the floor right then, but he didn't. He rose, and bowed his head, every lesson so deeply ingrained into his being he could do nothing else.

'*Madame.*'

And then he was gone, turning his back on her, leaving that damned cottage, and walking as far and fast as he could.

Never once looking back.

That would only worsen his curse.

It's done. It had taken all of what little strength she had left, but it was done. Now… Now she could rest a while. Rebuild. Piece back together all she'd destroyed with her own selfish folly. The task was daunting, but she would manage. She always managed. It would take time, and it would take strength she didn't have right this moment, but she would pick herself up soon, and be right as rain.

Right as rain.

It may not feel like it, it may feel like she was lost again in the land of nowhere, tired, desperate, alone, and hurting, and so she may be. But she knew the land of nowhere well. She may be lost, but she would find her way from it again.

Even if it didn't quite feel like it just now.

Even if it felt like she was bruised and bloody, her own heart torn from her chest to be thrown at the feet of a man who didn't even have the decency to stomp on it. No, he had to go and just look at her with that devastating understanding, that horror, and go and just leave.

No raging, no fight, nothing.

Just a polite bow, and that damned word, *ma-dame*.

She'd seen hurt and betrayal in his eyes too, but then apparently it hadn't even been enough to force him to relinquish all he was, as she'd been so tempted to do just for a chance to be with him a little longer, safe and warm. She'd nearly balked at telling him once he'd taken her hand. The last line of defence she'd built against him and the world had been swept away with that, and she'd wished she could remain there, in that moment, for ever.

But the land of *warm* and *happy* and *safe* was even more terrifying than *nowhere* because she didn't know that land.

And so you never will. Not like that. Never again.

In time, she might be lucky to find a land where she was happy and warm and safe, with Elizabeth and Jules, content in the knowledge that *they* were happy and safe and warm. It was why she'd done all she had. But it would not be the same. There would always be something missing, a piece of herself *he* had taken with him.

Still, it will be enough. For all will be right with the world.

'His Lordship left?' Juliana asked as she appeared in the kitchen. Genevieve sighed, and looked down at the cup of cold tea, unable to meet her eyes. Yet her friend knew with one look what had passed. 'You told him,' she said, settling herself in the chair the Marquess had left, taking her hand much as he had. 'I am glad.'

'So am I,' she said, forcing conviction into her words. If she said it enough, it would become the truth. She downed her cold tea, and met Juliana's gaze, her forced certainty making her bold. 'It's done now. He shall not return. We can go back to the way things were. The way things should be.'

'He rejected you?'

'He recognised me.'

'After the shock subsides, he could return,' Jules said reassuringly.

'I don't want him to.'

'I see.' She nodded, removing her hand from Genevieve's, and rising. She went to the window, and shook her head, as if she had every right to be angry. 'You made sure he wouldn't.'

'I did what was best for everyone,' Genevieve corrected, despair twisting itself into righteous indignation.

Did Jules not understand suddenly, what was at stake?

And what did she expect, for Genevieve to beg the Marquess to stay and accept her? So that what? They could live together in the delusion of a future for a bit longer? What right did she have to cast judgement on Genevieve's decisions?

Her decisions kept them safe, kept a roof over their heads, food in their bellies and—

'Truly, Ginny?' Juliana spat, whirling around, incredulity mingling with anger. Genevieve wanted to rise, to stop the flow of words she never wanted to hear, but her friend kept her pinned with her gaze. 'For who? Him? I've seen the way he looks at you, and I rather think that's what scared you. Perhaps it was for Elizabeth you behaved thus,' she offered, nearly scoffing. 'Though I've not seen her as open nor comfortable with anyone, not even us, as she is with him. For the love of the Almighty, she let him call her Lizzie!' Juliana exclaimed, her temper rising.

Genevieve was frozen now, the words cutting straight through all the pretence, all the excuses she'd made for what she'd done.

How she'd done it. She didn't want to hear them, she wanted to continue on, in her world of illusions, where she could believe she'd made the right choice.

For the *right* reasons.

'Or did you do it for yourself? You are so miserable, Ginny,' Juliana cried, looking at her as if she did not recognise her.

'I enjoy my life, with every breath!'

'You enjoy your life, but you are not *happy.*'

'That is nonsense.'

'It isn't. And you know it.'

'I do not need a man to be happy.'

'Do stop trying to twist my words, Ginny,' Jules warned. 'You know that I, of all people, would *never* propose that. I do believe, however, that *that* man, could bring you happiness.' Genevieve turned away, but her friend would not relent. 'You hide your own desires under pretence of indulgence, but then sacrifice all that truly matters under guise of doing what's right because you cannot bear the idea of being happy. You know misery too well, and so you would dwell there. Perhaps, you might say you do it for me? But I cannot bear your pain, just as Elizabeth cannot. Stop pretending you pushed him away to help others,' she said, disappointment dripping from every syllable. 'You did it to *protect* yourself.'

'Of course I did,' Genevieve seethed, letting the anger yet again take over, masking the sharp, bright, searing pain the truth brought. 'Every time I felt a sliver of happiness in my life, it was snatched away. I cannot bear it again.'

The two stared at each other for a long moment.

Genevieve's anger slowly melting away under the compassionate understanding of her friend. And when the anger was gone, and she was only left with pain, when she returned to the place she'd begun, she dropped her head in her hands, and willed the tears to come and release her.

Only they didn't.

They never do.

Juliana did, coming to Genevieve's side and enveloping her in a tight embrace.

'If you'd seen how he looked at me,' Genevieve

muttered. 'Regardless of how I might've told him, he could never understand.'

'Then he is not the man any of us thought him to be.'

They remained there for a long while, until finally Genevieve extricated herself from her friend's reassuring embrace, and went to sit with Elizabeth.

Her daughter was sleeping soundly, tightly snug and warm, no sign of fever nor ill-effects from the day. Genevieve settled herself by the window, and watched, watched her chest rise and fall, for hours. If this was all she had in the world, her daughter, safe, then that would be enough. The pain she felt would be, in time, soothed by her child's happiness, as it had been before. If all she could be was Elizabeth's mother, that was enough.

More than enough.

Because it was the most exceptional privilege she'd ever been granted.

No one could ask for more.

So we shall begin again.

Chapter Thirteen

Spencer was drunk again. And he was glad of it. In fact, he'd worked very hard at being drunk most of the afternoon, and now evening, aided by Bella the Buxom Bar Wench as he'd taken to calling the provider of his alcoholic beverages. Apparently in his inebriated state he enjoyed creating such nicknames; case in point two of his other companions, Gerard the Gouty and Alasdair the Angry. He might be clever—but no poet.

The fact was, yes, he was drunk, but he still had far too much of his mind left.

He wished for oblivion, to forget everything that plagued him, but at the same time, he couldn't stop thinking about it all, and really, he *wanted* to think about it, because he wanted *answers*. His mind, heart, and body had seemingly made a compromise therefore, agreeing to be drunk— but consciously so. It was a state he'd managed to maintain since he'd ridden here in the early afternoon, unable to bear the walls of Yew Park any longer.

He'd just needed to get out, expend the hurt that had transformed into pure, white hot anger, so he'd gone for a blistering ride, and somehow arrived in town, and when he'd seen the inn, he'd thought well, perhaps another experience like the one he'd spent near Lincoln might be just the ticket. All his peers vaunted the brilliant effects of liquor on numbing whatever ailed them—so why shouldn't he give it another try? Subsequently, here he was, enjoying round number, well, only Bella the Buxom knew.

Still, despite the copious amounts of ale and whisky, he only had partial relief from the anger coursing through his veins; found the most obvious answers to his questions. The more important questions, well, those remained unanswered.

Why did she lie to me?

She didn't lie to me—she lied to the world.

Why wouldn't she?

She was protecting herself. From more censure and scandal.

Why do I care so much?

Why does it hurt so much?

Why do I see it as betrayal?

Why am I so angry?

After all, she had the courage to tell me the truth.

After she'd taken what she wanted.

Still...

Why can I not agree with her?

A fleeting fancy. Satisfaction of needs. A discreet tryst.

Things she was known for. The adulteress.

A divertissement.

Why can I not stop thinking of her?

For even the knowledge of who she was, did not diminish his...interest. He couldn't care less if she were the Great Whore of Hadley Hall or a Whitechapel prostitute. Because she was...the woman from the gardens. The woman from the loch.

The woman I—

At least he'd thought so. He'd thought he knew her, was getting to know her, had seen glimpses of her soul... But he'd been wrong.

That was what enraged him, what troubled him, disgusted him.

She lied to me.

So have many others. Move on.

Widowed or divorced, either way—a relationship was impossible.

Indeed, there were much more important things that should be taking up space in his thoughts. Thoughts of when he would return to face his mother, and Society, and the mess he'd made. Thoughts of *what* he would do then. Thoughts of the future. Thoughts of anything *but* her. Her, and that damned dower house.

It was in his dreams again.

Scowling, Spencer downed his whisky, and huddled deeper into the worn but comfortable armchair set by the large hearth he'd claimed as soon as he'd entered, and barely moved from but to relieve himself. He was full of whisky, the fire was blazing, the room was full to the brim with people, all laughing and talking and in Alasdair's case, arguing, but still, he felt that chill down to the bone. The chill of fear, simmering there, beneath the anger that had kept him safe from it for a short time.

Despite his exhaustion from the day and its revelations, last night again he'd dreamt of yellow doors, screaming maidens, blood, and a loss so real, it couldn't be imagined. He hadn't felt anything like it since he'd lost his father, and even then...

He hadn't been so affected. They'd never been close; his father but a shadow hovering at the edge of his life. The loss had been hard, yes, but he'd also still been at school, no longer the heir, but the new Marquess of Clairborne. Everyone, even Reid had treated him as such, and he'd had to live up to that role.

Now, what he felt in his dreams, however...

It felt...*free*. Born in a time when the shackles of breeding hadn't kept his emotions tightly bound.

A loss I felt as a child.

In the dreams, he *was* a boy; as he'd been that

last summer here. Full of sunshine, and love. Before he became a little lord, and everyone, down to the scullery maids, changed how they behaved. How his own parents behaved with him, and each other, and—

Why couldn't he remember something so painful?

Because it was a child's loss.

Perhaps the loss of a toy, or a dog, nothing more. Those losses that felt like the end of the world to a child.

No—

A fountain of raucous laughter from Bella brought him back to the room, and he rubbed his eyes wearily, finding his refreshments, refreshed.

Cheers, Bella.

Sampling the ale, he watched her, as she bustled about, totally invested in her world. Entirely a part of it. Whereas Spencer... He was a part of Society; but not *part of*. He remained on the outskirts, moving about like a giant vessel on the waves.

Even his own family. They weren't close. They were civil to each other, but where was the affection, the togetherness? He was closest with Mary, but she'd been a babe when he'd been sent off, and in the rare moments he'd been allowed with her, he'd been forced to maintain a distance, as her brother, her keeper.

Where is home?

There is none.

Those things are not for you. The price of privilege.

Yet he'd felt it. For an instant. What he'd seen, envied in Reid and Rebecca, he'd felt a flicker of it, when he was with Madame de l'Omont. He'd felt the idea of affection and togetherness with her, and Lizzie. When they'd laughed and run with abandon through the maze, and wondered at the marvels of the grotto. When she'd come to him at the loch.

So we're back to her.

It doesn't add up.

That was the problem. *She* didn't add up.

Yes, why she'd been reluctant to foster an acquaintance, kept her distance, that made sense. But who she was with *him*, it didn't match the tale of the Great Whore of Hadley Hall. Likely why he hadn't made the connection.

The scandal had been one of the greatest of the past few years; only Reid's and that of Rochesdale had forced it back from the front pages, despite the matter having been settled for nearly a year by then.

Lady Stapleton—*Countess Stapleton*—wife to the Earl, mistress of Hadley Hall, had been divorced on the grounds of adultery. And not simply one instance, oh no. Dozens of her former lovers had testified to her depravity, her godlessness and wantonness. The case had lasted well over a year, as Stapleton lobbied support, and had his private act passed. Caricatures of Lady Stapleton had been plastered across London, and beyond, despicable renderings of a grotesque version of her in her myriad of sinful encounters.

Likely why she looked familiar when you first met.

Everyone had heard how she'd dishonoured herself, her husband, and their child.

A daughter. Elizabeth.

He'd not made *that* connection either.

Idiot.

In truth, the affair had disgusted him. All such did. Not the facts in and of themselves, but the gossip, the slander, the bloodlust. He had no taste for it. Affairs such as that reminded him of the dangers of marriage made for power, and fortune. His only opinion was that if someone wanted to be separated from another that badly, they should be.

And God have mercy on the child.

How did Madame de l'Omont—Lady Stapleton—keep custody of Elizabeth?

One of the many things that did not add up.

Just as the Great Whore of Hadley did not add up to Madame de l'Omont. Some might say it should, he thought wryly, thinking back on how she'd come to him, but no. When she'd come to him, there had been...

Hesitancy. Desperation. A search for something unknown. Pain.

For someone so blatantly wanton, so free in her

favours, she'd been quite hesitant indeed. There was a courageous boldness, not a boldness born of experience.

And he remembered a little of Stapleton. They hadn't associated—the man was an ass—and Earl in name only. Pockets to let, a penchant for gambling and women, an estate always plagued by some trouble. Not that the man's habits or attitude absolved *her*, still...

Something niggled at the back of his mind. Much like the dower house.

Downing his whisky before returning to the ale, Spencer cast his mind back over the years, trying to recall any instance of encountering the Earl or the Countess. There were none. Perhaps they'd been at some venue together or that, he'd seen Stapleton around the House surely, but they really hadn't moved at all in the same circles.

The tankard in his hand caught the flames and glittered in his eye.

Vauxhall.

The lanterns at Vauxhall.

A balmy summer night.

Stapleton—though I did not know him.

A woman, with child, but no life in her.

The memory speared through him, sure and true.

Yes, he remembered her. And the sorrow, the pity, he'd felt that night, returned and washed over him. It had marked him, that sight of her. He'd

been what, five and twenty then, enjoying his evening with friends, as one did at Vauxhall, as one
was expected to. He'd seen her, and the curtain
had been torn back, revealing the other world mir-
roring that which he dwelled in. The true land behind the mirage of Society. He'd already felt like
an outsider, but that vision, of a woman, who had
husband, money, child, position, looking like a
shade... She'd been an omen, warning him, reminding him of what the true price of such a life
was.

It was her ghost that had fed the seeds of doubt
already in his heart, sewn by the memories of
his parents' marriage. It was that vision of her—
though over time he couldn't recall her face—
along with memories of a cold, quiet house, devoid
of love but full of placid nothingness, that had
made his inevitable future harder and harder to
swallow.

He didn't want a marriage like that of his parents. He'd always known love was not for him—
marquesses didn't not marry for love—but he'd
resolved that at least he could find a match which
came with respect, and affection. Where he and
his wife could exchange more than two words with
civility, and where he wouldn't be a silent presence in his own children's life. He did not want to
look up from the paper one day, and see his own
wife looking as *she* had that night.

A spectre. A lifeless doll.

And now you are here, free and alive.

She had been dead—but now she lived.

She had her child, when no other woman on a path such as hers would.

There was a reason he couldn't reconcile the Great Whore of Hadley Hall with Madame de l'Omont.

Because one of you does not exist.

But how does that change anything?

Another answerless question.

Spencer tucked it away with all the others as he rose unsteadily. He might've toppled back to his chair, or to the floor, had Josiah not appeared, helping him to stand.

When did you get here?

'A while ago, my lord.' His valet smiled, guiding him steadily through the crowd, answering the question Spencer hadn't realised he'd spoken aloud. 'Thought you might need assistance to find your way.'

'Good man, Josiah,' he managed to slur as they reached the door.

Spencer felt as if he'd dived into the frozen loch when the brisk night air hit him.

Dizzy, nauseated, he swayed, and they stopped for a while until the air became more tonic than shock, then Josiah slowly led him to the waiting conveyance.

'There you go, my lord,' he said gently, settling him with a blanket and a bucket he'd obtained from God only knew where. 'We'll get you home. You'll have a rough morning, but will be right as rain after that.'

'Right as rain.'

Yes, Spencer thought as they began their way. *It will all be right.*

I will make it right.

I have to.

Chapter Fourteen

Spencer yet again found his quarry in the gardens of Willowmere, though this time she was hard at work in her *potager*. He yet again took a moment before approaching, watching her toil in the muddy soil. She was filthy, and damp, both from sweat and the light drizzle that wafted down from the Heavens, and her hair was an absolute mess. She looked stronger than she had that day in the kitchen, but still diminished, and he knew it was his doing. But he would make it right.

Because he knew now that every inch of her was real. The realest thing he'd ever known, and the grey light illuminated her as he'd never seen before. As she'd always been, but as he'd failed to see her.

Until now.

Grasping his courage, he made his way to her, stopping a few feet away.

If he got too close…

If he got too close, all that he needed to say, ask, confirm, well, it wouldn't be said. And he needed to hear it from her, hear the words come from her own lips before he could dare venture any further.

All I want is the truth.

'I thought I recognised you the first time we met,' he began. Lady Stapleton—*Madame de l'Omont*—stopped, set down her trowel, and sat back on her heels. She waited, silently, stoically, for whatever blow he might bestow. 'But I just couldn't put my finger on it. I remember a young bride. At Vauxhall.' He caught the tiny frown, his memory not at all what she expected. 'You were with child, yet there was no glow of joy surrounding you. That's what caught my eye. I remember looking over, and seeing you, standing at his side, so fragile, as if a light touch might crack you into a thousand pieces. And I thought, what a sad, broken thing.'

Madame de l'Omont flinched, her hands tightening into white-knuckled fists, but Spencer forged on. He knew she was hurting, by God he could feel it, but it needed to be said.

All of it.

'I thought, here she is, in the glow of the magnificent lanterns, heavy with child, life within her, and still, there is death, and nothingness in her eyes. I asked my friends who you were, but you'd disappeared.'

'Not many from my life before would recognise me now,' she gritted out, her voice tight with emotion. 'Or so I like to think.'

She turned to look up at him, her eyes searching his, begging to know *why*.

'I've been trying to reconcile you, with what Stapleton and the papers made of you,' he answered. 'And that girl I glimpsed at Vauxhall all those years ago.'

'And have you been able to reconcile them all?' she asked tentatively, no hope shining through, as if she were as afraid of his answer as he was of the consequences.

'I have a notion that might.' He took a deep breath before continuing. 'I was never well-acquainted with your—Lord Stapleton. But I heard enough. And I recall that look in your eyes. Nothingness.' With a strained nod, Madame de l'Omont turned away from him again. 'I would wager you found a way to obtain a divorce, at the cost of your reputation.'

A sniff, and she swiped her sleeve beneath her nose before brushing her hands off on her apron, and rising to face him.

'A wife may begin proceedings for an act such as I required only in the case of life-threatening cruelty,' she stated flatly. 'I would argue that what I suffered was such, however, those in power would not have agreed. My husband never raised a hand against me.'

She sighed, and turned her gaze to the horizon for a moment.

Spencer felt the urge to go teach her former husband a lesson in what it meant to be a gentleman—or rather, a man—but he tampered down his feelings towards the worm, and focused instead on the woman before him, who was sharing the tale he'd asked for.

The tale he hoped might free them both.

'He never thought much of my wits,' she continued, turning back to him, steel in her eyes, still bracing herself for judgement. 'Particularly not after all that time. Thought he'd quashed my intelligence along with my spirit perhaps. Fortunately, that was not the case. I found…leverage. And I made a deal. If he obtained a divorce, and let me have Elizabeth, I would keep his secrets, and leave what was left of my fortune to him.' She smiled a mirthless smile and shrugged, as if it had all been nothing at all. 'And so the Great Whore of Hadley Hall was born. His final act of cruelty and humiliation. But there is not a day I regret my choice,' she told him, almost in warning. 'What he did… No one would say it was wrong. That it was anything other than the *guidance* of a husband. And so I told myself for many years. But I felt it. Here,' she said, placing her tight fist against her belly. 'I knew it was wrong. And when I saw his cruelty turn to Elizabeth… I could deny it no longer. I would suffer the shame for a thousand years if I saved my daughter's soul. God will judge me, but I like to think He shall be fairer than any man might be.'

The echoes of her words rang loudly in the silence that followed.

He knew she was challenging him, challenging him to deny her again, judge her as so many had; walk out as he had not days before. But he would not; could not. Everything she'd said, tore his heart apart, and built it back up again. She was precisely who he'd thought, and more.

I am in awe of you, madame.

'There is no shame in what you did,' he said finally, and her eyes widened with disbelief. 'I look at you, and I see only courage, and strength, beyond that of anyone I've ever known.'

I can't breathe.

Genevieve tried sucking in tiny breath after tiny breath, as Jules had taught her, but she just couldn't breathe. There was the most incredible weight pressing on her chest, tightening her ribs so they could not expand. Tears pricked at the back of her eyes, and she turned away, turned away from the man who had just said words she'd never dreamt of hearing. Not from anyone. Even Jules, well, they'd never spoken like that. They had both put their pasts behind them, and that was that.

When she'd first seen the Marquess appear, she'd expected a confrontation. A demand for explanation, the reckoning perhaps he'd not given the day she'd confessed her great lie. The very last thing she had expected was for him to say... All he had.

That memory he had... She remembered that night. She hadn't wanted to go. She should've been home, resting, on the doctor's orders, but Stapleton had wanted to parade her about, and then when she hadn't been amusing enough, he'd humiliated her, as always. She remembered all the people around her that night. She remembered wondering if she screamed, would anyone truly hear? If not for Elizabeth in her belly, she might've ended it, there, and then. Walked down to the Thames and let it take her away.

The past, the present, all of it flooded her heart and mind like a great tidal wave, the weight crushing her until finally she sucked in a huge gulp of air, only when she tried to expel it again, a sob wrenched free instead. And all she'd kept so tightly coiled inside for years, it unravelled, unwound, and she couldn't stand. She fell to her knees, all those tears that she had refused to cry for years tumbled out.

The unbearable hurt mingled with the unbounding relief of being understood. Of being *seen*. Of being acknowledged for all she'd faced, by *him*. She'd dreamed of his acceptance, yes, but not of his admiration. And she knew she had it, she'd seen the truth in his eyes, and that had been her undoing.

I am not alone.

One moment she was there, her knees entrenched in the mud, clutching herself in the vague hope it might lessen the hurt tearing through, tearing her apart until she would no longer recognise herself, and then he was there, holding her, tighter than she could, encircling her with himself, and it broke her a little bit more, his comfort. The last vestiges of her armour disappeared into the air, just as she'd known it would.

Everything that she had been, the shell she'd crafted so perfectly, was gone, and she was left only with the most fragile, truest part of herself.

Genevieve clung to him, and he shifted his hold, sitting in the mud himself and pulling her onto his lap, rocking her gently as she released all she had within. There was no cold, there was no rain, there was only him, his warmth, his scent, his strength, carrying her, protecting her, and though it was terrifying, Genevieve knew it was as it should be.

How long they remained there, her in his arms, being whispered to sweet reassurances, was anyone's guess. After a very long while, the tears finally subsided, and she was left with nothing but an aching throat, and a weak languor that felt dizzying, but also, wonderful, and freeing.

And then she was being lifted, and she was

floating on air, safe, and there were hushed voices, and nothing but warmth, and her exhaustion called her to sleep, and so, she did.

Chapter Fifteen

If he were facing a firing squad, Spencer thought it might look and feel a lot like his present situation. Yet again, Miss Myles had seen to it that he was redressed, refreshed, and given tea, before seeing to Genevieve, who Spencer had brought in and been instructed to leave in the drawing room. Now, Miss Myles, and her stern partner, Lizzie, sat across from him at the kitchen table, eyeing him with as much severity as the harshest judge. He waited, doing his best not to literally squirm.

His mother would be very proud of these ladies.

They had enough mettle to bend the strongest man to their will, and the fact that Spencer understood they were Madame de l'Omont's gate-keepers—*I really need to ask her name*—made them all the more fierce. Should he wish to have another chance, he would have to convince these two he was worthy.

Again.

He began to straighten, but Lizzie narrowed her eyes, and he froze.

Damn. Why is this so difficult?

'What happened out there?' Miss Myles finally said, looking decidedly intimidating in the fire and candlelight.

Like some ancient goddess, come to pass judgement on him.

Athena herself...

'We spoke of the truth of her…divorce.'

'You will have to do better than that,' Miss Myles said flatly.

Spencer glanced at Lizzie, trying to find suitable words considering her presence.

He wasn't about to start repeating her mother's infamous nickname—

'You need not censure yourself, my lord,' the girl said, surprising him. '*Maman* was always honest. About everything, even what she had to do to get us away.'

Oh, Hell.

His heart twisted in his chest. The way she said it, so dispassionately, as if it were nothing at all, not only to be witness to what she must've in her own home, which should've been a refuge, but to have to be made aware of all the monstrous things said about her mother, to be in the midst of such a separation… She'd been forced to grow up so fast—much like him—though for very different reasons.

Nodding, he added, *Give Lizzie a proper childhood* to his list of things to do with his life.

'I left rather abruptly,' he said after a moment. 'When your mother revealed the truth of your situation. I was shocked, and admittedly, angry.'

'And Ginny did nothing to soothe the blow,' Miss Myles said blithely.

Ginny. Interesting.

Lizzie cast her a quelling glance and he continued, somewhat heartened by the fact that he apparently had some support from Miss Myles.

'I came today,' he continued, his attention on his most reluctant interlocutor. 'Because I could not believe your mother was what she was made out to be. I needed to know the truth of who she was.'

'Why?' Lizzie asked sharply.

Asking all the difficult questions, aren't you?

'Because I've come to care for her,' he confessed, willing the truth of it to shine in his eyes, holding the gaze of the young woman who would make or break his future. 'For you both. I could not leave it where we had, but neither could we move forward with half-truths between us.'

He couldn't tell whether she was satisfied with his answer; she simply turned to exchange a look with Miss Myles.

'What precisely are your intentions?' the latter asked, steepling her fingers on the table, doing quite the impression of *disapproving father*. 'You say you wish to move forward, but the truth is, my lord, you will be leaving soon. What precisely do you expect to happen?'

Everything. Anything.

Spencer took a deep breath, trying to find an answer which was both truthful, and yet which would not alienate her.

All or nothing old chap.

'There are limitations,' he said. *And I hate that, and I sound like the Society stiff-neck everyone believes me to be.* 'See here, Miss Myles,' he began again—*too casual, but there we are.* 'The truth is I don't know. But as I've expressed to your friend, I wish to get to know her better. Her, and you, Lizzie,' he said, turning back to the young girl. 'I've known you both barely a fortnight, however in that short time, I have…' *Become addicted to your company. Longed to be part of your little circle. Been changed for the better. Found a place I feel myself.* 'Well, the thing is…' Dash it all, but he really was squirming now. 'I just want to enjoy what time we have together. I can make no promises, I think we all know that. However, I will regret it my entire life if I walk away now.'

Sighing, he shrugged, his cards dealt and played. Now, he awaited judgement.

The ladies exchanged a look, and Lizzie nodded.

'It will be Ginny's decision,' Miss Myles declared finally, and his heart skipped a beat.

Thank God.

Thank you, ladies.

'Thank you.' He smiled. Miss Myles offered him a small one back, which he took as a resounding victory. 'Inappropriate though it may be, may I go to her?'

Really pushing your luck...

'Until she wakes,' was Miss Myles' pronouncement. 'Then, if she decides you should leave, so you will.' *Or else*, she left unsaid. 'Come, Lizzie, let us to bed.'

He bowed his head in acquiescence and gratitude, and rose as the ladies did.

'Wait,' he said, remembering something very important as they made for the door. 'I... I don't know her name. Her Christian name.'

Miss Myles threw a glance at Lizzie before exiting, and the young girl turned to him.

'I will tell you, but there is a price.'

'Anything.'

Genevieve woke as she'd fallen asleep. Enveloped in a haze of gentle, soothing warmth. She let her mind slowly revive but kept her eyes closed, enjoying the wondrous feeling. Slowly, she pieced together all that had happened; all that had been unleashed.

Where once had stood the final impassable barrier within her, constricting and limiting, now there was only openness. She could feel the heat from a fire, see the flicker of it behind her eye-lids, and her body rose and fell with every breath of another being.

The Marquess.

Though perhaps she should call him by some-thing else now, considering all they had become. What it was that they'd become, precisely, she could not name. Nor did she wish to, for fear it might still be snatched away before it could even become real.

But it was real. *He* was real. Holding her against his chest as he lounged in what she presumed was the drawing room sofa.

Henry Spencer.

Henry.

Spencer.

She wondered which he might prefer.

Only one way to know.

Peeking open her eyes, she stirred a little, and felt the arm banded around her waist tighten as the man behind her stirred to life as well. It was dark, and glancing at the clock on the mantel she spied that it was well past nine in the evening.

I've slept away the afternoon.

And he stayed.

'You stayed,' she whispered, and the arm around her tightened again, as his other hand found her own tucked beneath the blanket over them both.

'You doubted me.'

At every turn.

'Elizabeth? Jules?'

'They are well,' he said softly, planting a kiss on her hair. 'Tucked away in bed now I presume. Lizzie was quite concerned, but I spoke with her, and Miss Myles, about, well, everything. They agreed I could remain until you had awoken and pronounced your own judgement.' There was a smile in his voice, and Genevieve found one forming on her own lips. 'Are you hungry? There is some bread, cheese, and cider if you'd like.'

Genevieve found that she was actually quite starved, and so she nodded, making to move, but Spencer—*Henry?*—would not allow it.

'Here,' he said, unlacing the hand which held hers and reaching out to grasp a plate on the table. He set it on her lap, and then handed her the jug when she had removed her arms from beneath the confines of the blanket. 'Unless you really wish to move that is?'

Genevieve shook her head and proceeded to nibble on the food.

Henry—*Spencer?*—proceeded to steal a morsel or two, as he stroked her hair gently.

'You are thinking very hard, Genevieve. Would you like me to leave?'

'No,' she said, and felt his relief. 'I was actually wondering what I should call you. In my mind, I've kept you as the Marquess, but it doesn't seem right. I see you learned my name,' she added, not bothering to hide the grin in her own voice.

'Lizzie told me. For a price.'

'Which was?'

'That I should take care with it. And you.' A lump of emotion tightened her throat, and sensing it, most likely, Spencer—*Henry?*—dropped another kiss on her head. 'A fair price, I think. And in answer to your question, Spencer. My mother is the only one who calls me Henry, and I admit, it feels almost foreign.'

'Spencer,' she repeated, liking it very much. It suited him, and she understood all too well the power of names. 'What now?'

'I don't know,' he admitted, but somehow the prospect didn't sound so terrifying when he said it. It sounded...exciting. Full of possibility. 'Likely not the best answer, but it is the truth, and if there is one thing I will promise you, it is the truth.'

'Thank you.'

'I wondered at the question whilst I lay here. Perhaps, the best first step would be to take time, to get to know each other, now that the need for pretence is gone.'

'I should like that.'

'I know a little, admittedly. Pieces I remember from the papers,' he began as she sipped the cider, letting it warm her insides. 'Your family was French, as I recall?'

'Mother's side. Minor aristocracy, from Normandy,' Genevieve said, placing the empty plate back on the table. The papers had loved that—it demonstrated that blood will out—and that French women would always be at heart wanton whores. *Bastards.* 'My grandparents left during the Revolution, when Mother was still a babe. They came here, and tried to rise again. They did, somewhat, when Mother married a fortuned English baron.'

'Did she teach you how to make lace?'

'Yes.' Genevieve smiled. 'She learned it from Grandmother, and so on. *Dentelle de Bayeux.* It is unique, and very special, and someday I hope to teach Lizzie, just as I taught her French. It is a small heritage, but it is hers, nonetheless. We were not very close, my mother and I,' she continued, letting the memories wash over her. For so long, everything had been pushed aside to make room. To make space for all she needed to move onwards. 'She had high hopes for me, and pushed me to be everything I should be to rise higher than she had. But when we worked on the lace together, conversing in French, it felt...like she was well and truly, my mother. Only that.'

'You are lucky in that.'

'You and your mother are not close?'

'We were, once, I think,' he said, his voice drifting off slightly as he brought his own past to mind. 'But not for a long time. It is not the way of things, for people like us.' Genevieve slipped her hand over his. 'May I ask how Miss Myles fits in?' he asked, and she accepted his reluctance to reveal more.

He would, in time, she felt.

'She was Elizabeth's nursemaid. Seven preceded her. They could not bear life at Hadley Hall. But Juliana...' Genevieve trailed off, the memories of that time, of the fear that grew each time a new maid came, fear of being removed entirely from her child's life, or of her husband inflicting himself on yet another innocent girl, as rife as ever. 'Juliana could not be driven away. She had this way of dealing with him... After a while, he simply let her be. I was so jealous... But then, she befriended me, slowly. I grew to trust her, and she allowed me much that had been denied by others under my husband's orders.'

'Your husband denied you Lizzie?'

'She brought me joy, so yes, naturally. And when time came for a governess... He made it clear I was to have no contact unless it was expected in company. He couldn't risk Elizabeth becoming like me. She was going to be what he needed her to be. What I'd been. A bargaining chip for fortune and advancement.' Genevieve clenched her jaw—the anger as fresh as ever. *That* fear, as fresh as ever. 'That's when I knew I had to leave. Already the light was dimming within Elizabeth, and I knew it would be snuffed out, as mine had been. Juliana helped me leave, and face all we did.' Spencer laid another kiss on her head, and she felt herself relax again, the fear ever-present—but not paralysing. 'It's why we remain removed. Not only to avoid scorn, but because I fear one day *he* will enforce the rights I can never take from him, and come for Elizabeth. No matter the consequences.'

'We won't let him,' Spencer promised.

Genevieve nodded, though something inside her still refused to relinquish that fear.

To relinquish it, meant to trust that Spencer would be there, always, and that was not something she could envisage.

Because you know it is impossible, no matter anyone's feelings.

All she'd thought in the beginning, all that had kept her away from Spencer, returned to the forefront of her mind. It was still true. They might have something wonderful, for a time, and she felt ready now, powerless really, to accept that and the inevitable heartbreak that would follow. But one day he *would* leave, marry the proper woman, and they would be alone again, to fend for themselves.

And I must be ready.

'So Miss Myles left with you?'

'She needed a safe harbour as well. Without her... She is a sister to me, and she knows so much... She teaches Elizabeth, and I, so much, that I was never allowed to learn for it was not for us women to know.'

'May I ask,' Spencer began hesitantly, and Genevieve knew what he would ask.

But she was ready now—ready to speak of it.

She'd never breathed a word before, Juliana had been witness to it all, but there had never been anyone else to speak to. Even her parents had believed the tales of her sins. In time, she hoped to discuss it with Elizabeth, but she'd already had to disclose so much, had to ask Elizabeth to grow up so quickly… She'd done the best she could, but there was no book on how to handle what they had. But until the time came when Elizabeth was older, and ready to be burdened with more, all Genevieve had lived was doomed to remain hers alone. All the regret, the anger, the despicable memories, they were hers, to keep, festering in her own breast.

Until now.

She wanted Spencer to know, for the ugly poison was part of her.

'May I ask what he was like, your husband?'

Spencer knew he shouldn't ask, so bluntly, like this, after all Genevieve had been through today. He knew, *enough*, to paint a picture—a despicable picture he wished he could burn, erase from existence and replace with a perfect, beautiful one. But Genevieve, Lizzie, Miss Myles, they'd all been forged in the fires of that Hell they'd dwelled in for so long, *too long*, and he wanted to know them all. Know all of them. He had from the first.

Not for any other purpose than that.

If Genevieve did not wish to, so be it. However, he had a feeling that she too needed to voice her experience; he doubted she had ever before. Who was there to listen after all? All those who had known her before sided with Stapleton, including her own parents.

Taking one of her hands in his, he toyed with her fingers, waiting, giving her time and space to make the decision, and to find the words if she wished to.

'At first…charming,' she admitted finally. 'Likeable. Handsome. I thought I was lucky indeed to have been given such a match.'

'He was not your choice?'

'Are many husbands young ladies' choice? Or that of their fathers?'

Spencer nodded; he could think of very few ladies, particularly those of their class, who were afforded freedom of choice.

He himself would be expected to make a choice of a certain order, but still, he had a *choice*; something he'd always made sure Mary had too. How many others, however, had been cajoled, forced, blackmailed, drugged even? How many had been simply engrained with the knowledge that they knew nothing at all? Taught to trust their keeper's judgement, when their welfare was rarely even on the list of requirements for a good marriage.

He knew that, had always known, but somehow today, he felt the bitter truth.

'I was not angry, nor resentful of it,' Genevieve continued, seemingly following his own thoughts. 'I was not stuck on romantic notions of marrying for love, though I hoped to pledge my life to someone I could like. And I believed wholeheartedly that my father knew best, even now... I think he thought it truly was.'

'When did it all change? You don't have to answer. I just want to understand. I want to know you. All of you,' he confessed.

'It is good to speak of it,' she said, and he looked down to find a small smile on her lips. 'I haven't...' Spencer clasped her hand, appreciating more than he could express that she would trust him enough to speak of it. They were alike, he thought. Taught to keep emotion out of everything, taught to silence the heart, the soul. 'Little things began that first year. Comments about my behaviour, or my looks. I thought he was trying to improve me. I wanted to be a good wife. Slowly, it worsened, as I failed to bear him a child. Then Elizabeth was born, and... Everything disintegrated. I had failed in giving him a son, and that was only the greatest in a long line of sins. Nothing I said, or did, was right. His control grew with every passing day. I could not go out, for fear of

who I might meet. How I might embarrass him.
He controlled what I ate, what I wore, and the
slightest word or gesture would awaken his ire.
He would cut me down in public, flaunt his mistresses, and when I finally refused him my bed…
He had me moved to the attics, and installed his
latest mistress in my place. This once, whilst we
entertained his friends, a footman served me a
ladle too many of parsnips. Stapleton forced me
to eat them all, off the floor, like the pig I was.'

Spencer forced himself to breathe, to relax, to
be nothing more than present.

He'd wanted to hear the ugly truth, and so, here
it was.

His anger, his resentment, his outrage, would
serve no purpose.

Only comfort, and stalwartness, for Genevieve,
would do.

'His friends, I imagine they said nor did nothing?'

'One of them, Merton, testified to being my
lover,' Genevieve offered. 'He sent me a letter
after, and said he'd done it as a kindness. To help
me get my freedom. His testimony was one of the
more luridly entertaining, and I think was done
to ensure I would get what I needed.'

'The way your husband treated you should've
been enough.'

'Of course.' She shrugged. 'I lived in fear
of him, every minute, of every day. He would

threaten me sometimes, always in private, and if it hadn't been for Elizabeth, I think I might've welcomed such a fate. Perhaps why he resisted the urge after all. I lived in shame, of who I was, until I was nothing anymore. And such behaviour, it will kill. A little more, every day. Until you are a living ghost, as you saw me, at Vauxhall. You said once,' she continued, swallowing hard. 'That I allow Elizabeth anything. The villagers say as much, and I know they think I indulge my own every whim. Perhaps it is indulgence. But for so long, we were both denied. I would not do that to her again. Not to myself. It has taken me long enough to understand that I am allowed to want. To choose. To understand, what things I want, and who I am.'

'I envy you that,' Spencer admitted.

'Wanting? Or indulging my whims?'

'Both, I suppose,' he said seriously, and she turned a little in his arms to look up at him, disbelieving. It was his turn to shrug. He took a moment, trying to put into words what he'd felt, but only truly discovered coming here. Meeting *her*. 'Some might say my title, my sex, my fortune, afford me freedom to indulge in whatever I wish, but I was raised to believe that a good name, and reputation, were paramount. Not to be… Mere illusions. But that I, we, my sister and I, should live by the strictest codes of honour, and morality. To be a shining example to those beneath us.' Spencer scoffed; he'd believed it, all of it, save for being someone's *better*. At least not how most meant it; *better* to him, meant better than those who lived to harm others. 'Coming here, was the first thing I've ever done for *myself*.' He hesitated, wondering how she might feel about the reason why. But then, he'd promised honesty. So he would give it. 'I had an attack of the nerves if you can believe it. I was to meet a potential bride, and I just... couldn't. I knew taking that step, meant I would wake one day and find myself in a home as cold as the one I was raised in. I always knew, I never wanted that. But when I came here, I realised... I couldn't offer anything else, because I'd become the mask. No longer a man. That's why all the experiments. To find who I am again. How to be... happy. How to feel, again. I envied you from the first, you know. You had this...air about you. As if you knew what it meant to enjoy life. I wished to bask in your light. Learn from you.'

'You are a man, Spencer. The best I've ever known. Kind, affectionate, with so much to give.'

He swallowed hard, her words touching him more than she could know.

When she said it, he believed her. That he *did* have much to give; that his truest self had been buried. Not that he was empty.

They fell into a comfortable silence for a moment, Genevieve relaxing against his chest again.

They breathed together in time, and all he could think was how very extraordinary that was indeed.

'Was I,' he began after a long moment, not sure why he needed to know, only that he did. 'Was I one such thing? That you wanted? Is that why you came to me?'

'Yes,' Genevieve breathed, and his heart stilled a little, the disappointment harsher than he'd expected. 'You are that which I have wanted most,' she continued, and just like that, the disappointment was snuffed out like a candle. 'So much so it terrified me.'

'I know the feeling well,' he said softly.

It still terrifies me.

For what future could they truly have?

Do not think on endings before beginnings have even flourished.

Spencer agreed with himself, and pushed the thoughts away.

'What were you like as a girl?' he asked, moving them to what he hoped was safer territory.

'Quiet,' Genevieve said, chuckling softly. 'Restrained. Dutiful. Never a hair out of place, or a stitch awry.' She looked up at him again, mirth dancing in her eyes. 'What were you like as a boy?'

'Wild, once.' He grinned. 'Until I understood who I must be. Then, much like you.'

'Never a stitch awry?'

'I think we've established that my needlework needs improvement.' Genevieve laughed, and the sound filled that place that had always been a void within him. It filled him with beauty, and wonder, and light, and he knew he would never tire of hearing her laugh. Of making her laugh. 'It is a great gift you give Lizzie, you know,' he said seriously after a moment. 'Freedom. Choice.'

'Thank you,' she whispered. 'For saying that. Seeing it.'

There were a thousand words, a thousand thank-yous on the tip of his tongue.

Thank you for being with me.

Thank you for trusting me with yourself and Lizzie.

Thank you for bringing light to my life.

But he couldn't say the words. Instead, he bent down and kissed her, and willed all of them to flow through to her. He willed all that he felt, joy, hope, wonder, elation; all of it, to be felt in that kiss, so different from those they'd shared until now. For it wasn't simply a kiss of desire. It wasn't a kiss of heat, and mindless passion. It was a kiss that stripped you bare with tenderness, and something more.

It was a kiss that answered all of life's questions, and gave you faith.

It was a kiss that changed fates, and made blind men see.

And so, it did.

Chapter Sixteen

Spencer felt like he was floating. There was a spring to his step, a lightness in his feet, indeed, in his whole body, his heart, that he'd never felt before. It was the joy that came with feeling as if you were right where you belonged. As if the future had a thousand different prospects, each more titillating than the next.

It was a joy of *possibility*.

Before, there had never been possibility. Only certainty. And he should truly be terrified by the *un*certainty that now descended on his future like mists, obscuring all but glints and shadows. But he wasn't. Not in the least. The languishment, the uncertainty within, was gone.

As Spencer made his way along the loch, his mind strayed back to Willowmere, to all that had happened today. Had it truly only been a day? A day since he'd woken, troubled, and yet somehow

sure of one thing and one thing alone; his need to
get answers from Genevieve.

Genevieve.

He liked the sound, the taste, the movement of
his lips when he said her name. And the way she
said his own… It was special. *She* was special.
Lizzie was special. Even Miss Myles. How lucky
he was to have found them. He'd not wanted to
leave, when he'd carried Genevieve up to bed, and
tucked her into her own sheets, and looked down
at her… He wanted nothing more than to remain,
to slip beside her and just have her melt against
him. Wanted nothing more than to breathe with
her; exist with her. He wanted to wake up to her
face in the morning, and have breakfast with her,
and Lizzie, and Miss Myles, there in that kitchen
that felt like what *home* should.

But staying there… It was a risk, and still too
early. What they were…*whatever* they were, was
still fresh, and fragile, and he wouldn't risk shat-
tering it. He would not push, and risk her slipping
through his fingers again.

*Though one day soon, you will need to release
her to grasp another's hand.*

Letting out a heavy sigh, Spencer stopped, and
turned to face the loch. He forced himself to be
there, in that moment, to see, and hear, and breathe
in all the world offered him.

The glint of moonlight on the water.

The white sparks at the tip of the tiny waves as they rise and fall with the wind.

The wind, crisp, and clean, though I feel only warmth, radiating from within.

Pine, heather, salt, and moss.

A whistling, in the mountains, and through the trees.

The groaning of the centuries-old woods.

Animals, scurrying in the dark; a hoot of an owl, echoing in the night.

The lap of water at the shoreline, the gentle slide of rocks moving to and fro.

A heartbeat; the heartbeat of the land.

Spencer remained there until his own heart beat with it. There was something about this place. It soothed him. Restored his equilibrium. Reminded him of his place in the world. Not Society, but the world. The elation he'd felt earlier, it was still there, shooting life through his veins, awakening every part of him, but it was settled now.

Nodding his thanks to the landscape, he began again, his steps quick, but sure; strong, but respectful. Before long, he was back at Yew Park, standing below the cascade of terraces, looking up at the house. Only a dim light shone from the windows of his own quarters, and those of the servants, both above and below, and in the moonlight, with only the outline of its eccentricity visible, it looked dreamlike. Something from an old tale

where a princess waited, or a strange monster who
was not a monster waited for his love to come.

*Since my princess is across the water, then I
must be the monster...*

Smiling slightly, Spencer tipped his head to the
house which he felt he owed a thanks to as well.

Thank you for bringing me here.

*For providing me safety from the world out-
side, an escape—*

What the Devil?

A brighter light appeared in the darkness at
the edge of the house on the north-west corner.
The lantern was shielded, to bring light only to
its bearer, but still a beacon. He couldn't quite tell
who it was, but he was certain it shouldn't be *anyone*. No one should be creeping out of the house at
well past midnight. Something wasn't right.

And he was intent on discovering what. With
all he'd just found, well, he wouldn't risk any harm
coming to it.

Bounding up the terraces, careful to remain
silent and unseen, Spencer kept his eye on the
beacon as it disappeared around the back of the
house. He caught sight of it again as he topped the
hill and rounded the house, bobbing like a will o'
the wisp. It kept on the path closest to the house,
and so did he, winding through the gardens until
it reached a small clearing.

The chapel.

And the family graveyard. Long-abandoned,

once used only by his Catholic ancestors, just like the chapel itself. He'd seen them both on his travels, but not paid them much attention other than to admire the stonework.

But it seems someone is.

Indeed, his will o' the wisp had stopped. And was now laid to rest beside a grave at the back. Keeping to the shadows in the edge of the trees, Spencer snuck around until he could see who his midnight wanderer was. Murmuring reached his ears, a voice filled with sorrow, and grief.

A woman's voice, chanting the Hail Mary.

Mrs McKenna.

There she was, kneeling before a simple block of stone, that no one would notice except for the fact it was spotless, devoid of moss, or wear, clean but for a fresh posy of daisies. Spencer stopped, and watched, waiting, trying to understand. In the low lamplight, her grief was unmistakable, the pain of loss he'd noticed on occasion in her eyes, etched deep into the lines of her face. Her agelessness was gone, and now she looked as if she'd been born with the world. The shadows dancing on her as the fire flickered with the wind revealed her true self—not the strong, proud, woman, but simply the woman, who suffered so greatly.

But whose loss does she mourn?

It must be someone close to her, but who? Her husband still lived, and as far as he was aware, she had no children.

Did she?

If she did, why would they be buried here?

Just wait. And you will know.

Yes, he would wait, until she'd finished, and left, and then he would go see if the name etched on the stone would provide answers. He felt somewhat of an intruder, standing there, watching her in her most private moments, but at the same time, he felt part of it. As if he were not a casual observer, but *meant* to be there. To share in the grief. Even if he didn't understand why.

After what seemed an hour or so, Mrs McKenna crossed herself, kissed her fingers, and placed them on the stone. She rose, with difficulty, but as much strength as he'd seen in her, and disappeared back into the night. He waited until long after the light had gone to emerge, letting his eyes get accustomed to the dark. The moon shone brightly, no clouds obscuring it, and he had no trouble making his way through the iron gates into the graveyard, back to the spot at which his housekeeper had knelt.

He knelt before it too, minding the freshly laid daisies, and ran his fingers over the indents in the stone.

"'Here lieth the body of Muire McKenna'," he breathed, the name tugging at something in his mind. "'Daughter of Hugh and Morag McKenna, who departed this life June 17th 1801 in the twenty-fourth year of her age.'"

June the seventeenth.

So, this was Mrs McKenna's daughter, and today was the anniversary of her death.

Muire.

'Muire, wait for me!'

The echo of the voice was so clear, so tangible, Spencer turned his head, seeking its source. Seeking the source of the childish laughter that followed.

But there were no children.

Only ghosts.

'Muire, wait for me!'

Spencer shivered.

He knew that voice.

It was his own; the voice of his five-year-old self.

And he remembered *her* laugh, radiant, like the sun. She used to tip her head up to it, and bask in its rays, as if gathering power. She was beautiful. Long blonde hair, that glinted in the sun like gold silk. And blue eyes, light blue with hints of grey, always laughing and full of…

Love.

He felt it, there, he remembered that too.

He remembered chasing her through forests to the dower house.

To the yellow door that was always open in summer.

They would play, him and Muire.

And Mother, and Father too.

On the lawn, by the loch. Bowls, and badminton, and they would go swimming too.

He'd learned to swim here, with her, she was like a selkie.

And then he felt it, the pain, knifing through him afresh.

Spencer doubled over, clutching his chest, it burned so fiercely, and it hurt, God how it hurt, and there was no more love, only fear—

'*Muire!*'

Terror in the night. Screams, drifting through the nursery windows on the wind.

He'd padded through the house, following them, and he'd known they were Muire's.

He'd got outside—*how?* He couldn't recall, but he could remember the breathtaking terror, and he'd called for her, and for his mother, little bare feet trampling through the woods, cut and torn on rocks and sticks, but it didn't matter, because Muire, Muire was hurting, and she was going to leave him, and where was Mama, and where was Papa—?

'*Muire!*'

He couldn't breathe, the pain wringing his heart, his lungs, twisting them into terrible shapes. Hot, burning hot tears were streaming down his face, but he couldn't stop now. He couldn't stop remembering it all even though he wanted to. He wished he'd never come, he didn't want to see, to know the rest, but there it was, the yellow door, still shining in the darkness of that night, and her screams, and then, the door opened, and—

'*Mama!*'

Mother was there. There was guilt in her eyes, he knew that, even then, and blood, so much blood, on her hands, and her dress, even her face, and she stopped him as he went to find Muire, but the screaming was gone.

The yellow door was closed and would never open again.

It was quiet then, only his own crying and screaming rent the night air. And then Mr McKenna was picking him up, and he was kicking and screaming, he had to find Muire, had to save her, but Mr McKenna wouldn't let him, and then there was no more.

Only his own sobbing in the night, this time, not a memory, but very real. He curled into himself, and mourned the loss of someone he'd loved. He mourned the loss of simple innocence he'd dwelled in his entire life, and mourned the loss of peace he'd found for a brief moment.

'*Our secret, Henry...*'

Mother, what did you do?

That question repeated endlessly as Spencer wept until he had no tears left.

Chapter Seventeen

'What on Earth is this,' Genevieve asked, unable to stop smiling at the man currently on her doorstep, holding up a large parcel, a broad smile of his own, and a glint in his eyes. It had been a day, *only a day*, since she'd cried her heart out in his arms, and they'd talked, *and kissed*, well into the night, and she would be lying if she said she hadn't worried that despite his words, he might not return.

He hadn't come, sent no word, and what came next was as murky as a mud puddle. She wouldn't have blamed him, either, if he'd decided it was best to cut his losses, though it might've truly undone her.

But now he is here.

'What are you doing here?'

She searched his eyes, for any hint, but all she found were shadows and sadness she didn't remember. There were circles under his eyes, as if he hadn't slept. His smile seemed genuine, not the one he wore with the mask of joviality, but still. He was troubled by something. Reaching out, she stopped herself just in time.

How am I meant to behave with this man?

'I have come to collect you, Lizzie, and Miss Myles,' Spencer said, his smile faltering but for a second as she took her hand back. He quashed any question of *how to behave*, when he leaned down and kissed her, not so much chastely as briefly. *Much too briefly.* 'I have it on good authority from Mr Ross, the bootmaker, that today's sunshine is set to last. And I have tested the waters,' he added, slipping inside the corridor. 'They are cold, but as warm as I think they shall be for a while. I am going to begin your swimming lessons.'

'Dare I ask what's in the parcel?' Genevieve asked, with the smile that still, *always,* refused to fade.

'Swimming *accoutrements*,' Spencer said, wiggling his eyebrows. 'I admit, I thought about suggesting you all swim in your gowns, or your chemises, it is a quandary, but then I decided, some dedicated clothing that will aid your movement. Shirts and breeches for everyone,' he finished, holding up the parcel as if it contained the best invention of the century.

I think it does.

'How utterly shocking.'

'I thought you'd approve. Now, here is more

shocking still. Lizzie,' he shouted, so that literally the entire house could hear. 'Lizzie!'

Rapid little footsteps, doors opening and closing, all sounded as Genevieve stood there, staring at the man, completely thrown off balance, and yet, as comfortable, as certain as she'd ever been.

He threw her a glance, as if he knew precisely what he did to her, and then turned to the stairs as Elizabeth, and Jules descended, the former less like the young lady she always was.

Still, she curtsied, as did Jules, and Spencer bowed before handing over the package.

'What's this,' her daughter asked, picking at the package's strings, excitement and pleasure in her eyes too.

We are both undone by this man—and this is only the beginning.

'Uniform, for today's lesson,' Spencer informed her gravely, though he winked, and her daughter grinned. 'We, are learning to swim.'

Elizabeth looked to her questioningly, and she nodded, still smiling.

'Truly, my lord?'

'Truly. Though today, and henceforth, I am Spencer. To all of you,' he added, with a significant look for Jules. 'Now, get dressed, and when you are ready, we shall to the loch!'

The joy, the excitement that filled her daughter's eyes, and her own heart, made her dizzy.

Made her completely forget everything else, the world, her past, her sorrow.

Oh dear. What have I agreed to?

What had she agreed to indeed? Genevieve thought some time later, after they'd all changed into their new 'swimming *accoutrements*'. They stopped at the edge of the cove—*cannot believe the rascal brought us here*—she, Jules, and Spencer, who carried a delighted Elizabeth on his back. The clothes had demonstrated preparedness, which was touching in itself, but what awaited them truly sunk any hope she ever had of surviving the heartbreak she would suffer when this man left her.

A bonfire blazed as it had the last time, only this one was huge, fit enough for some pagan rites. Beside it, pillows and blankets, and a little to the side, beside a privacy screen, were tables laid with covered dishes, urns of what must be hot drinks, fruit and all manner of other surprises. Spencer really hadn't left anything to chance.

Genevieve looked over at him, hoping the gratitude and amazement would shine in her eyes, for his solicitude rendered her completely mute.

He dipped his chin and smiled.

'Ladies, you will remember Josiah,' he said, turning his attention to the man emerging from the woods, who bowed as he approached them. 'I needed some help treating you, but I also didn't think you would like too many witnesses to our folly. The screen there is for you to change once you've had enough of the cold water, so do pass him those gowns you've brought with you.'

Genevieve and Jules passed Josiah the bundles they'd prepared, having obeyed Spencer's orders blindly.

'If my presence disturbs you,' Josiah said carefully, shooting his master a glance. 'You may say so and I shall disappear until later.'

After a quick look to Jules, Genevieve smiled and shook her head.

'Your presence will not disturb, sir.'

With a bow, and a thanks in his eyes for the title, he left to busy himself by the tables.

'Well now,' Spencer sighed, regarding them all. 'We shall have to do this in turns. Lizzie, I suppose you volunteer to be first?' He glanced over his shoulder at her daughter, who grinned and nodded vigorously. 'Excellent. Then, Genevieve, Miss Myles, won't you make yourselves comfortable. We have swimming to do!'

And without another word, he tore off, Elizabeth giggling as Genevieve hadn't heard her do so in a very long time, if ever.

Spencer ran straight into the water, Elizabeth still on his back, and then dashed about the shallows until they were both properly soaked.

It felt like her heart might burst then, watching them together, and rather than mar the wonderful feeling with thoughts of such days never coming again, Genevieve simply smiled.

'You made the right decision,' Jules said quietly, yet again reading her mind.

But then, some friends have that ability, don't they?

'Yes, I think I did,' Genevieve agreed.

They smiled at each other, and made for the bonfire. Josiah appeared, served them tea, and together they watched as Spencer began his lesson with Elizabeth.

I truly think I did.

'Just relax, and breathe, Genevieve,' Spencer said soothingly. Oh, that was *so* easy for him to say, wasn't it? He wasn't the one trying to lie back on water; trying not to feel terrified anytime his legs dipped too far into the depths, or the cool water lapped at the corner of his eyes. Elizabeth and Jules had had their turns, and both managed to move on from floating to paddling about, and now it was Genevieve's turn, while the others warmed themselves by the fire and feasted on the goods Josiah provided. 'I've got you.'

I know.

That was half the problem with the *breathing* and *relaxing*. He wasn't the one doing it whilst being gently supported with a hand at the small of his back, and another on his stomach; hands that made her feel and think of delectably wicked things. That made her heart race and her blood turn molten. And God was it beating. She could hear it, so much louder now, the rest of the world dulled by the water in her ears.

Spencer wasn't the one lying back, feeling, when he got the balance just right, that he was floating on air.

No, I am.

And *she* was the one doing it whilst gazing up into his eyes, strong and reassuring, keeping her steady and calm. She was the one doing it whilst gazing up into the face of the man who had stolen her heart.

Yes, no doubting that now. Here, in this moment, everything but his touch and gaze grounding her to the world, there was nothing but certainty that what was left of her heart to give to anyone, was his.

It was a strange feeling, one she'd never felt before. She loved Jules, as one did a sister. She loved Elizabeth with all her heart, her soul, everything she was, and ever would be. And loving *him*, it felt, somewhat like that, only different. Terrifying, and joyful, but differently. There was still the same fear of loss, but also of rejection. There was joy and excitement, yes, but *very* different kinds. And her love for Spencer, it seemed to fill in the blanks, the voids within her soul. Who she was as a person. Not just as mother, friend, daughter, wife. But as *Genevieve*.

She wasn't quite sure when it had happened. Perhaps the day he'd been attacked by Galahad. Or when she'd been with him, here, in this cove. Perhaps when he'd held her, told her that he saw the *real* her. Perhaps it had been that first moment, in his gardens. Perhaps there hadn't ever really been any choice, but simply by meeting his gaze that first instant, she had relinquished part of herself to him.

It didn't matter, really, when it happened. Just like it didn't matter when she'd realised.

Earlier. When he and Lizzie swam little lengths through the water, and he looked so proud of her. And she looked so happy, and safe.

It didn't matter because she knew she couldn't fight it. It should terrify her, knowing that she was giving him her heart, and that he would leave her, but she was at peace with it. Floating in a cold loch, held steady by the man you'd fallen in love with, it gave you a sense of peace. Of rightness. It would hurt when they parted, yes, but she would've felt this. *All* this.

And actually, it would be better than never feeling it at all.

A tiny smile curled the corners of her lips, and a knowing smile appeared on his.

'If ever you're in trouble,' he said, his voice low and intimate, as if they truly were the only people left in the world. 'Just float like this.'

He released his hands slowly, his eyes never leaving hers, and her body felt as her heart did.

Free. Floating on endless sky.

'I will,' she promised.

'Would you like to try swimming?'

'Not just yet. I like this.'

'I do too,' he said, licking his lips. 'I shall do the same, right here beside you if you feel comfortable as you are.' Genevieve made to nod but floundered in the water a little. 'Steady on,' Spencer laughed, helping her back to position gently. 'Ah, yes,' he sighed once he'd slid beside her. She couldn't see him, but she could feel his presence, feel the ripples of water coming from him. 'If you do wish to swim, you can just move your hands, like little oars, gently.'

Genevieve felt a swish of water from his own hands, then a tip of his finger toying with hers. Experimenting slowly, she felt herself glide a little, and that was rather extraordinary too.

'Wonderful, isn't it?'

She could tell he was smiling, and lord, but was it contagious.

'*Wonderful* doesn't even begin to describe it. I can't tell you what a gift you've given us, Spencer,' she said after a moment, trying to put into words some of the intense feelings in her heart. Not the part about it belonging to him; best for both of them if she kept those words to herself for now. *For ever.* 'Losing Elizabeth… I cannot think how

I would continue on without her. I've always been terrified to let her too near the water, for fear of what might happen. For fear of what nearly happened. Knowing she will be able to survive, enjoy it even, it is incredible.'

'Anything I can ever do, to assuage your fears, or ease her way, tell me. It will be done.'

'Thank you.'

Spencer's fingertips brushed hers again, only this time, they took hold. They glided slowly over the water together, the white puffs of clouds above seemingly so close they could touch them.

'What are you all doing tomorrow afternoon?' he asked after a while.

'We don't have any plans. Typically we read, and eat, and rest. Play games sometimes.'

'May I take you all to the falls?'

'Only if you promise to wear another of your vibrant coat and waistcoat combinations,' Genevieve laughed.

'I think that can be arranged,' he chuckled, tugging playfully on her fingers. 'I shall consult with Josiah.'

'May I ask about those? Is it the colours you like? Or is it colourful camouflage like a peacock.'

'A peacock! I should be offended for that comparison,' he said, his tone filled with amusement and false outrage. 'The truth is, both I think. People see, what they want to see,' he continued seriously. 'They wished to see an extravagant marquess, a charmer, with little substance, so that is what I became. Over time, I enjoyed finding new combinations. It felt as if I could express myself, be unique, in that small way.'

'I like them,' she breathed, trailing the tips of her fingers against his palm.

'You never did believe the illusion, did you?' he asked, and it seemed the most important question to him. 'You know which smile is true, and which is the mask.'

'Yes. And which is for me. Which is for Elizabeth. Which is for Jules.'

'They are all very special.'

'So are you, Spencer,' she admitted quietly.

The only sign that he'd heard was a gentle tightening of his hand around hers.

Genevieve never did make it to the part of the lesson where she could swim little laps. They simply floated, glided around for what seemed an eternity, together, in quiet harmony, suspended between earth and sky.

And it was wondrous.

'This place is magical,' Genevieve said as the sun began its descent. Lizzie, Miss Myles, and Josiah were engaged in a vicious duel with sticks by the water, whilst he and Genevieve sat basking in the warmth of the fire, tucked in blankets, bonetired. And well, there really was nothing more to ask for. Sitting here with her, the others happy, he had everything he needed; everything he'd ever wanted but never known could exist.

The time they'd spent together in the water... Well, suffice to say, it was not simply the place that was magical, but this woman, beside him. Not that he felt quite ready to tell her that. Tell her all she meant to him. He wasn't even ready to admit that fully to himself.

Just enjoy the day. And each day thereafter you are lucky enough to have.

'Did you come here often as a child?'

'For a time, every summer, I think. And then... Never again.'

'Did something happen?'

Yes.

I don't know.

Spencer sighed, pondering what to say.

Everything. You are not alone anymore. She will hear you.

Though wary about spoiling the day with darkness, he knew he needed to speak to someone about what haunted him, and she was his light. It was why he'd come here today. Yesterday...

Yesterday he'd whiled away the morning raging, crying, searching frantically, the house, his mind... He'd thought he was going mad, that he would go mad from the pain, the nightmares, the memories. And then he'd thought of Genevieve, and Lizzie, and the promised swimming lesson, and he'd had purpose again. Something to chase

away the darkness. So to town he'd gone to pur-
chase their clothes, made the preparations with
Josiah, and last night when he'd laid his head on
the pillow, he'd dreamt not of dragons and blood,
but of this. Of this perfect day.

It had made him realise, that he was not alone
anymore; though he'd not understood how alone
he'd been until he'd met her.

'I… I think so,' he admitted finally, turning to her. She studied him with those knowing
green eyes, softer now, less full of shadows. He
continued, unable to resist the openness she offered. She had entrusted him with everything;
he could, *would*, do the same. 'I had forgotten,
until…recently. Even now… What I remember,
I doubt it. Fear it to be true.' Genevieve's hand
found his, and she squeezed it lightly, as he had
her when she'd laid out her past before him, and
he drew strength from her. 'I recall happy times
as well,' he said, a wan smile curling the corners
of his lips as he glanced back out at Lizzie and the
others. 'It's why I came here. To remember what
being happy, and free, felt like. But even those
times, they seem unreal. My father playing with
me. My mother, happy—both of them—in love.'

'Were they not so otherwise?'

'No… When I was five, shortly after Mary was
born… Everything changed. After we came here
for the summer. My parents drifted apart. As if…'
He trailed off, his mind travelling back to that time

again. He'd thought on it often these past days, the succession of events, the changes. None more so than the past day. But he'd not been able to find the words to describe it until now. 'The love was gone. There was a coldness in our house then. I was entrusted to a tutor, then sent to school before Lizzie's age. My father shut himself away, and Mother tried to carry on as before, I remember that, but... It was as if he weren't even there. For a long time, I thought it was because of me,' he whispered.

That too, he'd forgotten. Or rather, it had transformed into the belief that the change had been to prepare him. From boy, *son*, to little lord.

Just as the belief that his closing off to emotion had been born solely of his need to be that little lord. Now... Now he realised much of it must've been his own mind protecting him from the pain, just as it had protected him by taking away the terrible memories.

'The memory,' Genevieve asked quietly. 'The one you fear... That's what has been troubling you.'

'Yes. It is of my mother,' he said flatly, though he felt the tightness in his own voice. 'Screams in the darkness. Blood on her hands, and guilt in her eyes.'

'You don't think...?'

'That she killed someone,' he finished for her. 'Yes. I find that I do. There was a woman here.

Muire. The McKennas' daughter,' he said. 'I found her grave, by the Yew Park chapel. I don't know what happened, but I know... I know that I loved her,' he whispered, the grief he'd felt that night still so fresh. 'And I think, my mother killed her.'

'Spencer...'

'Fantastical, the conjurings of a boy's imagination, I know,' he sighed, shaking his head. Oh, how he wished it were that simple. 'Still, there is something in that house...'

'I was only going to say, that is a terrible burden to carry.'

He turned back to Genevieve, searching her eyes for any dissemblance.

It was too unbelievable, she had every right to discredit what he said, to diminish it, dismiss it, only she wasn't.

'You believe me,' he breathed, incredulous.

'I do.'

He couldn't help but reach for her then, take her face in his hands, and kiss her, no matter who saw. He had to taste her, to lose himself in her for a moment at least, to thank her, for being on his side.

For being *by* his side.

'You should ask her,' Genevieve said gently as he released her from the kiss, but not his touch, keeping her close, losing himself in the depths of her mossy eyes. 'Your mother. You said that you feared she killed someone, but you did not say murder. You cannot carry that doubt with you.'

Spencer nodded, and kissed her forehead before tucking her into his side, lifting his blanket to cover her shoulders as well.

She was right, naturally. He'd known he would have to pry the truth from his mother, though he'd hoped there would be another way.

And she was right; killing, and murder, were two very different things.

Which I wish to think on no longer.

No. Now, he wished to be here, to enjoy his time with Genevieve, and Lizzie.

He did not want to mar the present with the past.

'Thank you,' Genevieve said wistfully. 'For today. I shall treasure it, always.'

'I should like to give you many days like today.'

I should like to give you a lifetime of them.

Yes, the past could wait.

It had waited long enough. It could wait a little longer.

Just like the rest of his life.

Chapter Eighteen

Genevieve had thought she knew what freedom tasted, smelled, felt like. She'd thought she'd known what it meant to enjoy her life. For them all to be free. Because she'd never known the land of *happy* and *warm* and *safe*; she'd fooled herself into believing *contentment* and pleasure were enough to feed one's soul. Simply because they were better than *nowhere* and *nothing*.

How very wrong she'd been.

How very right Jules was.

Not that she would admit it out loud. Her friend was an insufferable know-it-all on the best of days. Besides, the know-it-all knew very well indeed that Genevieve had learned the lesson these past days.

The know-it-all would have to be blind not to see that the final shackles Genevieve and Elizabeth wore, known, and unknown, were dropping, like discarded garments by the wayside. Genevieve could see it in her daughter, and in herself. Hadn't she bemoaned that some lessons Stapleton had inflicted refused to be unlearned? Hadn't she still seen shadows in the depths of her daughter's eyes that first day they'd encountered the Marquess?

Now, the lessons were being unlearned. Slowly, yes, but surely. Each act of kindness from Spencer, each careful word, and new lesson, chipped away at the old words seemingly carved into flesh and bone. Each laugh, each new experience, pushed back the shadows a little further; in them both.

Every so often, Genevieve would catch herself thinking: *what did I do to deserve this?*

But then she would chide herself, for she knew, that kindness, affection, those were not things people *deserved*. Love was not a prize to be won with good deeds and a pure heart. That was its nature. And even though she knew better, she had to admit, what Spencer showed them all, it felt a lot like love.

They'd been to the falls at the other end of the loch, where it met the river, and enjoyed another sumptuous picnic.

They had, well, Josiah had, unearthed two boats, and all of them had gone fishing, before enjoying the fruits of their labour that evening at Willowmere. It had felt so natural, so intimate, to sit around the kitchen table, altogether, laughing and talking until the moonrise beckoned Spencer and Josiah home.

The weather had continued to hold, and so there had been the trip to Ben More, and even Elizabeth had made it to the summit, though Spencer had carried her down. There had been numerous walks, around the loch, and up the surrounding hills. There had been outdoor lessons on farming, agriculture, biology, and entomology. There were games of balls, and badminton, and hide and seek. There were picnics, and evenings of song and quiet reading at Willowmere.

The weather had turned on Thursday, and still, Spencer had remained with them. Genevieve wondered if he was using them to escape the terrible memories he'd told her of, but then, every day his own shadows seemed to lessen, and so, even if he did, it didn't matter. So long as they could bring him as much peace and joy, as he did them.

He came every morning, helped with the chores, helped with Elizabeth's lessons, or simply read on his own as Genevieve worked on her lace. There were still games, of chess, of piquet, even charades. It never felt as if he spent time with them in order to gain anything but their company. Though he still touched, and kissed her freely, the subject of more had not been broached. Genevieve, for herself, longed for *more*, only after all they'd shared, she knew it would mean so very much more. And though her body screamed *yes*, her heart screamed, *give me time.* Perhaps Spencer sensed that, and she was grateful to him for that too.

And just like that, an entire week had passed since they'd been swimming. As if in celebration, Spencer invited them all to dine at Yew Park, and so, here they were, taking the final steps towards the imposing front door.

So this is the land of happy and safe and warm, Genevieve thought, when the door was opened, not by the butler, but by a smiling Spencer, aquamarine waistcoat and midnight-blue coat and all.

I think I like this land after all.

'Where did all this come from, Spencer?' Lizzie asked, awe and excitement in her voice, as they entered the laboratory-cum-specimen room. The room Spencer had taken to calling the Chamber of Monsters, and which he'd hesitated at showing Lizzie, but the budding scientist had been insistent once hearing the word *specimens.*

Miss Myles had declined joining the tour altogether, settling herself in the library with Josiah and a game of chess after the lovely, and lively dinner they'd shared.

A tortuous, but lively dinner.

Tortuous, for he'd had to endure the sight of a breathtaking Genevieve, drinking and eating and generally being unwittingly sensuous, throwing him heated looks all evening.

But otherwise he could not truly complain. The food had been scrumptious, the table set as if for royalty, the McKennas having outdone themselves, something which, even considering his current feelings regarding them, *confusion, anger, hurt*, Spencer could recognise, and appreciate.

In fact, his entire little household had come together with the promise of guests, seemingly enthralled at the fact that not only was he having company, but at the company itself. It was always odd, sensing that servants approved or disapproved of certain people. Spencer had learned early on to pay attention to those subtle signs, shifts in mood. A glance, a lean, a narrowing of the eyes, they could tell you whether this lord or that was handsy; this lady or that was kind.

And strangely, the fact that this household, which was his own, and yet, not truly, approved of Genevieve, Lizzie, and Miss Myles, warmed his heart, and made him bolder. Bold enough to open doors himself, and even sneak Lizzie an extra cherry from his plate. Then again, maybe it was their company that made him bolder; bold enough to be himself. To be relaxed, and free, and open, and intimate. Without care nor concern for convention, people's thoughts, or even duty.

This past week in their company had been filled with what he'd always wanted and never had. A sense of family, and home. Of fun, and quiet contentment. Life finally felt like that. *Life*. Days playing, and learning, and simply *being* had filled him with a sense of rest. A peace, in his heart that quietened the terrible noise. When the dragons and nightmares came, fierce shield-maidens that looked like Genevieve chased them away. When his own voice from boyhood screamed in the darkness, Lizzie's laughter answered, telling him to come play, and leave his sorrows behind.

He'd been concerned, bringing them here; it was why he'd avoided formally inviting them for nearly a week. Concerned that the darkness might take over them. That the staff would judge, and wish them gone. That...something, anything would put an end to the glorious reprieve. That somehow changing the status-quo would...change the status-quo. But when he'd seen them all on his doorstep, dressed in their very best clothes, fine gowns, if a bit out of date, he'd known, he need not have worried.

They belonged anywhere he was.

'I admit, I don't actually know,' Spencer said, a faint smile on his lips from that final thought. He watched as Lizzie made her way around the circular room, cramped with shelves upon shelves of jars, books, scientific instruments and all manner of unknown oddities. 'One of Great-Uncle Jasper's ancestors was an alchemist as I recall, so I suspect most of it comes from him. There was also a cousin, though he dabbled more in the occult, and was forced to leave the country to avoid meeting with a bonfire. I think others, including Jasper, picked up the scientific appreciation, if you look there,' he said, pointing to a shelf to Lizzie's right. 'That particular octopus is dated 1772, so likely Jasper found that beauty.'

Lizzie held her candle up higher to better see the monster, and made a little sound of appreciation.

'How did all this survive the wars?' she asked, eyeing more gruesome samples. 'There are so many wonders in this house.'

Yes, there are. Even more so tonight.

But it was a valid question. The art, the silver, the furnishings, even the house itself, had survived remarkably well the last tumultuous century and a half.

'Not to disparage the dead, but let us simply say that Jasper's side of the family knew how to keep themselves on the winning side of things.'

Lizzie nodded, understanding very well the diplomatic understatement.

In truth, it had been blood, and betrayal, that bought security for his ancestors. One of the many reasons Spencer had to *be the best man he could be*, always, and for ever. Only honour, and a good name could wipe away the sins of the past.

As Lizzie continued her rounds, Spencer glanced over at Genevieve. She'd stopped at the centre of the room, where a giant desk sat piled high with parchment, books, and more implements of experimentation. Her fingers swept delicately over the pages of a Renaissance manuscript, careful to respect the ancient pages.

This week had changed her too. The weight she carried seemed to lessen each day, and her light grew stronger and stronger, as did Lizzie's. Until they were both so blindingly bright, it was nigh-on impossible to gaze straight at them, lest you be scorched.

Like right now, for instance. In the flickering of the candle beside her, in that rich emerald and blue, nearly iridescent silk, oddly reminiscent of a peacock's feathers, the thin gold filigree of the chain around her neck glinting with every breath, her hair in a loose, seductive pile of curls, she looked utterly celestial. Every day, she took his breath away. Every day, she seemed to grow more beautiful, and every day he wanted her more.

He knew from the heated glances she bestowed on him that the feeling was mutual, but he'd sensed she needed time. Before she could take that step again, before they could share passion and pleasure again. And if he was honest, so had he. For this time would be so much more. He intended that there would be nothing between them now. She knew him, and he knew her. More than he would've thought possible in a week; though he knew not even a lifetime would be enough to know her entirely.

A lifetime with this woman would not be enough, though it would be something extraordinary.

'You've found the bestiary,' Spencer said quietly as he slid beside Genevieve, letting her warmth seep into him.

His fingers brushed her own, and they tangled together, as they often did now.

It was the little touches, the little tender signs of affection he'd never known that he seemed to crave most. That meant, the most.

And with her hand in his, he felt a man ready to conquer the world.

'It's beautiful.' She smiled, meeting his gaze. *Oh, that I could live in the universe within you.* 'The craftsmanship is extraordinary.'

'Quite.' He smiled, leaning over to brush a kiss on her lips. 'Ah the rhinoceros,' he said, glancing back down at the page.

'There was a rhinoceros in London in 1684,' Lizzie offered, coming to peek from Spencer's other side. He moved back a step, and let his other hand fall on her shoulder. 'It cost a shilling to see it.'

'Would you have liked to see it?' he asked.

'No. I should like to see one in the wild some-day. Not in a cage. It died a couple years later,' she added, and Spencer felt his heart do that little twist. 'Nothing is meant to live in a cage.'

'So you shall be an explorer, then? Like Mr Von Humboldt, perhaps?'

Lizzie had spent some time vaunting the man's *Personal Narrative of Travels*, which she'd apparently devoured in a matter of days, in the original German, naturally.

The girl was a wonder, and just as her mother did, surprised him every day.

'Perhaps.'

She looked up and smiled at him, before turning her attention to the other books on the table.

In that moment, Spencer wanted to promise her that she could be whatever she wished. That he would take her anywhere, fund her expeditions to whatever end of the world she wished to go to. He would make sure she saw those rhinoceros, if it was the last thing he did. He wanted to offer that they go right now, even if just back to London so they could find her more books, or attend some scientific lecture.

Only, he realised that he couldn't. Yes, he would watch over her, always, ease her way, make her dreams reality, but something as simple as a trip to London...somehow that was the dream he could not make real. This past week, they had consciously, or unconsciously, avoided Aitil. The relationship he was fostering with Genevieve, had its limits.

He would leave. They both knew it. He would leave, and they would remain.

So he could not jeopardise the life they had, nor could he jeopardise his own, the one which waited for him in the South, and that he dreaded more with every passing day.

'Or perhaps I shall become an astronomer,' Lizzie said with a cheeky little grin as she spied a telescope, tearing him from the bitter thoughts. 'Or a painter.'

'Perhaps all three,' Spencer offered.

'All three, then.'

'Well,' he said, picking up Genevieve's candle, and steering them all to the door. 'If you are to be a painter, you should see the pieces Jasper brought back from his Grand Tour.'

So on they went, to see the paintings.

Then the sculptures, the orangery, the armoury, then every other wonder Spencer could think of. Sadly, not even his house was big enough, nor full of wonders enough, to keep them there eternally.

And it was far too soon that he was bidding them goodnight at Willowmere's door.

For I wish this night, this day, this summer, would never end.

Chapter Nineteen

A storm was coming. The scent of rain was on the wind; the unspoken, and yet unfulfilled crackling of lightning on the air. Outside, the night creatures were silent, only the violent rustling of wind through the leaves, the creaking of the boughs, and the whistling of the pines was to be heard. The excited cresting of the water against the point before Willowmere.

Lying in bed, Genevieve could hear the deafening silence of the wait, the anticipation, and though she loved a good tempest, she had to admit, waiting for it was beginning to set her nerves on edge.

Or perhaps that was the evening at Yew Park. The low light of the candles, the twisty corridors… Even the room full of jarred creatures and ancient books. They'd all set her imagination on fire, when Spencer was not doing the job himself, glancing at her with such looks, vowing pleasure beyond her wildest dreams.

Each glance was a caress, a promise, which she still waited to see fulfilled.

Each touch of his hand, little brush of fingers, meant that now, she couldn't sleep.

All she could do was lie there, watching the fire writhe with every gust of wind that swept down the chimney. The howling that accompanied it was ominous, and threatening, as if heralding the arrival of demons.

When she was a girl, she'd never been frightened by storms, even when they rattled the shutters and flung open doors. Perhaps because fear like that, was a luxury. She'd known even then no one would come to comfort her. Not her mother, not her nurse. So instead, she would imagine that it was gods on mighty steeds with wings, charging the walls to take her away to some faraway kingdom. The kingdom wouldn't necessarily be beautiful, and magical, but it would be…

Anywhere but where I was.

Sighing, Genevieve curled tighter into the covers. Neither had Elizabeth ever had the luxury of being afraid of storms. She'd have nightmares occasionally, and now would sometimes dare to creep into Genevieve or Jules's bed, but the lessons taught by Stapleton, and the nurses before Juliana had been well taught.

No crying. No fear. No one will come to comfort you.

Bastards.

Genevieve would've comforted her, had she been allowed to—

Don't think on that.

Think on wonderful things. Or think on those gods coming forth again to fetch you.

Smiling, Genevieve did just that.

And look, the rain has started.

There were few pleasures greater than being tucked in a warm bed, a fire roaring, the sound of rain on the glass—

Oddly singular rain.

Frowning, Genevieve listened carefully, and realised it actually didn't sound like rain at all. This sound was sharper, almost as if someone was—

It can't be.

And yet it was, she confirmed a moment later, having thrown the blanket over her shoulders, and half-tripped, half-scrambled to the window in eagerness.

Spencer.

There he was, beneath her window, with handfuls of pebbles. He grinned that dangerous grin when he saw her, and she thought that perhaps the gods had come after all. He looked like one in the shadowy moonlight, a god of mischief perhaps, his hair wild in the wind, shirt flapping, coat unbuttoned, and no waistcoat. Dropping the pebbles, he approached, as she unlatched the window and leaned out. The wind whipped her furiously, and she should've been cold, but she wasn't. Not in the least.

I am alive, and afire.

'I couldn't sleep,' he said, in a voice loud enough to be heard over the storm, but not loud enough to wake anyone. 'You can send me away, if you wish. But I had to see you.'

'I will come unlock the door,' she said without hesitation.

'You will do no such thing! I shall climb up to you, Princess.'

'You're mad, the stone is slippery—'

Spencer raised a hand and she stifled a giggle. The man was mad.

For me. As I am for him.

'Be careful,' she hissed as he began the climb, nimbly navigating the uneven stones, and the occasional hook and ring along the wall.

He reached her in moments, and she pulled back slightly as he reached the window.

'Hello.' He smiled, his eyes alight with boyish playfulness.

'Hello.'

They remained there, him suspended outside her window, she there, wrapped in her blanket, staring at each other for a long moment before finally he leaned in and stole a kiss.

Some of the tension within Genevieve uncoiled, and she sighed, contented.

This. This is what I've been waiting for.

'Come in,' she said, moving aside so he could. 'You must be quiet, though Jules is at the other end of the house, Elizabeth is between us.'

As he latched the window shut again, Spencer threw her a glance over his shoulder and raised a brow that seemed to say, *I shall not be the one needing to be quiet.*

Genevieve waited, her fingers tightly curled under the blanket as they held it, more nervous than she'd thought she would be. It wasn't as if they hadn't *done this* before, only this was different. He was in her home, in her room, filling it with his presence, warming it more effectively than any fire. He was asking, and she would give more, than she had that day by the loch. She couldn't hide anymore, behind pretences of *quick trysts* and layers of clothes; not that she'd been able to hide from him, well, ever.

Spencer stood before her now, towering, and yet, unthreatening in every way.

Behind him, the rain did come, pelting across the glass.

And then, the thunder, and lightning.

'Say the word,' he whispered, need infusing his voice. 'And I will stop, or I will go.'

'I want this.'

'One does not preclude the other.'

Nodding, more grateful than he could ever know, she released the blanket, nervous no longer.

His eyes skimmed the outline of her form,

which she knew would be rather visible in the firelight, the hunger in them growing with every curve and turn. His brow furrowed slightly, and he bit the corner of his lip, as if debating where to begin.

Anywhere, so long as you begin.

Her silent prayer was swiftly answered when he slid a finger under each side of the drooping neckline, sliding it ever further, over her shoulders, down her arms, and—

'Damn,' he muttered, frustrated when the fabric caught on both arms, effectively trapping her, not quite wide enough to be taken off so. 'I thought that would work.'

They laughed, the lightness of the moment welcome, and wonderful.

'Here,' she said, bunching up the bottom, and sweeping the whole nightdress over her head.

'Much better,' Spencer agreed seriously, his eyes darkened to the colour of night.

With the lightness of a feather, his fingers traced the line of her collarbone, the slope of her shoulder, the length of her arms, all the way down to the tips of her fingers. Then back up, swirling across the lines of her palms, jumping over to the slope of her breasts, following the teardrop to its very end. Genevieve couldn't move, too dazed by the delicate, sweet touch. Her skin had gooseflesh, but she wasn't cold, no, she was burning again, scalding hot from the inside out. It felt like warm treacle in her veins, melting them, oozing out into flesh, making her boneless, and malleable wherever he touched.

It didn't matter that his fingertips barely brushed across her skin; the touch had more impact than if he'd grasped her outright.

Down still he travelled, along her ribs, over the rounded slope of her belly, across her hips, then, falling to his knees, down her legs to the tips of her toes. She brushed her own fingers through the damp strands of his hair, unable to resist any longer. Only, they were just there, begging to be swept from his brow.

And when he looked up at her then, she felt her heart skip a beat as her breath caught. Because there was something else in the depths of those blue eyes, something more than *heat*, and *want*, and *need*. Something beyond care. Something that looked, and felt, a lot like what she held in her heart. A lot like love. Love for the Genevieve inside, the soul.

Bending down, as tall as he was, she needn't go too far, she willed her lips to say the words, to express the feelings she couldn't, not out loud.

I do love you.

His cheeks in her palms, his arms snaking around her legs and hips, they remained thus for a long moment, savouring the other's taste, the other's scent, and warmth. Speaking the slow language of love with their lips and tongues, and even teeth. And beneath the fiery passion, the desperation, the enjoyment, she felt it there too, what she would never admit to herself was *his* love.

The kiss broke, and then he was kissing her everywhere, making up for lost time it seemed, careful not to repeat any gesture, or visit any spot she did not react well to, concentrating instead on those places—*underside of the breast, nipple, meeting of the waist and hips*—that made her clutch him a little tighter. Made her release breathy little cries, and moans of approval.

And when she felt like she couldn't quite take it anymore, that she was simply too boneless, and her heart rushed too fast, and the fire in her veins was too much for her body to contain anymore, he wrapped his arms around her, beneath the buttocks, and lifted her before laying her gently down on the bed. A swift kiss, and he straightened, shucking his coat, and ridding himself of all but his underclothes.

Thankfully.

Now she could see *him*, in the firelight again, and still he seemed to glow, though there were no droplets to make him glitter today. Her fingers traced the paths she had before, over his chest, swirling over his nipples, down further, over the ridges of his stomach. And then she traced new ones, along his jaw, the column of his neck, down the arm that supported him as he leaned beside her.

Another kiss, swift, and far too chaste for her

liking, and he was disappearing again, and that was very disappointing, but then he was nuzzling the thatch of curls guarding her entrance, and she hesitated, unsure, a rush of nerves returning, but then he planted a kiss along the lines on her belly, the ones from Elizabeth, and she softened, tears pricking her eyes which she categorically refused to let fall. Taking a deep breath, she closed her eyes, and opened to him, and then his lips, and tongue, and deft fingers were everywhere, bringing her glorious waves of sensation she'd never experienced before.

Again, he listened, repeated when her body said *yes*, and pulled back when it resisted.

It was the strangest sensation she'd ever felt, the slick, moist heat of his mouth mingling with the molten honey within her, sending her further and further away from the world until it felt as if she was floating on clouds of stars. Yet she was not lost among them, he kept her grounded still, his fingers on her thigh anchoring her as she witnessed the beginning and end of galaxies, then crested back down to Earth.

Still, he was there, waiting for her, and perhaps that was the best feeling of all.

Knowing that someone cared enough to worship her, to *listen* to her, then to wait for her, as if nothing mattered more than being together. Than holding each other, as he did then, ridding himself of his final piece of clothing before slinking back up her body, and curling himself around her back, arms around her waist, and her neck, his stiffness between them, but still, *waiting.*

Spencer kissed her hair, her earlobe, the line of her jaw, as she slid her fingers down the lines of corded muscle in his arms, the bumps of his knuckles; tucked herself tight against the wall of strength and stability he provided. As if he would always be there, *could* always be there, at her back. And when her blood had returned to a gentle simmer, she slid her leg along and over his, the soft bristles of his hair tickling the pad of her foot and making her smile.

His hands were moving then, understanding the silent entreaty, one coming to her hip while the other turned her head so he could claim her lips again. A moan of satisfaction vibrated through her, him, or perhaps, them both, a shared sound, as they shared breath for a moment. She slid her own hand between them, arching as best she could without severing the connection to guide him where he belonged.

His grip, his kiss, everything tightened then, as he slid into her, and she'd been right.

This is different.

Holding him inside herself now, everything that he was surrounding her, their skins nearly fused together with lightning and slick heat, this is what it meant to join, to merge, to unite. She felt his own soul in his touch, *his* opening, and giving; not simply taking or receiving.

They moved together, the kiss breaking as their passion and pleasure grew, as the need to find the highest summit together grew. Still he kept her close, and tight, nimble fingers sliding down to that hidden bud again.

And she knew he would withdraw again, when he'd seen her to completion, but tonight, she wanted it all.

I can have it.

'Don't release me, Spencer,' she managed to gasp out, as they rolled higher, and higher, holding on to that final shred of reason so she could let go completely. 'My courses ended yesterday. It's safe.'

There was the tiniest sliver of hesitation, and she understood, but then he was grasping her tighter, closer, which she might've thought was impossible without fading into the other, not that she would mind.

He peppered her with open-mouthed kisses, until finally she was soaring, and he followed right behind, and she willed her heart to speak through her body, for her flesh to speak to his, for her breath to carry with it the words *I love you.*

Whatever left of myself to give, I give to you.

Outside, the storm raged on, forbidding, and yet, soothing. Yet again, Genevieve lay enveloped in the warmth of the blankets. Yet again, the fire roared and danced as the wind howled and moaned on its descent through the chimney. Thunder and lightning boomed and crackled, and centuries-old wood creaked and groaned.

Only this time, she wasn't alone. She was surrounded by more warmth. *His* warmth. Genevieve smiled as she recalled the rest.

They'd lain together on the bed for a long time, breathing the other in, lost in the haze of their coupling, in their mingled scents, in the heat of their togetherness. And then he'd taken her again, lazily, almost clumsily, both so drunk on ecstasy. They had washed each other after, and she'd slipped her nightdress back on as Spencer slid on his underclothes and shirt, and he'd begun to reach for his coat, but then she'd asked him to stay.

'The rain...' she'd said, though both knew that storm or not, she would've asked him to stay. In the morning, he could disappear into the dawn mists, but she wanted every second she could have.

For there will only be so many.

Dreamily, Genevieve pushed away the unwelcome thought, snuggling closer to the body behind her, and tightening her hold on the one in her arms.

Wait...

There was another?

Genevieve's eyes opened, and in the darkness she spied the glint of familiar eyes. Tonight apparently was one of the few times Elizabeth had decided to seek her out. She stiffened slightly, fear invading her heart.

What will Elizabeth think?

What will Spencer think?

But one question at least was answered.

'It's all right, *Maman*,' Elizabeth whispered, closing her own eyes.

And rather than disturb either of her loves, Genevieve followed her example and drifted back off to sleep. She would deal with the consequences in the morning.

For now, she would fall away to that distant kingdom, whose benevolent god was beside her, and where she and Elizabeth would roam free, and happy, always.

Chapter Twenty

*H*ome. He knew what that felt like now. What it tasted like, what it smelt like, what it sounded like. It wasn't remembered, as it had been for so long. Echoes of whispers of memories, ghostly sensations he'd known once but couldn't find again. This wasn't the home he remembered as a boy, fleeting though it may have been, tainted with darkness, and unanswered questions. No. This home, was real. It was his present, and it was quite literally within his grasp.

Here, there were no unanswered questions. Because *she* contained all the answers, known and unknown, spoken, and unspoken. She contained the answers which allowed one to live a fulfilled life; a life of happiness, and love.

Love. Yes.

He knew what that was now too. Not the dutiful love of a son for his mother, the remembered love for a stranger, or the love for a sister. This love, was one of passion, and understanding, and choice, though he doubted he'd really had any choice but to love her. To love them both. For there, in his heart, alongside the love of a man for a woman, was the love he had for her daughter too. He felt it, as surely as if she'd been his own flesh.

Spencer inhaled deeply, burying his nose a little further into the mass of Genevieve's hair, holding her tight. He was loath to open his eyes, to acknowledge the sun streaming in, brighter and clearer, for the storm having passed. He only wanted to revel in this moment, and the memories of last night.

Yet again, Genevieve had surprised him. By being more than he could've imagined, her body lush, and welcoming, and beautiful, and real. A man could get lost in a body like that; far too much to explore. Not that he hadn't tried. But just like the rest of her, it would take a lifetime to catalogue her wonders.

And when they came together, when they moved as one, and rose to the furthest heights of pleasure, it was what poets wrote about. What he'd wanted, without ever being brave enough to believe in it, let alone admit it. It was the sharing of souls, a connection of spirits. Genevieve had opened herself to him, opened her heart, shed those final defences, and let him in. And so had he. He'd let her see all of him; and how terrifying and liberating that was.

He smiled, finally unable to resist the day, slowly lifting his head from the crook of Genevieve's neck to peek over her head, revelling at how *right* it felt to be here, like this. Lazing late on a Sunday morning, the woman he loved in his arms, sleeping soundly, the girl he loved just there, her hand entwined with her mother's, sleeping just as peacefully.

What he wouldn't give to have this every day, for the rest of his life.

What wouldn't you give?

Nothing.

That was the brutal truth; there was *nothing* he wouldn't give.

Certainty filled his heart then. A calm, but terrifying certainty, that he would do, sacrifice whatever he must, to share a life with these women, to make them his family, and to become theirs.

His life had been led for duty. This wasn't the future planned for him, that which he'd agreed to himself. But it had to be his future. For if it wasn't, he would suffer the fate he'd always feared.

A cold, empty life of bitterness and torment.

One could not experience this sort of love, this belonging, and simply cast it away. That was heresy; hybris. Fate had brought him here, given him that which he searched for: *happiness, home, myself.* And he would not reject her gift. For once, he would not let his head rule. He would give in, surrender to his heart, let it lead the way. After all, it had brought him here.

I will go to Stirling, tomorrow.

Yes, and then he would—

'Good morning,' Genevieve whispered sleepily.

'Morning,' he breathed, nuzzling her again, just because he could.

'Do you mind, about Elizabeth?'

'Why should I mind?'

'Because…'

Genevieve trailed off, her unspoken thoughts loud.

Because she will know you spent the night in my bed and somehow that means more than kisses and touches.

Because it is too intimate, too much like something we are not.

Because it means we are a family.

'I love you,' he said simply. Her breath caught, and her heart raced beneath his palm. 'You don't have to say anything,' he reassured her.

And it was the absolute truth.

He didn't want her to be frightened, to feel as if she had to say the words, to say anything at all. He knew he loved her, and for now, that was enough. He knew in his heart that she felt something for him, love, he liked to think, for he might've sworn he'd seen it in her eyes, felt it in her touch. But taking that step, saying the words, giving them reality with voice, it was taking a leap. And if she wasn't ready to, well, God knew he understood. Another reason he must go to Stirling. If they were to move forward, she had to know, there was weight, and intention behind the words he spoke.

They are not empty as I once was.

Spencer felt her relax again, breathe again, and so he closed his eyes, revelling in the feeling of having arrived.

Precisely when and where I was meant to.

They remained there for a good while longer, until Lizzie woke, and declared she was famished. Then they all retired downstairs to breakfast, in their nightclothes, and feasted, and laughed, and simply lived.

This shall be my future, Spencer thought as he helped Miss Myles dry the dishes when they'd finished. *And I could not ask for more.*

'I must to Stirling tomorrow,' Spencer said, drawing her attention from the lace she was working on. She'd felt him staring for a while now, not that she minded, he did that often, and if she was honest, she indulged often enough herself to be unable to cast any stones. Glancing up, she found him still lounging in the chair across from hers, as he'd been all evening, dark shadows flickering across his face as the flames danced in the hearth. The book he'd pretended to read for a while, before Elizabeth and Jules went to bed, lay discarded on his lap, and there was a seriousness about him that concerned her.

All week, he'd seemed happy, and unburdened.

But now, she wondered if the life he'd pretended didn't exist, if those dark memories he'd seemed to wilfully push aside, were all coming back to haunt him with a vengeance.

As troubles often do on Sunday eves.

'Is everything all right, Spencer?'

'Never better,' he said, with a smile that was a shadow of the false one he used to don.

It struck her heart.

He'd not used that smile, that facade for a long time. Not with her, at least. Not this past week, ever. This past week, he'd changed, giving free rein to himself to *be* himself, and the fact that he was donning it again worried her. For him.

Could it be because she hadn't said the words? Returned his declaration this morning?

He'd said she needed not, and he'd been himself all day, well, the Spencer she knew now. Laughing, and playing games, helping to do the chores as if it were the most wondrous occupation he could ever have. But now, in the darkness of the evening, the culmination of the day, could he be feeling pain, anger even at her silence?

It wasn't as if she didn't love him. She'd hoped he felt it, last night, that he knew even if she didn't say the words. Because she couldn't. She wanted to; oh, how she'd wanted to this morning as she'd lain there in his arms, snug and safe, Elizabeth beside them, like they were a proper family. A family who loved each other.

But that was precisely the problem. They *weren't* a family, and could never be.

Not anywhere outside of the world created here.

And that was why she'd been unable to speak the words. To say, *I love you, Spencer, with all my heart*. Because there had to be something. Something she held on to, one final step she didn't take. If she did, when he left her, there could be no illusions. There could be no rewriting of history, no self-preservation. She would've admitted the truth, made it real, and there would be nothing left for her. She might've said it, a thousand times, when she touched him, kissed him, lay with him, but it wasn't the same. It wasn't the same as saying *I love you* to the world; knowing that the world would then take that love away.

Because love wasn't enough to break the curse of impossibility.

'You can tell me anything you know,' she said, bracing herself for whatever came next.

'I know,' he said, a little frown of confusion furrowing his brow. He searched her eyes for a moment, then, seemingly understanding her concern, relaxed slightly. 'I will,' he promised, and what could she do, fool that she was, but believe him. 'In time. Just not tonight. Don't worry, Genevieve,' he said, rising, a true smile on his face. 'It will all be right as rain soon enough. You'll see.'

Spencer closed the small gap between them and laid his hand on her cheek.

Unable to do anything else, she leaned into it, closing her eyes to truly revel in every sensation that trickled through her any time he touched her.

'I'll be back tomorrow night. Tuesday morning at the latest,' he added, before bending down for a kiss.

It began innocently, a sweet brush of the lips, but quickly transformed into something far more heated, and filled with promise.

And then the fire burning in her veins turned to ice in an instant when he broke the kiss and leaned his forehead against hers. A strange feeling filled her heart as she gazed into the clear depths of his eyes. It was similar to the one she'd experienced when he'd first arrived. A sense of impending change, only this time, there was a whisper of doom, and endings, that seemed to squeeze her heart. It felt as if that kiss would be their last.

Nonsense. Utter hogwash. You're merely tired.

'I'll see you when you return,' she said, forcing a smile to her lips.

'You will.'

With a wolfish grin, he straightened, and made his way out.

Some time later, Genevieve went and locked the house. Still, she could not shake the feeling that everything was about to change again.

This time for the worst.

Chapter Twenty-One

It was disconcerting how quickly Genevieve, how quickly all of them really, had become accustomed to having Spencer in their lives. How much of a hole he left in the short day and a half he'd been gone. Their lives went back to what they were before he'd begun spending so much time with them, which in actual fact weren't all that different to what they were when he was around. They still did chores, Elizabeth still had lessons, they still played games and had pleasant walks, Genevieve still worked on her lace, or tended to the *potager* as she did now. Except that it didn't feel the same as before.

It felt like something was missing.

They missed Spencer.

Not just her, she knew, but Elizabeth, and even Jules. The two had found a pleasant camaraderie over the past week, laughing and speaking of art and music to their hearts' content, and for someone like Jules, who distrusted men as a general rule, that was really quite something. But it was overall disconcerting to mark his absence so, to feel it so, for it showed just how much of a loss it would be when he left for good. It wasn't that they needed him to be happy, it wasn't that they needed a man in their lives, but it did feel as if their lives would not be whole, as if their family would not be whole, without Spencer.

Which was utterly foolish, and nonsensical, really.

Genevieve had given the man her heart, and Elizabeth surely had. Jules had given her friendship, but they didn't need anyone to be whole.

Right?

We were absolutely fine before, and so we shall be again.

Fine. Content.

Yes. But not happy, and fulfilled, and—

Sighing, Genevieve tossed down her trowel, and swiped a sleeve across her sweaty brow. She'd been like this since he left. That feeling she'd had when he'd walked out of Willowmere Sunday eve hadn't left her, not truly. And she'd been going in circles, trying to prepare herself for the day when he *would* leave for good, whilst reminding herself of her promise to enjoy what she'd been given, for the time she'd been given it, with no regrets.

You do not need a man to be happy. Spencer

simply showed you what the land of happy and safe could be, but you can build it yourself some day.

Yes, but—

Her thoughts were interrupted by the sound of a carriage and horses. Frowning, Genevieve rose, half expecting to find Spencer, though why he'd be arriving in a carriage would be anyone's guess. For half a second, her heart filled with dread, that it might be Stapleton, come for Elizabeth as she'd always dreaded.

But then she spotted the woman emerging from the carriage, indeed the carriage itself, and utter dread was replaced by wariness, and curiosity.

Well into her middle age, the woman was beautiful, of the same height or so as Genevieve, with a fine figure and features, silver hair, and exceptionally turned out in forest green travelling clothes, as befitted only a peeress, or a member of the wealthy elite. The carriage itself was doubtless the latest model, and the man in livery handing her down from the vehicle marked her as likely aristocracy.

But why is she here?

The woman did not look familiar, apart from the raised chin and stiff back, reminiscent of so many Genevieve had known. There were other lords in the area, naturally, so perhaps the woman was lost?

Wiping her hands on her apron, pushing away

as many stray hairs as she could, Genevieve made her way to the garden gate.

'My lady,' she greeted with a pleasant smile and a curtsey. 'May I help you?'

The woman approached, but not too closely, eyeing Genevieve as though she were something foul. Her dark brown eyes shone with disgust, and reproach, and though Genevieve was used to such looks, something about this lady's whole manner immediately raised the hackles on her neck.

Does she recognise me?

Let us pray not.

'I am looking for my son,' the woman said in clipped, cultured, biting tones, and Genevieve understood at once.

Spencer's mother.

Though why she'd come *here* to find him, that was another question altogether. Spencer had promised his staff were discreet, no one in the villages or Aitil knew of their association as far as she knew, but then again, faced with a dowager marchioness, one as potent as this, Genevieve doubted many could hold on to their secrets for long.

However she'd come to be here, in truth it mattered not. She was here now. Genevieve hoped that Jules would keep Elizabeth inside, and not come investigate. She had a feeling this interview, visit, well, whatever it was supposed to be, would not be pleasant.

Stiffening slightly, her lessons in deportment shining through as she readied for battle, Genevieve studied the woman before her again. She felt an odd sort of resentment, on behalf of Spencer, for all the woman had kept from him. For what she might've done, that still haunted her son.

For a split-second Genevieve wanted to call her out, ask her precisely what had happened at Yew Park all those years ago, but luckily she managed to bite her tongue.

'I was told he was likely to be found here,' the Dowager continued, eyeing Willowmere as critically as she had Genevieve.

Well, as much as I love you, Spencer, I'm sorry, but I won't make this easy for her.

The time for cowing, and bowing, and ceding to every person's wish was over. She'd sworn never to let herself be treated as filth ever again, and just because this was Spencer's mother, well, that did not mean Genevieve owed her anything but a lesson in manners.

Her anger on Spencer's behalf, mingled with the urge to remind this *lady* of her place, and she plastered on another sickly-sweet smile.

'As we are not acquainted, my lady, I am afraid I cannot guess who your son might be.'

'Do not play games,' the Dowager snapped, taking a step closer, her eyes boring into Genevieve's. 'You are not stupid, for if you were, you would not be attempting to secure your future, and that of your daughter, by attaching yourself to a marquess.'

Though she'd expected something of the sort, it didn't stop the sting.

Had the woman slapped her, it might've had the same effect.

The effect of reminding you why you and Spencer can never be.

'Your words remind me of the world I left behind,' Genevieve said steadily, and the Dowager at least had the grace of looking somewhat taken aback. 'And for that I thank you, my lady. As for your son, he is not here.'

'Where is he?'

'It is not my business to divulge his whereabouts if he does not see fit to inform you. Good day, my lady.'

Turning her back, Genevieve made for the garden again, forcing herself to breathe, in, and out, in, and out. Forcing the urge to be ill, and to cry, and scream, back down, so she could retain some dignity.

'How dare you?' the Dowager raged, her voice rising to a very unladylike volume. 'Who do you think you are to deny me?'

'She's the woman I'm going to marry, Mother.'

Both women whirled around at once, to find Spencer, still astride his mount.

Neither had heard him arrive, though neither had missed his words.

Genevieve stared at him in shock, her stomach plummeting down to her boots.

God, Spencer, no, why?

This wasn't how it was supposed to go. Any of it. Spencer had had a plan. A *good* plan. A flawless plan. Well, there were flaws in any plan, but his plan had been as devoid of visible flaws as one could make it.

He'd gone to Stirling, and got the ring. Normally, he'd be expected to propose to any potential bride with a piece from the Marquessate's collection. Something with history, and meaning, perhaps even the ring his father had proposed to his mother with. But that would all be expected if he proposed to a woman as he was meant to. A young debutante, with impeccable breeding, and a sizeable dowry. Which is not who he would be proposing to, so that is not how he wanted to do it. He didn't want to taint his future with the past. He wanted to mark a new beginning, a new history with Genevieve. Both for himself, and the Marquessate. For Society, even.

So to Stirling he'd gone, to find a ring that represented that new beginning, and also the special nature of his relationship with Genevieve. Hours he'd spent in the few jewellers in town, until finally he'd found it. A simple silver band, with an emerald as its centrepiece, and two tiny sapphires by its side. They were linked by silver leaves, and he thought when he saw it, that it was perfect. Even Josiah had agreed, and the man's opinion had come to mean something. It had been too late to return then, as much as he'd wanted to, so instead he'd returned this morning, practising his speech in his head as the miles faded behind him.

It was full of declarations of love, of promises, and wishes for their future together.

And they'd all faded into the wind as soon as he'd seen his mother's carriage. And she and Genevieve talking, not pleasantly from what he could tell.

Whoever spoke of Genevieve to Mother will pay dearly, he swore as he hurried towards them.

This isn't how it was supposed to go, he kept thinking, as he travelled the short distance that seemed like miles. He was *supposed* to get Genevieve's acceptance in the first instance. They would talk, make plans, and then, *only then,* would he inform his mother, and deal with the aftermath.

Not this.

Neither of them noticed as he rode up, Genevieve too busy walking away, and his mother too busy berating her. He hated her, truly hated her in that moment, for the past, and for the present. For ruining everything. He was so angry, he let his mouth run before his mind.

And now they were both staring at him, mouths agape, and he knew he had to fix this, because it wasn't pleasant surprise in Genevieve's eyes, it was sheer panic.

Taking advantage of their shock, he slid off Simpheon, and strode to Genevieve's side, to face his mother. He laid his hand on the small of Genevieve's back, willing her to stop staring at him like that, willing her to trust him, and not stiffen, and praying for her to give him a chance to make it right.

Please, Genevieve.

'Henry!' his mother gasped, finally coming to.

'You heard me, Mother,' he said, as proudly, as steadily as he could manage.

'Henry, you can't possibly think to marry her— wait... I know you,' she murmured, her eyes studying Genevieve, and—*damn it all to Hell.* 'Lady Stapleton.'

Hell and damnation, indeed.

There was no denying the disgust in his mother's eyes, and he was about to tell her precisely where she could go right this very moment while he made things right with Genevieve, when the latter spoke.

'You should go.'

Something in her tone, *is it heartbreak*, warned him that the words were not meant for the person he wished them to be.

He turned, and found her looking straight at him, as fragile and distant as she'd been the day she'd revealed her truth to him in Willowmere's kitchen. She took a meaningful step back, out of the circle of his arm, and then he felt the panic grow, the heartbreak in his own chest dawning.

But he refused it, refused to recognise it, convinced that he could still fix it.

'Genevieve—'

'Henry—'

'Mother, please—'

'Go!' Genevieve shouted, and the pain breaking her voice speared through him. 'You need not concern yourself, my lady,' she said flatly, turning to his mother. 'Your son and I will not be wed. Good day to you.'

With a curtsey, she turned and went back into the garden.

'Henry—'

'Go to Yew Park, Mother.'

'Henry!'

'Go to Yew Park, Mother,' he ground out, making for the gate himself, willing himself not to lose his temper. 'You've done enough.'

'Henry!' his mother shouted again, raising her voice uncharacteristically high, but he didn't care.

Genevieve was nearly at the door, and he knew that if she shut it, he would never be allowed inside. He would never be allowed to make it right, and he could, he just needed to speak to her.

'Genevieve, wait!' She tried to hasten her steps, but his legs were blessedly longer, and he made it just as she opened the door. 'Genevieve,' he said again, softer, and she finally stopped, turning to face him. Her eyes flicked to the leaving carriage, but he kept his gaze affixed on her. *Please, hear me out.* 'Will you allow me inside? We need to talk.'

'Why?'

Her gaze finally met his, and there it was again, that wall, that veil. He felt the coldness as surely as he would death one day, and wasn't this death, being shut out of the universe within her?

'Genevieve, I meant what I said. I was coming here to propose,' he said weakly, taking out the ring he'd bought.

'I know.' She shrugged. 'That is precisely the problem.'

'I don't understand.'

'You don't understand,' she repeated dully, searching his eyes for something she apparently did not find. 'You don't understand that I might take umbrage with you declaring—not asking, but declaring—that we would be wed?'

Yes, he did, of course he did, and he would've told her so, but she forged on, when his lips refused to move.

'You don't understand that I might take issue with you making such a momentous decision without us even having spoken of such a future? You don't understand that I might not *want* to marry you?' she asked, her voice rising in pitch as she fought back the emotion rising within her.

So at least she does care.

He felt his own throat collapsing, his lungs, his heart, everything stopping.

No, he hadn't considered that she might not want a life with him, as he did her. Sure, they hadn't spoken of the future, because there had been an understanding that he couldn't offer one, but then, he was going to offer one—

'You don't understand the scorn and disgust your mother already feels towards me?'

There was a commotion on the stairs behind her, and they both turned to find Lizzie and Jules watching them.

'Take her back upstairs,' Genevieve ordered, and he saw the hurt on both the others' faces. He looked to Lizzie, willing her to forgive him the mess he'd made of everything. 'Please, Jules!'

'My mother does not have a say in this,' Spencer said, when the others had disappeared again. He had a chance, before Genevieve shut him out again, truly, and for ever, to speak, and he wouldn't waste it. 'This is about us. And I will fight her, and anyone who dares speak against us. Against you.'

'It is not your battle to fight!'

'It is! Your battles, Lizzie's, are mine,' he cried, daring to take a step closer. If only he could take her in his arms, he could make her feel what they had again, and it would all be worth it. 'I love her, and I love you!'

'Love is not enough!' Genevieve screamed, and Spencer flinched, frozen, in mind, body, and soul. 'You are a foolish boy, Spencer. I never thought you of all people would be so daft as to think otherwise, but the fact is, love is not enough in this world.'

'It can be,' he pleaded. 'If you are brave enough to let it.'

Wasn't that what he'd learned?

That you could let your heart rule your head, when it was worth it?

That you could take a leap of faith, and it could all work out?

'Let us imagine for a moment this future of yours, Spencer,' she said coldly. 'Let us imagine what it might be like for us to face Society. What it would be for your mother, your sister. For deny it as much as you like, you know very well that your actions have consequences for them both. Our actions would have consequences for Elizabeth, and any children we might have. It would be a lifetime of cuts. Of shame, and scorn, and rejection. Of closed doors and hurtful whispers. Will love be enough then? For you, who have lived your life for duty, and honour, and ensured your family's name is as bright and polished as a king's armour? God, Spencer—'

'I would face it all for you,' he breathed helplessly.

She was right, and he knew that, but he just couldn't…

I cannot live without you.

'I believe you,' she said sadly, the veil falling from between them, until there was only hope-lessness left in her eyes. 'I do. But would you ask them all, your family, your friends, to face it too? To sacrifice their futures, for us?' He willed him-self to answer, but no words would come. 'I didn't think so. If you could, you would've told them, written to them. Instead, you came here to pro-pose to me in secret. And then what, were we to marry in secret? Live here, always? Or would you leave us when you had to return to London, your dirty little secret?'

'Of course not—'

'What we had…' she said, quietly, but force-fully, forestalling any more debate.

Finishing the job of cutting his heart into a mil-lion pieces, and throwing it to the wind, like the future they could've had, had he not been so stu-pid.

Grasped too tightly, again.

'I will be grateful for it the rest of my days, Spencer. But our time has ended, as it was al-ways going to. Let it go. Let me go,' she pleaded, tears in her eyes he longed to brush away, to kiss away. *No more. This is the end.* 'Like a wonder-ful dream, let it fade away into time.'

'I will always love you,' he whispered as she

turned away. 'You will for ever be the answer to all I ever have, and ever shall ask.'

He saw her shoulders rise and fall, saw her hesitate for the briefest moment, but then she closed the door, without ever looking back.

Spencer might've stayed there all night, staring at the closed door, hoping, praying, begging God for some way to get back inside, to make it right, to find the future he'd thought was within his grasp. Only Josiah came, set his hand on his shoulder, and guided him slowly back to Yew Park.

But it isn't within your grasp, and never was.

Chapter Twenty-Two

If there was one thing Spencer liked to think he was not, it was a coward. He might've been called many things, *cheerful*, *somewhat odd*, *annoyingly perceptive*, *an uptight obstinate pain in the backside*, but, much like *impetuous*, *coward* was not something anyone would've called him. Not to his face, and not in private. Spencer had that unique character trait that meant he would always, always, face the consequences of his actions.

Which is why he was letting Josiah lead him back down the drive to Yew Park, towards the front door, and not slinking off into the trees to find the servant's entrance and disappear into the bountiful bowels of the house.

Even though that's all he really wanted.

To be alone, to lick his wounds, to mend his broken heart, and reconcile himself with the fact that he was back where he'd started. Worse. Because when he'd started, come here, he'd known

love, and beautiful futures full of it were not for
him. But then he'd allowed himself to feel, to
dream, and lost it all, and that was much, much
worse. And instead of being allowed to find a
hole to heal himself in, he would be forced to
face the music.

In times such as these I wish I was a coward.

'Spencer,' cried a voice he'd not expected.

He looked up, focusing on the open door, and
the form running from it.

'Mary?'

So mother had brought her too.

Fantastic.

Though he had to admit, as annoyed as he was
to face more people, he was glad to see his sister.
It was unlike her to be so demonstrative as she
was being now, yelling his name, and rushing towards him with the eagerness of a toddler. But
that too, felt good.

There had always been that barrier between
them, because of the role he was to play in her life,
and because he'd been sent away from her so early.
They'd never been allowed to be siblings, to have
fun, and play together, to be close. To be friends.

Perhaps I can have that at least.

His sister stopped before him, flushed, hair
slightly unbound, and searched his eyes.

'Spencer,' she said, a small frown creasing her
brow. 'Are you well? We were so very worried!

What happened? Why are you here? What even is this place? Mama would not say much else other than it is ours.'

'Mary,' he sighed, folding her into a tight embrace, promising that if he could not have Genevieve, and Lizzie, he could at least make up for lost time with his sister. *I can still have a family.* 'Mary…'

After an awkward moment during which she simply stood there, her arms finally curled around him, and held him tight. Vaguely, he heard Josiah muttering something about *horses*, but all he cared about was Mary.

'Spencer,' she murmured softly. 'What's happened? What can I do?'

'Just be here,' he whispered into her hair.

The smell of it hit him like a wave, so long had it been since he'd been this close, touched, his own sister. He remembered…

Holding her the first time.

It was some months after her birth, wintertime. Though why it had been that long, he'd never known. He vaguely recalled mention of illness, but it had been so long. He'd not even remembered this much in…for ever.

It was late, he'd been sleeping, but crying had woken him. He'd gone to the room adjoining his own in the nursery wing, where Mary and her wet nurse had been kept since their arrival. A fire had blazed, making the room so very warm, and her nurse had invited him over to the chair she sat rocking his sister in. He'd marched over, with serious intent, and yes, a little fear.

'Would you like to hold her?' the nurse had asked. And at first he'd been apprehensive, but she'd reassured him. Taught him how to hold Mary properly, and told him she would be right there, just in case. And so he'd taken the bundle in his arms, as instructed, and rocked her, and smelled her hair, just as he did now.

How could I forget that?

He'd made a promise then, as he had with Lizzie that day in the water, to always be her protector. To always be her brother.

Slowly releasing her, he kept hold of her shoulders, and looked into the eyes that mirrored his own. There was concern in hers, and surprise, but also love.

'How are you here?'

'Mother and I left London in pursuit of you,' Mary said. 'She was out of her mind, Spencer, after you just left that ball. She was waiting with Lady Laetitia and the Duke, and you just left.' Mary's nose scrunched, and he could only imagine what she'd had to endure these past weeks. 'Mother was ready to call the Peelers, but Freddie and I managed to convince her that considering your note, nothing foul had befallen you.'

'Freddie?'

'Yes.' Mary nodded with a smile. 'He's come too, he'd just made his way back to Clairborne House when we received word you'd come here.' *But who sent word?* 'Freddie volunteered to chaperone us, not that we needed it, but I was grateful for his company, and thought you likely would be once Mother found you. Did she find you? She said something about fetching you before she left, and she came back in such a mood... But you are all right,' Mary asked again, lifting her hand to cup his cheek. He leaned into the embrace, like a man starved of affection. *I was.* Like a man in need of affection, as he'd just had his heart broken. *I am.* 'Aren't you? You seem...different.'

I am, in so many ways.

'I'm fine,' he managed to say, offering her a smile which was in no way convincing. 'I...suffered a disappointment, that's all. I just need some time to gather my thoughts.'

'Very well,' she said, unconvinced, but gratefully unwilling to push.

With a smile, she slipped her arm into his, and together they made their way into the house.

For a brief instant, Spencer thought he'd escaped the aftermath with his mother, but no sooner had they set foot into the hall, than she came barrelling down the corridor behind the stairs, still in her travelling clothes, and a look he knew well, *complete and utter disapproval*, on her face.

'Henry!'

Spencer patted Mary's arm, and she released him.

'I'll go see what Freddie's up to,' she said, disappearing behind a door he was almost entirely sure was a closet.

'Henry.'

'Not now, Mother,' Spencer said, making for the stairs.

He *would* have to face her, about the business with Genevieve, and everything else he'd wilfully forgotten these past days, he knew that, and so he would, just not *right now*. He was still too raw, and seeing Mary, holding her, it had soothed him, but also, troubled him in a way he couldn't explain.

'Henry Walter Fortitude Edmund Spencer,' his mother scolded as he set foot on the first stair.

'What?' he bit back, turning to face her.

'What?' she repeated, incredulous.

Not now, Mother, please, I will say things I regret. He took a deep breath, hoping to simply *endure* the tirade. Putting back up the shield he'd held up to the world, to his family, for so long— that now felt so heavy.

'You dare to ask me *what*? That woman, Henry! Have I taught you nothing? Did your father teach you nothing? We must be above such reckless behaviour! I will not stand by and watch the legacy we have fought for years to rebuild go up in flames because you had the sheer stupidity to fall for some adulteress whore.'

'Do not speak of her thus,' Spencer warned.

There was only so very much he could endure right now, and words against Genevieve, that was something he would *never* tolerate.

'You will not marry her,' his mother decreed, the force that had always bent others to her will, on full display. 'By all I hold dear, by God above, I swear, you will not marry that woman!'

'You need not concern yourself,' he drawled, willing his anger and pain to hold steady, tamp down, just a little longer. 'You heard it yourself, and then again, she refused me.'

'Thankfully, at least *she* has some sense,' she sighed dramatically, without losing any bite. 'I cannot even begin to speculate as to what you were thinking, though I suspect you were not doing so with your head. How you could endanger us all so recklessly, honestly, Henry. I barely recognise you.'

'The feeling is mutual, Mother, I assure you.'

The words were spoken before he could register them.

The look of shock, and hurt, on his mother's face made him feel a complete and boundless scoundrel, and he regretted it instantly, though truth be told, he meant the words. Coming here, he'd remembered another woman than the one stood before him. A woman full of joy, and love, and playfulness, not this scolding, uptight, judgemental matron he now faced.

What happened to you?

Someday very soon, he would ask. And apologise for the rest.

For now, he needed that blessed solitude he'd been after since Genevieve had shut the door on him; shut him out of her and Lizzie's life.

How precisely does one mend a broken heart?

Chapter Twenty-Three

G enevieve was asking herself the very same question. She had been, since she'd closed the door on Spencer; closed the door on the precious, beautiful thing they'd had. Closing that door, somehow it hadn't been that hard. In a way, he'd made it easier, behaving as he had. Not that he'd set out to hurt her, she knew that. He'd simply got swept away with the dream, she could understand that, and forgotten who she was, who they both were, at the same time. He'd thought...

Well, only he and God knew what he'd thought, but Genevieve could guess.

He hadn't.

Or if he had, he'd thought his station, his money, would make everything all right. That she would simply say *yes*, like some witless fool, and then by some miracle all would resolve itself with a wave of his powerful hand, and then they would be living happily ever after like in the storybooks. For a man of reason, he really hadn't displayed all that much.

Love will truly make witless fools of us all.

And latching onto the hurt she'd felt, that he'd not thought for one second how she might feel about a man taking control of her life again, without asking; to the hurt she'd felt after meeting his mother, well, it made the rest easier to bear. The nameless, breathtaking cut she felt when he looked at her, pleading, begging her to make it right, to say yes, to give them a chance… The heartstopping, wrenching pain she felt when he vowed to love her, always…

Because she knew, he meant it.

And she would love him, always, but it just wasn't enough.

Oh, that it were.

She was glad she'd never said it. Then…then she might've caved. She might've let herself be swept away with the dream too, and then where would they be? Precisely where she'd said. Years from now, discarded, sneered at by Society, Elizabeth, his family, all limited by the selfish choice the two of them had made.

Yes, it was a good thing that it had ended as it had. Painfully, but swiftly. Now, she could move on. They could all move on.

It was simply proving a bit more difficult than she'd expected, because well, she'd never experienced heartbreak like this before. She'd thought it would be easy, well, no more difficult than what she'd already endured, but it was not the same beast. It wasn't fighting for yourself, for your child, for a new future, for hope. It wasn't fuelling yourself with years of rage, and desperation, and pain, to keep moving. It was abandoning all hope of a future, of possibility with someone, and moving on.

How does one cure heartbreak?

Time, she'd heard. Friendship, distraction, most likely. Looking across the table at Elizabeth and Jules, she knew she had all she needed to move on.

Yes. Quite. Just as before. The same, only, different.

They hadn't said anything all day, she'd disappeared into her room, cried her little broken heart out until it was wrung dry, because now that her body remembered how to cry, it refused to stop, and then she'd gone downstairs to prepare something for dinner. Elizabeth and Jules had given her a wide berth, reappeared only when dinner was ready, as if summoned, and sat down, and so they'd remained, all sipping the soup that tasted like absolutely nothing in strained silence.

First things first. Apologise.

Summoning her courage, Genevieve took a deep breath, and set down her spoon.

It wasn't like she had any appetite anyway. She'd been forcing herself to swallow spoonfuls, and bites of bread, when really she wanted noth-

ing more than to curl up and forget about everything but the pain threatening to fell her.

Focus.

'I'm sorry,' she said quietly, and the other two
froze, spoons lifted to their mouths. 'For earlier.
I should not have spoken to you as I did.'

'Thank you for saying that, Ginny,' Jules murmured, setting down her own spoon, and meeting
her gaze. 'You were upset, we understand.'

Genevieve flicked a glance towards her daughter, who nodded, though she studied her soup as if
it contained all the answers to the universe.

Would that it did.

'The woman, in the carriage, was Spencer's
mother,' Elizabeth said after a moment.

'Yes,' Genevieve answered, though it hadn't
been a question.

Her daughter was too perceptive by far.

She grew up too fast. Because of me.

'He's not coming back,' Elizabeth declared,
meeting Genevieve's gaze with a look that wrenched
her insides all over again.

*I am not the only one who will suffer this sep-
aration.*

Elizabeth too, had loved, and been loved by
Spencer. It was not Genevieve alone who would
have to mend a broken heart. She'd known that,
but that too had been easier to forget. That too had
made the break much easier.

But we can do it. Mend our hearts. Together.

'No, he's not,' Genevieve said, willing her daughter to feel the truth, even though it didn't quite feel like the truth just then.

We can do it, together. Survive this. Thrive. Be happy without him.

Elizabeth simply nodded, and returned to her soup, though she merely stroked it back and forth, ingesting none of it.

Genevieve's breath caught, and she covered her mouth with a hand as discreetly as she could, willing the cry in her throat to disappear, forcing back the tears that threatened, *again, remorselessly.*

'The turnips and rhubarb will be ready soon,' Jules said, sensing Genevieve's need to speak on the matter no further, tonight, at least, whilst the wound was still fresh, and gaping. 'We shall have to make jam, perhaps the day after next, what do you say?'

'That sounds like a good plan,' Genevieve agreed, shooting her friend a grateful look.

Jules nodded, shooting her a compassionate smile, then returned to her soup as she continued speaking of the vegetables, and the chores, even Galahad.

A good plan.

Time, friendship, and distraction would cure their aching hearts. In time, it would all be as she'd told Spencer. The memory of a pleasant dream. Because they would move on.

They had to.

Chapter Twenty-Four

At Willowmere Cottage, the days which followed were quiet, and filled with industriousness. Genevieve applied herself to *distraction* and moving on, with fervour that verged on madness. The pain was as vivid as ever, it stole her breath sometimes when she thought of Spencer, of how he'd played with them, looked at her, held her. It refused to lessen even a little despite her best efforts, but she forced herself to wear the mask of stoic bravery yet again, for everyone's sake.

If she broke down, gave into her baser urges, and disappeared into her room to ignore the world, as she hadn't even, though she'd wished to, those first months after she'd left Stapleton, well. Nothing good would come of that.

So on she went, completing the chores, her lacework, those lessons she had with Elizabeth, with alarming verve. It seemed to fuel her that Elizabeth became quiet again, her sadness tangible, and unrelenting. Genevieve tried, to make her laugh, and lift her spirits, though the very last thing she herself wanted was to laugh, or smile, or pretend for one moment that it didn't hurt. But she couldn't allow Elizabeth to withdraw again, because then, it would all have been for nought, and it would all be her own damned fault.

Jules was a semi-willing participant in the game of *let's ignore Genevieve's obvious pain and try to make Elizabeth feel better*. She would try as hard as Genevieve to bring Elizabeth joy, she would attack the chores and lessons with as much energy and determination, but Genevieve would catch her sometimes, watching. Waiting, for Genevieve's inevitable breakdown.

It won't come.

She couldn't allow it to. If she did, then it would all fall apart. Yet again, she would be what kept them together, strong, and sane.

Distraction. Time.

And the truth was, as she'd told herself, she knew this land well. This land of nowhere may be different from the one she'd known, but it resembled the old one enough that she could navigate it. There was pain, and loss, confusion, regret, and hopelessness. But she'd conquered all those insurmountable peaks once, so she could again.

We can find safe, and happy, and warm again. Without him. I know we can.

And then, on the fourth day, as the sun rose, and Genevieve watched its streams invade her room, dust motes swirling aimlessly within, she had an epiphany.

We can.

But not here.

Here, there were so many memories. Beautiful, priceless ones, but haunting ones, nonetheless. They'd left London two years ago after the divorce had finalised, not only because Society refused to acknowledge them, but because of the memories. Because there was a terrible history in so many places, that they couldn't move on. They'd needed to start afresh, and so they would again.

It isn't like we could stay here for ever.

No, Genevieve had known that eventually they would have to move on, to give Elizabeth more choices for her future. It was earlier than expected, but it was the best thing. They had enough saved to go somewhere else, perhaps a city, Edinburgh or Glasgow, for a time, until they made arrangements for a more permanent home. Somewhere connected, but not so removed. They would have to break the tenancy, but then... Spencer would understand. Surely he could intervene, not that she wished for favours from him, but this could be good for him too. Cut the final tie.

It wasn't as if they were going to remain here for ever, wait until he returned some day with a new family, a wife, and children, and—

Yes. It will be good. A new start altogether.

She could begin the arrangements right now. Write all the letters, get them to Aitil before the post left this afternoon. Then she would speak to Elizabeth and Jules, and surely they would be thrilled, wouldn't they?

Yes. A new start. New memories. A good plan.

Genevieve did as she planned, writing all the appropriate letters, dressing, and riding off to Aitil before the others had even come down to breakfast. She felt, lighter somehow, as she returned to Willowmere some hours later, toffee in her pocket for Elizabeth, and a new book on Russian architecture for Jules. They weren't bribes, only tokens to lift their spirits.

Precisely.

Because they wouldn't need bribes. Leaving would be good. It's why she felt so much lighter. Because she was relieved at having found *the* way to move forward. To cure her heartbreak, and Elizabeth's. So she told herself, as she went to the kitchen, knowing Jules would be preparing luncheon whilst Elizabeth practised her harp upstairs.

A pot of potatoes was in fact boiling on the stove, though Juliana was at the window, looking out onto the loch, *and Yew Park*.

'Jules,' Genevieve began.

Only, that was as far as she managed to get.

Why is this so hard?

'We are leaving,' her friend said flatly, turning, an eyebrow raised in challenge.

'Yes,' Genevieve said, her lightness disappearing, and a knot forming in her stomach. Though she refused to acknowledge any of that. *This is the right decision.* 'We cannot stay here,' she said as if Jules were the daftest person on Earth. Only when her friend had that look…it meant she was about to say things Genevieve didn't want to hear. 'There are too many memories here, as there were in London. We always knew we would have to move on, that opportunities were limited for Elizabeth.'

There.

That about covered it, right?

'Oh, I understand, Ginny,' Juliana said, in a tone which suggested she did, all too well. That she knew something Genevieve did not wish to. 'I'll begin packing, and we can find somewhere else to hide.'

'This isn't about hiding,' Genevieve retorted, bite in her voice that betrayed the accuracy of Jules's words. 'It's about starting afresh.'

'It's about running away, and hiding again,' Jules exclaimed, literally throwing up her hands as she turned to face Genevieve yet again. 'There are too many memories here *for you.* Too much pain, *for you.* Yes, we said we would leave. *Some day.* Once Elizabeth had experienced a few years of settled quiet. Of *home.* And now you want to take her away, under pretext of doing what's best? You want to uproot us all because you cannot bear to remain here, and face your feelings? I thought you'd changed,' her friend pleaded. 'Learned to face your emotions, not bury them. Learned to *feel* again. But you are doing as you did before. Because it's easier.'

And there it was.

The core truth Genevieve neither wanted to hear, nor acknowledge.

'No one is forcing you to follow, Juliana,' she said bitterly, wanting to hurt as much as much as she was hurting, every day now, which was something else she didn't want to feel. 'You can go live your own life rather than simply follow us because it's easier.'

'I follow because I love you and Elizabeth,' Jules sighed, cut by the words, but aware of Genevieve's intentions. *Because she is your best friend and knows you better than you know yourself.* 'That doesn't mean I must agree with your decisions, nor keep my opinions to myself.'

So this is not only about the departure, but about Spencer.

Genevieve understood then that Jules must've heard quite enough that day, though she'd not approached the subject until now.

Likely Elizabeth did too, we weren't precisely quiet.

Damn.

'We'd never spoken of the future,' Genevieve exclaimed, the pain surfacing, taking hold despite her best efforts, words, feelings she'd kept tightly bound, rising to her tongue. 'He'd never considered the consequences,' she pointed out, as if making a case to a judge, yet again. 'You think I want this life? That I wouldn't like to stay here, and be as we were? That I wouldn't like to believe we could be more than that, happy again? That I wouldn't like to believe I could marry him and all would be well and perfect? I do not have the strength to fight the world, Jules!' she yelled, her voice cracking. Swallowing a deep breath, she forced herself to settle, focusing on her righteous justifications. 'Not again. So yes, I will move on, and do what I do best. Stay strong for Elizabeth.'

'What will you tell Elizabeth, when she grows to understand your life? That you had courage enough for her, but not enough for yourself? What example do you set with that? Is that not true cowardice, Ginny?'

With that, Jules simply turned heel, and marched outside to wander the edge of the loch.

Genevieve stood there, worse than she'd been for days, as Jules's words penetrated her heart. The potatoes boiled over, but she barely noticed, and she repeated the same little prayer to herself, on, and on again.

This is the right decision.

We have to leave, so we can move on.

This is the right decision.

Chapter Twenty-Five

Those days which followed Genevieve and Spencer's separation, were, at Yew Park House, filled with just as much fervent normality, though slightly less industriousness. They seemed, to those who dwelled there, infinitely sombre days, though apart from a select few, no one knew why.

Spencer had come to the same conclusion as Genevieve regarding the mending of a broken heart, insomuch as that it would take time. He also knew it would take immense will, and application, as any task did.

He did not wish to rise every morning, and yet, he did, like clockwork. The nightmares returned, with a vengeance, with Genevieve, Lizzie, and Mary, now appearing regularly, and so he rose more exhausted, if that was possible, than he was when he lay his head on the pillow each night.

He didn't want to leave his bed, dress, shave, make himself presentable, and yet, he did, thanks to Josiah. Josiah, who he knew, had many a thing to say, though he gratefully kept them to himself.

He did not wish to eat, and yet he did, twice a day, as required, though he also found anything that passed his lips to be tasteless, and unsatisfying.

He did not wish to be around anyone, not even himself, and yet, he met his mother, sister, and Freddie, at mealtimes, sometimes in passing for tea, as required. He would watch sometimes, as Freddie and Mary engaged in games of cards, or walked the grounds, heard them wandering the house when the weather turned foul. But there was nothing in any of it for him, and so he kept his distance.

He did not wish to converse, and yet, he did, words passing his lips without thought. Somewhere in his mind, he heard questions, and gave appropriate answers. He heard Freddie speak of his shipping business, of politics, even the weather. He heard Mary speak of Town, of the latest exhibitions and news. He heard his mother converse with them both, though he noted she gave as sparse and uncommitted answers as he did.

All was as before.

A great divide separated them, and yet, they continued on, speaking of everything and nothing, together in the same house, and yet as distant as people could be. Spencer hated every moment of every day then, though he found he did it pas-

sively, bitterly, quietly, as he no longer had the
strength nor will to do anything but simply, sol-
dier on.

Because his mind was so full. Of Genevieve,
and Lizzie, the pain of loss, fresh, and festering. He'd look out onto the loch and remember
their swimming lesson. He would look out onto
the grounds, see the others wandering, and remember that first day. How captivated he'd been.
How good it had felt to bring wonder, and light to
Lizzie's eyes. He would look into the distance, see
the mountains, and remember the day he'd carried
her down Ben More, Genevieve smiling beside
him, the wind whipping her hair. He'd felt so full
then. So complete. He would wonder sometimes,
if it *had* all been a dream. Or a beautiful lie.

Genevieve had never said the words; he'd not
resented her that, but as his mind turned their
short-lived tale over and over, he wondered if he'd
imagined what he'd felt. If his own feelings had
blinded him, if she'd cared, but not loved, as he'd
been so sure she had. If that was why she'd never
said it. He wondered why he hadn't forced them
to speak of the future before, why yet again, he'd
tried to grasp too tightly, and instead lost everything.

Along with that recent past, lived the past of
his childhood. Of his nightmares, of Muire. Little things would return to him, when it was not
the same images—*Mother's bloody hands, Muire*

screaming—taking up all the available space in his mind. He would remember that here, sometimes, his mother would leave her hair unbound. He would recall that Muire smelled of wild mint, and that he would steal a taste of the first strawberry jam. He would recall a melody, a song Muire would sing to him, and that he'd heard again, streaming into the nursery from Mary's room late at night sometimes.

So little and yet, so much.

Once, he'd felt lost.

No longer. Now, he felt as if he was in limbo, waiting, eternally, for something to give him grace so that he could move on, knowing all the while, that he was the only one who could ask for it.

Except he wasn't ready. He knew, that once he took the steps to resolve what needed to be, to speak of what had to be, that would be it. He could forestall the future's arrival no more, linger in limbo no longer. The time would come for him to return to the world, to his life, to be as he'd been before. And something within him balked at that.

Though things could not remain as they were. With every passing day, his mother's anger transformed even more into wariness, and unease. He would catch her watching him, as if waiting for him to strike, to address the proverbial elephant in the room.

The past.

Something told him she knew he remembered

something, that she feared the day he would demand answers. And he would. Before he moved
on, he needed at least that.

The truth.

Let it finish me, so that I can begin again.

Footsteps sounded on the hardwood of the por-
trait gallery Spencer was currently occupying,
staring listlessly out of the floor-to-ceiling windows onto the misty, rain-soaked horizon.

He sighed, recognising the tread.

'I'm in no mood to talk, Freddie,' he declared,
though the footsteps remained steady. A moment
later, Freddie's shape appeared beside him, mim-
icking his own pose. Didn't the man have business to oversee? Why was he still here? 'Nor to
hear anything my mother, or Mary, have sent you
to say.'

'Mary may have pushed me to come, but my
words and concerns are my own. I am worried
about you,' Freddie said earnestly. 'We all are.'

A frown dipping his brows, Spencer glanced
over at his friend.

Freddie's candour, indeed his approach in itself, was unusual. Not that he wasn't truthful, he
was just more thoughtful. More reserved, though
always fun, and a thoroughly good conversation-
alist, but like Spencer, he often resorted to speaking his mind indirectly, if at all. Yes, Spencer had
seen himself a little in the man, hence their *rap-
prochement.*

They were both watchers, outliers, though in all outward appearances, just as they presented themselves.

'There is no need to be,' Spencer said finally, turning back to the view, a symphony of greys. *As I am myself.* 'I will be myself again soon enough.'

'That is precisely what concerns me.'

Spencer turned again, the question in his eyes. Freddie met his gaze, and there was something…

He too has dropped the mask.

'We've known each other some time. I've never seen such emotion within you as I do now.'

Was he truly that transparent? And here he thought he'd done a good enough job of appearing as he'd once been. Spencer turned back to the window, infinitely less judgmental, and *seeing*, than his friend.

'Good, or bad,' Freddie continued, undaunted by his less than receptive audience. 'It worries me that you should go back to wearing the mask you donned before. Shallow good humour and relentless detachment for duty.'

Damnit, man, can you not leave me to rot in blissful, wilful delusion?

'You cannot understand,' Spencer bit back, a little more shaken by the man's perception than he dared admit. He needed to conclude…whatever this was. Quickly. 'It is what I must be to wear the title I do.'

'Duty, honour, those things do not preclude others such as happiness, or love,' Freddie retorted, refusing to take insult, *damn him*. 'I do know that much.'

'In this case, Freddie, that is precisely what it means.'

'Hmm. And here I thought you had more mettle,' he remarked, and Spencer clenched his jaw, lest he take everything bottled up inside out on Freddie. 'This came for you, by the way,' Freddie added, dropping something on the table by the window. 'When I saw the seal, I thought it best to bring it directly, rather than risk it being lost in that study of yours.'

On that, Freddie left, his footsteps sounding even more ominous than on his arrival.

After a long moment, Spencer's curiosity got the best of him, and he reached over for the letter Freddie had left.

From Thornhallow.

Freddie had been right again, little devil. Spencer's hands nearly trembled with anticipation as he broke the seal and opened the pages filled with Reid's messy scrawl. He needed his friend's response more than he'd realised. He needed wisdom, now more than ever, though at the same time he dreaded reading what was written.

When he'd penned his own letter, things had been so different, and now—

Dear Spencer,
Before I address the rest of your letter, I
shall address the query regarding myself,

Rebecca, and the babe's health. We are all well, as is everyone in Thornhallow. There have been other happy events, but I shall not bore you with them now. Suffice it to say we are well, and happy, though Rebecca grows more and more eager to meet our child, and admittedly, so do I.

I will confess I was surprised to read your letter—but glad. Glad that you trusted me with such thoughts. I know that must not have been easy, my friend. We were close once, as close as either of us would allow anyone to be. Then I left, and when I returned, we were both different men, in some ways at least.

This past year and a half, getting to know you again, getting to know my friend again, has been a great gift. I am not ashamed to say it. We are both very different men—but at heart, I think we are very much the same boys we once were.

You ask for counsel in your letter, and I wonder if I can give it. I hope that what I will say might help with all that troubles you. If it does not, disregard it as the ramblings of the Disappeared Earl. We all know what a strange bastard he is.

You write that you are lost, Spencer, and I would be lying if I said I hadn't sensed it for a while now. As has Rebecca, but we

*shall never tell her, for she will taunt me
with being right for the next hundred years.*

*Perhaps it takes one lost soul to recognise
another. For you know she was lost, and,
well, so was I, undeniably, for so very long.
I travelled the world to escape my grief, and
ended up finding peace only when I accepted
that I could not outrun my past. Rebecca
helped, naturally. She was my saviour, in
truth. Forced me to see those things which I
refused to, determined to live in anger and
resentment as I was.*

*It sounds to me like this woman you speak
of holds the key to something within you,
Spencer. As Rebecca held the key to my soul.
Perhaps I am extrapolating from very little,
but the truth is, I have never known you to
be so uncertain.*

*Our lives were very different, yes, but we
were raised a certain way, as many in our
world are. I shook off many of the shackles
of our kind when I left my life behind, still, it
took facing the possibility of losing Rebecca
to know that nothing was worth the price of
letting her go.*

*You ask where I found my courage? My
blind faith to leap into the unknown? I found
it in her. In knowing I would not be the man
I wished to be without her. I found my way
through my darkest days thanks to her. It*

cannot be up to another to claw us from the depths of our own Hells, but they can bring us light, and show us another path from that which we've known.

I cannot explain that certainty I feel with her; all I can say is, when you know, you know. For us, it is about partnership, about taking the leap together, and knowing that we will be stronger for the adversity we face. That hopefully, the world will be a better place for seeing happiness where before there was only cold duty.

I do not know how the situation stands with this widow and her daughter, if perhaps this letter is full of useless nonsense now. Perhaps your mother, who did visit and interrogate us, has forced you back to London, or you have returned to the life you left behind of your own volition. However, if you are still seeking answers, I will say this.

You are a man of great courage, and honour, and steadfastness. I admire you. I always have. You saved me too, you know, more than once, and I do not simply mean last year. You know people so well, you know what they need, but do not forget yourself. You cannot lead, cannot be the example you wish to be for others, if you are not yourself. You can change your path, if you wish to— no matter what anyone says.

*Be safe in the knowledge that you will
have at least two disreputable friends by
your side, three if you count a tradesman
such as Freddie to be disreputable, in the
event you decide to do something unfashionable.*

*There, I have said much, I hope a little of
it helps at least.*

*I will send news of the babe as soon as he
or she graces us with their presence.*

In the meantime, I remain yours,
Reid

*PS: Do not fear. I will not tell your mother
where you are.*

*PPS: I have reopened this missive to inform
you that our child, Halcyon Sylvie Reid, has
finally arrived. She is beautiful, Spencer.
The most incredible thing I have ever seen.
Come and meet her, soon, for we are making you her godfather. I must go now, but I
will add as a final thought that it was worth
it. Every single thing that led me to this moment.*

The paper crumpled in Spencer's hand as he
clutched it tight, tears he'd never wanted, nor
dreamed of spilling, falling onto his cheeks.

It is time.

Chapter Twenty-Six

The Dowager was thankfully alone when Spencer found her some time later, having searched what had become her usual haunts, the drawing rooms, the library, the conservatory. She sat, eyes closed, on a bench in the middle of the orangery, the dim grey light somehow reflecting off the bright fruits and flowers of the surrounding trees, bathing her in a soft, delicate light. She seemed so small, so fragile. Spread as thinly as Genevieve at her worst.

How had he not seen her withering away before his eyes? How had he not seen the sadness permeating her every pore? Had it not been there, or simply invisible, until now, when he observed her, unseen, and without the barrier of anger, and resentment to cloud his vision?

For it was gone now, that barrier. He didn't know how, or when, only that the fog had lifted with Freddie, and Reid's words. That he knew now, the truth *would* set him free, no matter how painful. That whatever he learned, his mother was still his mother. The one who had tucked him into bed, and told him the tales of George and the Dragon, and King Arthur.

Yes, I have remembered those nights too.

'Henry,' she said, looking over to him, finally back from the world she'd been lost in.

'We need to talk, Mother.'

'If this is about that woman—'

'It's not about Genevieve,' he said gently, settling himself on the bench across the aisle from her own. Something about his tone must've given him away, for her jaw clenched, and she stiffened, as she always did when readying for battle. 'This is about what happened here, twenty-nine years ago.'

'I don't know what you are talking about,' she said, rising.

'Mother,' he said, quietly, but firmly, and she froze. 'It is time. Tell me, what happened here. I *remember*,' he told her. 'Coming here…seeing that house… I remembered. I saw her grave, Mother, and I know, what I felt, what I saw… It was not a dream, but a memory. Did you kill Muire?'

'Yes,' she breathed.

Spencer's heart felt as if it had skipped twenty beats at once.

Though he'd thought it, felt it to be the truth at the heart of the grim memory, he'd prayed, somehow, that it hadn't been.

His mother sighed heavily, nodded, resolved, and slowly, sat back down, all defiance gone. Only that terrible, terrible sadness, emphasising the lines of her face, making her seem a century older than she was.

'You are right,' she agreed. 'It is time. Though I prayed today would never come. That you would forget, and that I might take the secret to my grave. Have only the Almighty to lay my heart before. It's why we never came here,' she said weakly, her shoulders rising as if to shrug, which was something she *never did*. 'Why I came for you. I'd hoped I would be quick enough, but by the time Morag's letter reached me, I suppose you had already begun to remember.'

Morag. Mrs McKenna. So she wrote of my whereabouts.

'What happened?' Spencer asked, as steadily as he could manage considering the present circumstances.

'Muire died giving birth to your sister.'

'My...?'

'Sister. Yes, Mary,' she said, and pieces began to fall into place, dizzying him, sending him spiralling. *Muire. Mary.* 'I did... All I could. But I could not save her. I should have called for the doctor, but by the time I realised... It was too late.'

His mother's voice broke on a sob, and she shook her head, trying to force back the violent emotion, much like someone else he knew had for so long.

Much as he had, always.

We are all so alike.

He longed to reach out, to hold her, only he couldn't just now. He was grappling with his own self, trying to keep steady when it felt as if the floor had just tumbled away and he was being hurled, headlong into the Pit.

The pieces, the clues, everything was falling into place, as the relief of his mother not being a murderess, or a killer, simply feeling the guilt of failure washed over him. And still, he knew there was more.

More to know, more to feel, more to accept.

'Mary was not Muire's only child, was she?' he said. 'I am too, aren't I?'

Eyes of blue and silver. Golden hair. A love beyond measure.

There was a long moment of silence as his mother breathed in and out, taking steadying breaths, trying to stem the flow of tears. Finally, she nodded, and Spencer might've sworn he heard the mighty click of the final piece falling into place.

Muire was my true mother.

'Why?' he croaked out. 'Was she Father's mistress?'

'Your father and I loved each other dearly,' the Dowager said fiercely, clawing herself back from the thrall of emotion, her need to be understood matching Spencer's need to understand. 'Our match, for all its other benefits, was one of deep, abiding love. We were fortunate in that. We were not, however, fortunate with children.'

She drew in a shuddering breath, and the pain of having been lied to, of having his origins concealed, faded slightly, as he understood what his mother's pain must've been. He felt for her, for that supposed failure at performing one of the duties of a woman in her position. For failing at giving the man she loved a child.

Of giving him an heir.

'After three years, we understood that it would never be for us,' she continued, distance in her voice that he knew preserved her. 'I offered your father a way out, but he refused. He would not allow me to go through that, and part from him. So we made an accord. We would find someone to bear his children. Someone we could keep hidden, while she conceived and carried the child. I would stay hidden too, carry out my *confinement* as far from prying eyes as possible, then claim the woman's children as my own.'

'Muire.'

'We came here to make a plan, find a woman, and that is when we met her,' she said, a sad smile that spoke of old disbelief. In Fate, in luck, in all the things Spencer had believed brought him Genevieve and Lizzie. 'I saw the spark of interest in

your father. She was beautiful, and kind, and...
I loved her too. We both did. We were the truest
friends, the three of us. The time we spent here
was the happiest of my life,' his mother told him,
tears streaming down her cheeks and down his
own, but they both let them fall. Now was the
time for catharsis, for release, and the unburden-
ing that came with truthfulness. 'But then... We
lost her, and nearly lost Mary. Something...broke,'
she said, urging him to understand, and he did, for
he remembered all too well how it had been. 'The
loss, was too much for either of us. We handled
it differently, and though the love remained, we
couldn't be as we were before.'

Spencer nodded, and dropped his head, staring
down at the tile.

He felt so much, and yet, so little. It was strange.
He felt betrayed, lied to, hurt, confused, angry,
yes. He felt frustrated, at the time lost, the energy
lost, the years of torment he'd endured watching
his parents drift away, growing up in a cold house.

Yet, he understood. And somehow, that lessened the pain, and the anger. It made it less potent,
less confusing. He'd known the truth, always, in
his heart. The pieces, the memories, had shown
him, only *he* had refused to see the pattern, because he was afraid to see it. Afraid to look at the
whole picture, and see a tale of woe, and loveless-
ness, rather than one of infinite love, and sacrifice.

It would take him years to sort through it, to
truly come to terms with it, but in his heart, there

was a calm settledness that he'd not known before, not even with Genevieve. Because the shadows, the secrets had still been there, and now...

Now I am truly free.

'Mary should know,' he decided, meeting his mother's gaze once again.

She looked a bit taken aback, as if she'd expected any reaction but that, then panic crossed her features.

'No, I—'

'No more secrets, Mother,' he said simply. It was a strange thing, freedom. It really did make everything clearer. 'She deserves to know. She's not a child.'

His mother nodded, either convinced, or too tired to fight.

'Do not hate me, nor your father,' she said quietly. 'We did the best we could, and never doubt we loved you.'

'I know,' he said, and he did.

The house had been cold, permeated by grief and loss, but he could see now, remember now, the love had been there.

In every gesture, every reprimand, every father-son talk. It had been in their concern, for his future, and Mary's, even if they hadn't known, or felt able to express it fully anymore.

But my house will not be cold. It will be as the summer days here were.

I will not settle for less.

'And I understand, Mother, I do. But now, you

must understand. I cannot do as you and my fore-
bears have. How long have we made sacrifices
only to destroy our worlds and ourselves further?
Is it not time we began making the right sacrifices? Nothing good is ever easy. And life isn't
easy regardless.'

'You mean to have that woman.'

'Yes, Mother.' He smiled. 'If she will have me,
after I fall to my knees before her, I mean to make
her my wife. Your daughter. Mary's sister. I mean
to raise Lizzie as my own. And I mean for you to
love them both, for I do. I ask much, yes, of this
family, of my friends, but I will ask,' he said.

And he would.

Genevieve had accused him of not considering
the consequences, well he had. So would those he
asked to support him.

But he would ask.

*She is worth the fight, this family is worth the
fight, and the world will be better for me fighting for it all.*

'The truth is, Mother, I would love her regardless of her past. For she is a glorious, shining light.
But you should know, her past is not what you
think. Genevieve is so very courageous. What she
did—what Society couldn't blacken her for—was
only to do right by herself and her child.'

Spencer then told his mother Genevieve's
tale, hoping his love would forgive him. Only, he
needed his mother to understand now, to know

her, as he did, and since Genevieve was not available for consultation, he would have to set the record straight for those closest to him, those he could trust.

As he revealed Genevieve's truth, he saw his own mother's understanding, and empathy, shine through, and it gave him hope that all could be right after all.

'Our family name may be tarnished,' he said when he'd finished recounting the tale. 'I'll not deny that. But our family will know love again. Pure, unfettered love. And I'll not live with regret. I'll be true to myself, and that is integrity, and honour, Mother.'

'Well, at least you need not worry about telling me anything and wasting time,' came Mary's voice, and both he and the Dowager turned to find his sister emerging from behind a rather thick bunch of citrus. 'I heard everything.'

'You always were fond of eavesdropping,' Spencer mused, and she smiled.

'I am not angry, Mother, nor do I hate you,' she said, turning to the woman who was, and always would be, their mother. Though now, they had another, to remember, and to honour. 'I regret it should've come to this for the truth to out, but what's done, is done.'

The Dowager nodded, and Mary laid a kiss on her cheek, before bestowing one on Spencer as well.

'As for what you said, Spencer, I would rather face Society's scorn, than see you unhappy. If I am to be disparaged, and unwanted, because you had the courage to follow your heart, well. Those who chose to do so are not people I should like to associate with.'

'Your chances—'

'Spencer, I am well entrenched in my spinster-hood,' she said wryly, shooting a glance at his mother he couldn't quite read. 'If ever there were to be someone… I should like them to risk as much for me, and you will for your Genevieve.'

'Thank you,' he said, rising, and enveloping her in a tight embrace.

One could really get used to this hugging business.

'Now, let us all to supper, for it has grown late,' Mary said, as Spencer released her, taking her mother's hand as she rose. 'We shall talk more, of all this. Freddie can be trusted, don't you think? Perhaps later, we can visit with the McKennas. And we shall make a plan together, for you to arm yourself with, when you go to your Genevieve.'

'You truly are the cleverest of us,' Spencer said, feeling the lightness of freedom, of secrets bared, and darkness conquered. 'Far too clever by half.'

Mary laughed, and twined her arms into Spencer's, and the Dowager's.

And together, they set off to do as Mary had decreed.

For though the healing of old wounds would

take years, their future began this very night, and they were all unusually eager to greet it.

'Gone? What do you mean gone?' Spencer asked, pushing past Josiah to see inside Willowmere for himself. He didn't understand. How could they be gone? It had been barely a fortnight since they'd separated. All right, so a little over a fortnight. He hadn't really seen time pass when he'd been…wandering the house like a shade.

Lost in limbo.

And then he'd learned the truth of his and Mary's birth, the truth of Muire, and there had been a lot to discuss. They'd all spent valuable time with the McKennas, *my grandparents*, making peace with the past and trying to find a way forward, so that they could all truly get to know each other, and be family, in some way. They'd even visited Muire's grave all together, the first of what he hoped to be regular visits.

There had also been plans to make regarding his future with Lizzie and Genevieve. He'd wanted to make sure he did things intelligently this time, not rushed; they deserved better. He, Mother, Mary, even Freddie, had made initial plans for, firstly, his apology and retrieval of Genevieve and Lizzie, and then secondly, for what happened next. Nothing firm could be put into place, he hadn't even sent a note to Reid yet, because the lady had to accept first, and so it really hadn't taken all that long. How then could they be gone?

How could he not have heard of it?

But gone they were, Spencer realised, as he wandered the empty, gloomy, house. Most everything was still there, part of the cottage, but the books were missing, and Genevieve's lacework, and all their trunks, and Lizzie's harp. He leaned against the doorframe of what had served as Lizzie's schoolroom, now restored to its original purpose of a plain, simple bedroom. It was sad, and lifeless, and he hated it.

They're gone.

The worst thing was, he knew why. Could he truly expect them to remain, after what had happened? Would he truly have been able to stand it himself, having Genevieve and Lizzie living within reach, but unable to have them?

No.

'I have to find them,' he breathed. 'Someone has to know where they've gone.'

This isn't how our story ends.

'Aye, my lord,' Josiah said reassuringly. 'I'll make enquiries. You should check the post at Yew Park, after all they were renting from you.'

'You're right,' Spencer agreed, already in motion. 'I'll meet you in Aitil as soon as I've done that. Oh,' he added over his shoulder as they descended the stairs. 'And find out what they did with Galahad.'

'Yes, my lord.' Josiah grinned.

No, Genevieve, my love, this isn't how it ends for us.

Chapter Twenty-Seven

This isn't right, Genevieve thought, as their cart bustled onwards, ever further south, bumping and jarring on every rut and hole, as if the road itself warned them this was not the way. Gazing out onto the horizon of rolling hills, valleys, and fields, occasionally punctuated by houses, or a kirk, all covered in a damp, grey blanket of misty rain, Genevieve couldn't shake the feeling that none of this, none of the decisions she'd made to arrive at this point, were right.

That *leaving*, wasn't right.

Yet she'd been so sure, so entrenched in her own conviction for days. Since she'd received word from the Marquess's man that as she agreed to pay for the cottage until autumn, she was free to end the tenancy and depart whenever she wished.

From then on, she hadn't stopped. Making final arrangements for the return of the key, paying one of the farmers she studded Galahad to to both take the goat and chickens, and keep an eye on the cottage until new tenants arrived. Ensuring their cart was ready for a long journey, packing, making arrangements for those things they couldn't take with them quite yet to be held in Aitil for a time, making preparations to stay in Edinburgh... All of it had kept her so busy, busy enough to ignore Jules's words, to ignore the warnings in her own heart that this *wasn't right*.

That she was running again. Hiding. Being a coward.

But really, it wasn't as if she could just go back to Yew Park, and say, *yes, please, do marry me even though I said no, and Society will destroy us and those we love, even though your mother hates me I'm quite sure, and...*

Well. All the rest.

It wasn't as if she could just turn back and say, *actually, I will fight, for us, for me, for the extraordinary thing we have, because I'm tired of Society dictating even now who I can be with, and what kind of life I may lead.*

That was preposterous.

And mad.

This isn't right, Genevieve, the annoying, troublemaking voice said, making a reappearance.

Go away, she ordered.

Only it wasn't just her own little voice that was telling her that. It wasn't just that her entire body was rebelling at the notion of running again.

Starting over.

Running.

It was the look on Elizabeth's face when she'd told her they were leaving.

Resignation. Blankness, like that which was there before.

It was how silent she'd been, a quiet little doll again, dutifully packing her things up, not saying a single word when the farmer came for Galahad. It was how she looked now, silent, and sad. Oh so very heartbroken yet resigned.

It was in the tightness of Jules's jaw, the solid set of her shoulders as she drove them onwards. It was in the disapproval she saw in her friend's eyes every time she dared to meet them.

It was in that moment, when she'd stood before Willowmere the last time. The cart packed, Jules at the reins, Elizabeth bundled up in the back. They were ready to go, and Genevieve had stood there, key in hand, every window and door tightly shut.

One last look, she'd thought.

Even though it is bad luck.

Yet she'd stood there, looking back on the home that had been a haven, and brought them so much. In the grey light of another wet day, it seemed cold, and forbidding. Resentful of their departure. Every stone, every blade of grass, every flower, every inch of the still, glassy loch seemed to turn away, forsaking her. Forsaking her for abandon-

ing all the wonderful memories. Forsaking her
for not having the strength of the land, to remain,
steadfast and unshakeable in the face of adversity.

So she'd turned her back on all of *them*, and got
in the cart, and driven off.

But then she'd looked again, throwing another
glance over her shoulder, and the chill had crept
up her spine, and dead weight had settled in her
stomach, and she still hadn't managed to shake
any of it.

Because it isn't right.

Shaking her head, Genevieve focused on the
road ahead. Had it not been for the misty sky,
they might've seen Edinburgh by now. The road
so far had been long, and tiresome, and that was
all there was to her feelings. She was tired. From
sleepless nights at inns. From pulling the cart out
of the mud countless times, and shivering on road-
sides as they all forced down morsels of cheese,
bread, and sips of cider.

*You always knew before when things were
right.*

So?

So what if she'd known the day Stapleton had
berated Elizabeth for daring to look at him with
'insolence in her eyes' when he'd reprimanded her
for daring to run to him for a hug? Known that
moment, that day, that soon it would all become
worse, and that she had to leave, and take Eliza-

beth, and go far, far away. Get out of his clutches, out of his control.

So what if she'd known the day the Great Whore of Hadley Hall had been born that it was all still worth it?

So what if she'd known that day they'd set off from their rooms in Fleet Street for Willowmere that it was *right*?

So what if she'd known the day she'd gone to Spencer by the loch that being with him was *right*?

It means nothing.

It means everything.

'Stop the cart,' Genevieve shouted, tears in her eyes, her breath coming uneasily. 'Stop the cart,' she repeated, looking to Jules.

Her friend slowed the horse, and they stopped. Jules watched her, waiting, and she could feel Elizabeth's eyes on her as well.

In that moment, the decision was made.

She would not be a coward. She would not be selfish.

Whatever arrangements she'd made be damned. They could be unmade, or made again. The life she'd wanted for them all was one of freedom, and choice.

So I make mine.

'I am willing to fight,' she said, turning to her daughter. 'He may not want us. But I am willing to turn back and try. If you wish to, Elizabeth.'

'Oui, Maman,' her daughter said softly.

'Jules?'

'I've come this far with you, Ginny.' She smiled. 'You won't be rid of me yet.'

'Then turn us around.'

'With pleasure.'

A little up the road, they found a spot to turn the cart around.

And as they began to retrace their steps, Genevieve finally felt it.

This, this is right.

They never made it back to Willowmere. In fact, they barely made it ten miles, to the next inn, where they decided to stop for the night, as the misty rain had turned into a downpour. Though the accommodations were no more or less than they'd experienced so far, all three slept like babes, and woke with excitement, and hope in their hearts.

Genevieve had woken well before dawn, restless and eager. She knew this gamble might not turn out in their favour, but she also knew that if she didn't do this, yet again, she would regret it her entire life. And Jules had been right. What would she tell Elizabeth in the years to come? That she hadn't tried for fear of failing? That she hadn't dared to fight for her own happiness even though that was precisely what Elizabeth should strive to do?

Preposterous.

So now here she was, ensuring their things were loaded and secured on the cart as Jules and Elizabeth finished breakfast. If the weather held, and the roads were only slightly muddier than on the way here, they could hope to be back at Willowmere, and Yew Park by overmorrow.

What if he's already gone?

What if he doesn't want us?

Then we will figure out the rest from there.

Everything will be right as rain in the end.

Because this is right.

Satisfied, both with her conclusions, which she'd already reached numerous times, and her job readying the cart, Genevieve nodded to herself, and gave the horse a nice scritch on the nose.

'Right as rain,' she told him, a smile curling her lips.

There was a bit of a commotion behind her in the yard, and she turned, hoping it was merely an overzealous coach driver or impatient traveller.

It was not.

Her jaw fell clean open as she realised the source of the commotion was a harried marquess driving a cart much like her own, his equally harried valet in the back, holding—

'Galahad?'

The Marquess stopped the cart, as gracefully as one could in a busy, muddy yard, and shot her a bright grin.

Shocked, her heart full to bursting with that

glorious, shining hope, Genevieve could do nothing but stand there and gape, as the man tossed the reins to a groom, jumped down, and sauntered, well, sloshed over to her.

He couldn't be here. He couldn't be here for her; for them.

Perhaps I am still asleep, and dreaming.

But if she were, she was pretty sure she might've imagined another reunion. One where they both weren't soggy, and wet, and in filthy, muddy travelling clothes, and surely, she wouldn't have imagined Galahad.

No, not likely.

Still, as she looked up at the man now standing before her, she couldn't quite believe it. Even though she knew he was real, knew those crystalline eyes looking down at her with hope, and love, and excitement, were the ones that had drawn her in from the first. She knew that scent, beneath the sweat and the road, was *his*.

'Spencer?' she asked weakly, searching his eyes for any clue that this categorically wasn't what she thought. 'I mean, my lord. How did you find us?'

'Not easily.' He grinned, and she couldn't help but choke out a laugh.

Finally I've found you, Spencer thought, as he looked down at Genevieve. He was glad to have her alone for this part, not that he didn't want to see Lizzie, only, he needed to say what he had to first, and then, hopefully, they could all reunite. He'd nearly lost hope of finding them, and in fact, he might not have, had Galahad not begun to devour Josiah's clothes again, and soil the cart. The restless demon needed a walk, why he'd even thought to bring the monster, was anyone's guess.

But now, he was grateful to the creature, because they'd been forced to stop, and here she was. He'd not quite believed it when he'd seen her, heard her speak the beast's name, and yet, he'd known. He wouldn't have imagined her like this, as bedraggled as he was, but still the most beautiful thing he'd ever seen. Or maybe he would've, because she remained real. Not some perfect vision, but the true woman he loved.

And the same emotions shone in her eyes that he held in his heart, bolstering his courage.

'And Spencer is fine,' he said, pulling himself back to the conversation. He could just look at her, enjoy her presence later. Right now, things needed to be said, so they could have the future they both wanted. That he hoped they both wanted. *That I know in my heart we both want.* 'We've been on your trail for two days. You might've hidden your tracks better, had you not been in such a rush to get away.' Genevieve swallowed, and looked away, but he tucked a finger under her chin, and bade her look at him again. 'Admittedly, I should've come after you days ago, weeks ago, but I think…now is better. My thoughts…are clearer now.'

'You spoke to your mother,' she said softly, ever the prescient.

'Yes.' He smiled, willing her to see the shadows had been chased away, and that only peace reigned in his heart now. 'I shall tell you in time. But we did not only speak of that, but of you. My future. The family's future.' Genevieve nodded, and he could tell she was bracing herself for the worst, but he willed her to see the worst wouldn't come, not this time. *Only the best, always.* 'We have decided, as a family, that should you and Lizzie, and Miss Myles should she care to come along, the more the merrier and all that,' he rambled on, idiot that he was, though Genevieve laughed, and he relaxed, gathering his thoughts again. 'Well, we've decided that we want you to be part of our family. That we are all aware, and willing to face what awaits us. I know I made a mess of things, Genevieve, and I am sorry for that. I did not consider the consequences, nor speak to you, to anyone, ask you your thoughts or opinion. And I am so very sorry,' he sighed. 'So very, very sorry. I never wish to decree, or order you, or make decisions without you. I wish to be your partner, in all things, you see.' Tears pricked his eyes, and he saw some shining in hers too, but there was more. *I need to say it all.* 'You said your battles were your own,' he continued, as steadily as he could. 'And believe me when I say, I will never question that. All I ask, is that you allow me to stand beside you. That is all my family wants. My friends too, I am sure, once they know. At least one already has agreed to support us. So, in case it wasn't clear, I now realise I have yet again forgotten to ask, but would you be my wife? Will you allow me the honour of being your husband, and a father to Lizzie?'

'We were coming back,' Genevieve whispered, her tears falling, and his too when he realised what she was saying. 'We were coming back.'

He smiled, his heart soaring, and pulled her close, and sealed the pact with a kiss.

A kiss of new beginnings, of endings, and loss, and discovery. A kiss full of the passion and love they shared; a kiss that promised a lifetime shared, and happiness.

'I will marry you, if Elizabeth agrees,' she said, and Spencer thought that was a fair deal.

A throat cleared, and he looked to his right, and found the girl in question standing there with Miss Myles, a calmer Galahad in her hands, and a dishevelled Josiah by their side.

Genevieve turned too, and Lizzie nodded, a big smile on her face.

'Thank you,' he told her.

'I love you, Spencer,' Genevieve said after a moment, taking one of the hands that held her cheek, and kissing his palm. 'I should've said it before, but I didn't want to believe, you were right. You are all I never believed I could have. All I could never even dare to dream existed. You lift me up, and bring me joy, and strength. I will face what comes next, with you, for I cannot imagine what I will be without you.'

Spencer allowed himself to indulge in another kiss before he released her, took her hand, and turned to the others.

'Josiah, would you be so good as to see the ladies' cart safely back to Yew Park? After you've had a nice meal,' he added, knowing he owed the man that much at least. 'Ladies, we can either see if there is a carriage to be had, or simply make our way back in my rugged conveyance.'

'Your cart will be just fine.' Genevieve smiled after a look to the others.

'Excellent.'

'Actually,' Miss Myles said. 'If you don't mind, I will ride with Josiah. I have no desire to ride with Galahad.'

'Very well then.'

With a nod for Genevieve, and a kiss for Lizzie, she disappeared into the inn with Josiah.

Whether the decision was truly because she would not suffer the beast for the remaining forty miles, or because she was offering the new family-to-be some time alone, it mattered not. Spencer was grateful.

'Let us get on the road, then,' he said. 'Mother, my sister Mary, and my friend Freddie cannot wait to meet you. Properly,' he added, considering technically his mother had already met Genevieve.

'Spencer,' Lizzie said once they had all installed themselves on the cart, securely bundled and ready to meet whatever lay ahead. 'Thank you for fetching Galahad.'

He looked over his shoulder and smiled.

'Anything for you, Lizzie. Though, if you ask for another goat, I may have to say no.'

They all laughed, and with a flick of the reins, they were off again.

The bright, shining future before them, illuminating the way.

The rest of our lives begin now. And how wondrous they shall be.

Epilogue

Yew Park House, June 1831

There, Genevieve thought, a satisfied smile on her lips as she dropped the last strawberry onto the cream. This wasn't her first time baking a cake, but it was her first time baking one so very delicate. Jules had always been in charge of Elizabeth's cakes when they'd begun celebrating her birthday again. And she always made them look scrumptious, and nigh-on impossible. Genevieve had never thought she would have occasion to try and out-do the master, but here she was, succeeding in doing just that, thanks to Mrs McKenna.

'It looks beautiful, my lady,' the woman herself said, and Genevieve straightened, hands on her hips, feeling prouder for the woman's compliment. 'Little Hal will love it, I'm sure.'

'I don't think little Miss Hal will quite know what it is,' Genevieve laughed. 'But hopefully she will like the colours. It will be up to the rest of us to decide whether it's worth it in flavour.'

She did hope everyone liked it.

Volunteering to take care of the preparations for Halcyon's birthday-cum-Reid and Rebecca's belated anniversary party had seemed a good idea at the time. Reid and Rebecca would be at Yew Park for the summer, and new parents needed to do nothing more than enjoy time with their babe. And Genevieve had wanted to do this for them, a small gesture after all they'd done for her family.

From the moment she and Spencer had made their vows to each other in September, in London, in full view of Society, they'd been there. They had stood by Spencer, and her, as the same vile tongues and vicious papers smeared her reputation, and his, all over again. But they'd stood strong, together, rising above the lies, the gossip-mongering, and the disdain. It hadn't been easy, but together, they'd made it through.

Though the truth of Genevieve's past was only shared with a very select few, rumours that *not everything was as it seemed*, spoken to the right ears, the right matrons, the right lords, the right journalists, and suddenly, doors that had been closed, opened again, ever so slightly. Not that Genevieve wished to truly be part of Society again, but for Spencer, for his position, and the good of the Marquessate, they did what they had to.

After a time, when they simply carried on as

before, and not even Stapleton, who had remarried, and seemed as uninterested in Elizabeth as ever; though whether a certain marquess, Disappeared Earl, or disreputable shipping magnate had a word with him as well was anyone's guess; when not even he rose to the poor challenge of berating the new Marchioness of Clairborne, things returned to a strange state of semi-normalcy. And, despite all the battles to be fought, and all the ill that came their way, there had been happiness. Spencer had found a passion for life, a new determination to change the world, and so had she. That, was all that mattered.

Living, with joy and love in your heart.

Spencer, Mary, and the Dowager had spent the year talking, finding a new way to be a family, healing from the past. It had not been an easy road, and it was long from at its end, but Genevieve liked to think that she and Elizabeth had somehow made it easier.

The Dowager for one had taken quite the shine to Elizabeth, and vice-versa. The Dowager seemed intent on making up for all she had missed with her children, and refused to be called anything but *Grandmother.* Mary seemed to have the most difficulty reconciling the fact that she was born of Muire McKenna, though she and Genevieve had become great friends, and she hoped that their talks, and time together, had helped Mary in some way. Genevieve knew Spencer worried about his sister, and indeed, so did she, but she also knew Mary would find her place when it was time.

Mary had also become close to the McKennas, who remained in their positions at Yew Park, but who had been accepted into the family as much as could be, or rather wished to be. Mary's own birthday, a bittersweet occasion this year, had been spent quietly, in their company. There was a longing to be part of their grandchildren's lives, but also a grief which could not quite heal.

Mrs McKenna had been an immense help to Genevieve since they'd returned for the summer, and though at first she'd found it difficult to accept the lady of the house wished to learn how to bake, and cook, indeed, even step foot in the kitchens, or sew her own fannions… Well, soon they'd come to understand each other.

And now I know all her secret tricks, Genevieve thought with a wry smile.

'Shall I take this one,' she said, returning to the task at hand. 'And you take the one for Reid and Rebecca?'

'Yes, my lady.'

Together, they did just that, navigating the stairs with caution as they made their way to the Renaissance terrace that was serving as the party spot.

They had been graced with glorious weather, and today was a brilliant example, all white fluffy clouds, and a bright blue sky that matched Spencer's eyes.

Though not his attire—today a lemon-yellow waistcoat and purple coat. A year later, and still he managed to surprise her with combinations—though she suspected Josiah was much to blame as well.

A cheer rose up as she and Mrs McKenna made their entrance, or rather, exit, and grinning, they set down the cakes before her friends; her family. She truly had so much now, some days she really thought she might burst of joy.

There was the Dowager, inspecting the cake with a glint of interest and a proud smile at the corner of her lips. There were Reid, holding his beautiful daughter Hal, who looked so tiny in his big arms, and Rebecca, her new dear friend, looking resplendent and fiery in the afternoon sun. There was Mary, looking settled, and beautiful, and content, Josiah behind her, a reluctant participant because of Spencer, who considered him a friend and seemed intent on cutting down as many rules of propriety as he could, at least when in private.

Soon, Mary too will be happy.

And Juliana beside her, looking as she did often now, at peace. Which was something very special indeed. The last year, she'd kept up with teaching Elizabeth, but also been a companion to the Dowager, a friend to Mary, and of course, to Genevieve.

More like a sister.

She was glad that Jules had found a place here

too, though she wondered if one day, her friend might leave, to forge her own path. If she did, Genevieve would be there for her. They were sisters in spirit, and nothing could ever separate them.

Freddie was missed today, business having detained him, but hopefully they would see him before the end of the summer. Spencer and she both valued him as a friend, and whatever had passed between the men during Genevieve and Spencer's initial separation, she knew had brought them closer. The man also indulged Elizabeth's love of science and travel, ensuring he brought her exotic treats and books at every opportunity.

And then there was Elizabeth, on Spencer's lap, bouncing and chatting as he toyed with her hair, and tickled her. He'd become her father in every way, a better father than Genevieve could've ever asked for.

Soon, he might be father to another; despite practising with unfettered indulgence over the past year, it was only recently that they'd decided to try in earnest for babe. They wanted to ensure old wounds were healed enough, for them both, to be the best parents they could to two children. And Spencer had harboured fear for her life, the knowledge of how Muire had passed weighing on him as he considered his own wife giving birth.

Elizabeth for one was utterly thrilled with the idea, and considering how well she took to Hal, well, Genevieve knew she would make a wonderful sister.

'It's beautiful, Genevieve,' Rebecca crooned with a huge smile. 'Thank you.'

'What do you say, Hal?' Reid asked, bouncing his daughter a little closer to her cake. The baby's fingers somehow found the cream, and everyone laughed as he then proceeded to wipe it off her. 'I guess so.'

'Well, happy birthday, goddaughter mine,' Spencer said, lifting his glass high. 'And happy anniversary to you both! Many happy returns and all that.'

'Charming, husband,' Genevieve laughed, going to sit beside him but instead being pulled onto his other knee, the champagne in his glass threatening to spill, but miraculously staying put. 'You truly do have a way with words.'

'Reid is a simple man.' He shrugged, kissing her cheek. 'And no words could do your cakes justice. Mrs McKenna,' he said meaningfully, raising his glass towards the housekeeper, and nodding his head.

She bowed hers, and slipped away.

'Shall we be eating these delicacies anytime soon,' the Dowager drawled. 'Or shall we have to listen to more bickering whilst they melt.'

Everyone laughed, and Rebecca began cutting the anniversary cake, passing a knife to Elizabeth so she could slice Hal's.

'Excellent,' the Dowager said when she'd finally been allowed her cake. 'Well done indeed, daughter.'

Genevieve smiled, and let Spencer feed her a bite, taking the praise, and the endearments, and tucking them away safely in her heart.

She had found the land of *happy*, and *safe*, and *love*, and made it her home.

And what a glorious home it is.

* * * * *

COMING SOON!

We really hope you enjoyed reading this book.
If you're looking for more romance, be sure to
head to the shops when new books are
available on

Thursday 31ˢᵗ March

To see which titles are coming soon, please visit

millsandboon.co.uk/nextmonth

MILLS & BOON

MILLS & BOON®

Coming next month

THE MARQUESS MEETS HIS MATCH
Laura Martin

"I'm sorry," he murmured. Never had he felt more insincere in his life. He wasn't sorry he had kissed her even if he knew it wasn't right. "I couldn't help myself."

"A moment of madness," Charlotte said quietly, but he could see the flicker of a question in her eye as if she were waiting for him to confirm why he had kissed her before showing her reaction to it.

"Exactly." He gave a little half smile and with great effort managed to step a few paces away.

Robert felt torn. Part of him wanted to pull Charlotte back into his arms and tumble her down onto the soft hay and damn the consequences, whilst the other part was screaming for him to make his apologies and leave as quickly as he could. The young woman in front of him seemed nothing like his late wife, but he had vowed never to become entangled with anyone else again. He'd learnt his lesson the first time.

Pushing thoughts of his late wife from his mind he turned his attention back to Charlotte.

"I should get to bed," she blurted out, trying to edge around him. "We have a busy day planned for tomorrow and I don't want Lady Mountjoy to think I'm not grateful for the opportunity to be here."

He knew he should say something to her, to explain

why he had kissed her, to check she really wasn't too upset by the situation, but before he could find the words she had slipped past him and fled the stables.

Charlotte waited until she had rounded the corner of the stables and then set out at a run, not caring if anyone saw her dashing through the gardens and across the lawn. There was still a hum of conversation from the drawing room but she couldn't face going in and pretending that nothing had happened, nothing had changed.

Everything had changed. She couldn't quite believe Lord Overby had kissed her, but what shocked her more was her reaction. She'd felt this deep, visceral pull, as if nothing could have made her step away from him no matter how bad an idea kissing him had been.

Shaking her head she tried to banish from her mind the memory of his hands running down her back and caressing her skin through her dress. It was just a kiss, a moment that had got out of hand. She didn't want to desire Lord Overby, she didn't want to desire anyone, and he'd made it clear it was a mistake.

She scoffed. Of course, it was a mistake for him. He was a marquess, one of the most influential men in the country, and she was the mildly irritating young woman who lived on the small estate bordering his.

Continue reading
THE MARQUESS MEETS HIS MATCH
Laura Martin

Available next month
www.millsandboon.co.uk

MILLS & BOON

THE HEART OF ROMANCE

A ROMANCE FOR EVERY READER

MODERN — Prepare to be swept off your feet by sophisticated, sexy and seductive heroes, in some of the world's most glamourous and ror locations, where power and passion collide.

HISTORICAL — Escape with historical heroes from time gone by. Whether your pas for wicked Regency Rakes, muscled Vikings or rugged Highlander the romance of the past.

MEDICAL — Set your pulse racing with dedicated, delectable doctors in the high sure world of medicine, where emotions run high and passion, con love are the best medicine.

True Love — Celebrate true love with tender stories of heartfelt romance, from rush of falling in love to the joy a new baby can bring, and a focus emotional heart of a relationship.

Desire — Indulge in secrets and scandal, intense drama and plenty of sizzling action with powerful and passionate heroes who have it all: wealth, good looks…everything but the right woman.

HEROES — Experience all the excitement of a gripping thriller, with an intense mance at its heart. Resourceful, true-to-life women and strong, fear face danger and desire - a killer combination!

To see which titles are coming soon, please visit

millsandboon.co.uk/nextmonth

JOIN US ON SOCIAL MEDIA!

Stay up to date with our latest releases, author news and gossip, special offers and discounts, and all the behind-the-scenes action from Mills & Boon...

 millsandboon

 millsandboonuk

millsandboon

might just be true love...

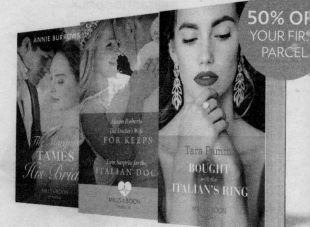